I0598241

THE ROBBER OF YOUTH

The CASA Chronicles – Vol 3

Keith Julius

Published by Keith Julius

Temperance, MI 48182

First edition - May 2017

www.KeithJulius.com

ISBN: 978-0-9969607-7-9

Printed by KDP Select

Cover Design - @pixon_design on fiverr

This book is dedicated to all the wonderful CASA volunteers everywhere. Without your dedication and commitment to the children you serve the world would truly be a sadder place.

Keith Julius

Also available from Keith Julius:

Remorse By Degree

The CASA Chronicles:

Volume 1 – Catch A Falling Star

Volume 2 – Born For Adversity

Volume 3 – The Robber Of Youth

Volume 4 – A Decade Aborning

www.KeithJulius.com
KeithEJulius@gmail.com

Chapter One:

OFF IN the distance, obscured by the night, the approaching train drew closer. The whistle made a mournful sound as the behemoth of steel entered the switching yard, maneuvering its nearly two hundred tons of steel through the congestion as its speed slackened. The CSX engine weaved past dozens of parallel tracks, temporary home to a wide assortment of rolling stock; dusty gondolas laden with coal, their mountains of black obscure in the darkness; box cars of assorted styles and colors, doors barricaded to conceal their contents; a bevy of tanker cars, white, black, and silver cylinders emblazoned with the names of various petroleum concerns.

Massive arc lamps stood as silent sentinels throughout the yard, throwing their harsh light over the environs. And while the illumination did much to reveal the surroundings it managed as well to cast dark shadows everywhere, shadows that merged with the night and concealed details.

Figures moved through these shadows.

The four teenagers kept close together, each of them gripping several cans of spray paint as they stumbled across the uneven terrain. From time to time they would stop in the shadow of one of the train cars, taking a few moments to scan the surroundings before continuing their journey. The progress was slow. They didn't seem in a particular hurry.

"All clear," Mickey announced, as he led the quartet from concealment. Mickey was the unacknowledged leader of the group, the one in the forefront of their activities. He achieved this position, not through any particular attributes or abilities, but rather due to the fact that he was the oldest of the four. As such he had long come to expect obedience from the others.

Tommy, his junior by three months, couldn't resist the urge to brook an argument. "What's wrong with where we're at?" He shook the can in his hand, the rattle of the agitator within sounding unnaturally loud in the gloomy surroundings. "Let's just do this."

It was too dark to detect the look of scorn Mickey responded with, though his tone of voice managed to convey his opinion of Tommy's suggestion. "We'll do it when I say we do it. Understand?"

"Sure, Mickey." Tommy hesitated, casting furtive glances around them, reluctant to back down but hesitant to resist further. "Whatever you say."

"You're not scared, are you?" Mickey suggested.

"'Course I ain't scared."

The question bothered Tommy. Most things about Mickey bothered Tommy. The older boy's status was an accident of nature that troubled Tommy to no end. It annoyed him, this feeling of subservience he felt around Mickey. To compensate, he took every opportunity to strut his stuff, his adolescent pride attempting to win the others over to his side for the slight he felt thrust upon him due to his age.

"Cut it out, you two," Jason interjected, hoping to forestall any further arguments. The constant bickering of the two boys was an irritant he could do without. He pushed his glasses back onto the bridge of his nose, then turned to look behind him. "You comin', Rosie?"

"Sure. I'm right behind you."

Rosaletta was the youngest of the group, over two years in age behind her brother Tommy. Though only fifteen she looked much older, having blossomed through her adolescence

6

into a striking young woman with raven black hair and a flawless complexion. She was aware of her physical attributes, as aware as she was of the undesired attention she often received from older boys because of her appearance, but she wasn't comfortable with it. Rosaletta tended to dress conservatively. She didn't like attention; she preferred to blend into the background.

This was difficult to achieve in most situations, but particularly so when it came to dealing with girls her own age. They seemed threatened by her somehow, as though her attractiveness was something she flaunted in front of them. But she couldn't help her looks. For a long time it had bothered her, this isolation from other girls her own age. But after a while she grew accustomed to it.

She no longer missed spending time with the girls. She didn't need them anyway.

At least she could be herself when she was with her brother and his friends. They looked out for her. They made her feel like part of the group, even allowing her to join them on their nocturnal excursions together.

"That train's getting awful close," Tommy remarked, feeling the beginnings of rumblings beneath his feet.

Mickey laughed at the comment. "What a wuss. Afraid the big bad train is gonna run you down?"

Tommy drew closer, feeling the need to defend himself. "I ain't afraid!"

"Yeah. That's what you say." A mischievous grin spread across Mickey's face. "We'll see. Follow me."

Mickey sprinted across the yard, crossing a set of rails, his shoes crunching against the gravel.

"Now what?" Tommy asked, to no one in particular.

Jason shrugged. "Who knows? Let's see what he's got in mind."

Then there were just the two of them standing there.

Rosaletta moved closer toward her brother, touching him lightly on the arm in an attempted show of solidarity. "Why do

7

you let him get to you, bro? Who cares what Mickey thinks, anyway?"

He shrugged the gesture off, as though finding it offensive. "Don't you start in on me."

"I'm not starting nothing. But you know Mickey likes to ride you. Just ignore him. It don't mean nothing."

"That's easy for you to say."

For several seconds they stood together in silence, watching their two companions moving away, the retreating figures blending into the shadows.

"So what you gonna do?" Rosaletta asked at last.

"What can I do?"

Tommy turned, walking briskly across the tracks, and his sister followed moments later.

Mickey was standing defiantly in the center of the train track. His arms were poised on his hips, his legs spread slightly; all he lacked was a cape to make the Superman stance complete. His voice matched the bravado presented in his appearance.

"I figger the train's comin' down this here track." His stare locked onto Tommy. "You willin' to stand here with me, and see who lasts the longest before movin' outta the way? Or are you chicken?"

Tommy hesitated, common sense getting the better of him. "I don't know...."

"That's what I figgered," Mickey interrupted, a smile of satisfaction crossing his face. "You don't have the balls for it."

Tommy spat on the ground, dropped the paint cans he had brought with him, then moved forward. "You wanna bet?"

"Tommy, don't."

Rosaletta grabbed for his arm but he shook the motion off.

"Stay outta this, Rosie."

A long-legged stride carried him across the steel rail to Mickey's location. A moment later both boys stood together, standing side-by-side on the creosote-soaked ties, staring down the line at the steadily increasing light of the locomotive as it moved toward them.

"Come on, guys," Jason urged. There was no denying the concern in his voice. He wanted to grab his companions, to shake some sense into them, but his reluctance to cross the rail held him back. He glanced down the line. "This is stupid."

"You callin' me stupid?" Mickey glared.

"Yeah, you're stupid. Thinking this is a good idea is crazy. Only thing this proves is you're both a couple a idiots."

The blast of the train's whistle cut off the last of Jason's words. The engine was slowing through the yard, in preparation for the coming stop, but momentum continued to urge the locomotive forward. It bore down on the group, relentless in its motion. Vibrations coursed through the rails, emanating from the diesel's motors. The ground shook, disturbing the ballast, sending tiny avalanches of stone cascading downward.

Mickey still smiled, the devilish grin he reserved for use while performing his pranks, but a somber look had entered his eyes, testifying to the realization of what he had gotten himself into. He chanced a look at Tommy, expecting to see fear etched in the other boy's features, but no show of emotion was revealed. Tommy stared straight ahead into the night, his attention captivated by the approaching contraption. He held his breath. He waited, immobile, like a statue.

"Please, Tommy." Rosaletta was crying, her body shaking. "Don't be doing this."

Her brother turned to face her. She could tell by the look on his face he had no intention of backing down. He had made his stand and was determined not to falter. She covered her eyes, refusing to look any longer.

The boys were bathed in light by now, the engine's triple headlamps seeking them out in the night, it's glow revealing the silhouetted figures standing on the tracks. Air brakes squealed. The whistle moaned yet again. Time seemed to slow, anticipating the inevitable conclusion of the confrontation between man and machine.

"Oh, hell!"

Mickey jumped to the side as the words escaped his lips, his wild leap throwing him to the ground. He rolled across the loose gravel, lurching to a stop and looking back toward the tracks.

Tommy smiled, confident in his victory, and walked casually out of harm's way. He came to a stop, barely off the tracks, as the engine hurtled past. The wind from the passing train whipped at him, slapping his coat against his body and tugging at the legs of his jeans. Loose stone and debris pelted him, stinging the back of his neck, but he failed to respond. A smile graced his face.

"Who's the coward now, big man?!" Even with shouting, his words barely carried over the racket of the passing line of cars. They rattled behind him; metal scraping against metal, aged suspension systems groaning in the night.

Rosaletta looked up, forcing her hands away from her face. She smiled at her brother, excited for him and what he had accomplished.

The smile lasted a moment only.

Somewhere along the line – somewhere between the switching yard in Chicago and the end of the line in Toledo – a rusted ladder leading up the face of a boxcar had captured a limb from a decaying tree. The branch had lodged in the rungs, riding the untold miles of rail in darkness, occasionally shifting position as the train jostled along its way. It had managed to stay upright for most of the journey. Only now, with the train's momentum slackening, the limb had shifted. It leaned to the side, threatening to fall to the ground, but somehow it's movement was arrested. Like a giant gnarled hand, the wooden obstacle reached out in the night.

Tommy never saw it coming.

The others, too horrified to do anything but watch, could only stare dumbfounded as the branch slapped across the young boy's head. He spun a complete circle, a pirouette accented by a sharp snapping sound, and fell to the ground.

No movement came from him other than the red flow that oozed from beneath, the rivulet of blood slithering toward the three remaining youngsters like accusatory fingers.

Rosaletta was the first to react, running to her brother's side and kneeling down beside him. Ignoring the loose gravel that dug into her skin, even through the jeans she wore, she reached for Tommy's face. The motion stopped, her fingers inches from his cheek. She found herself drawn to his eyes, staring into the lifeless orbs.

"Shit!" Mickey stepped closer toward the still form on the ground, spun indecisively about, then faced the siblings once again. "Shit!"

"We gotta do somethin'," Jason suggested.

"What we gonna do?"

"I don't know. Shouldn't we call somebody?"

"No sense callin' no one. Just look at him. It's too late."

"Maybe not. Maybe he'll be okay...."

"Just look at him, for Christ's sake. He's dead."

"No!" Rosaletta turned to face the bickering duo, the tears in her eyes glistening. She cradled her brother's head, stroking his hair. "He's gonna be okay."

"Forget it, Rosie." Mickey stepped closer. "He's dead. Ain't nothin' you can do for him now."

"No." Her head shook violently back and forth. "He's gonna be okay. I know it."

By now the string of train cars on the track behind them had coasted to a stop. The diesel engines still throbbed with life, like some sort of metal animal breathing in the night, but gone was the clatter of the couplers and the scraping of the wheels against the rails. Gone was the rattle and groans of the shifting rolling stock, the cars having settled into a peaceful slumber where they stood. It seemed almost quiet now, a still night disturbed only by the subdued roar of passing cars from nearby Interstate 75 and the sobbing of the young girl kneeling in the gravel.

Footsteps sounded, from somewhere down the track, of someone hurriedly moving their direction. Rosaletta failed to notice but both boys were drawn to the disturbance. Mickey and Jason exchanged knowing glances.

"I'm outta here," Mickey announced. Moments later he disappeared, swallowed by the darkness.

Jason touched Rosaletta lightly on the shoulder. "Come on, Rosie. We need to leave."

"I can't." She faced her friend. "I can't leave him. Not like this."

"You can't do him no good now. We need to leave."

"No." She turned back toward the still form cradled in her arms. "You go. I'll be okay."

Jason hesitated several seconds before making his decision.

And then Rosaletta was truly alone.

Chapter Two:

Benjamin Tuppelo arrived on the scene thirty-five minutes later. Several police cruisers were on site by the time he reached the train yard. The vehicles had their headlights on, the white light accenting the still form of the teenage boy sprawled on the ground, while the flashers on the roofs bathed the area in red and blue, lending a macabre carnival-like atmosphere to the surroundings.

Tuppelo strode from his car with the assured gait of someone who had served twenty-four years with the Toledo Police Department. The detective had seen death countless times while on the force. He had witnessed hundreds of accident scenes during his career. Each one struck him with the same feeling of regret, mourning the tragic lost he was called on to investigate on a regular basis. It all seemed so senseless to him.

Somehow a crowd had gathered already, a phenomenon about crime scenes that never failed to amaze the detective. It was well after midnight, in a location that could hardly have been more isolated, but that didn't stop the onlookers from congregating. Several had cellphones on the ready, hoping to catch a picture of the scene from where they were held at bay by a crew of uniformed officers.

"What do we have?" Tuppelo asked no one in particular as he approached.

A junior tech, someone Tuppelo recognized but whose name eluded him at the moment, answered. "Looks pretty cut and dry. Couple of kids fooling around." He kicked at one of the spray cans of paint abandoned on the ground. "Probably came here to leave their signature on some of the train cars."

The tech motioned to the body which lay on the ground, staring at the stars above with lifeless eyes that saw nothing.

"This one – the name's Thomas Guiterrez – got too close to where he shouldn't have been."

Tuppelo looked up and down the line of cars on the nearby siding, as though searching for something, then returned his attention to the still form at his feet. The blood had coagulated into an ugly brown pool that surrounded the youth's head, though there was no sign of bruising or lacerations. He must have bled from somewhere in back, the damage concealed now due to the position of the body.

It didn't look right to Tuppello. He made no attempt to disturb the victim as he considered the scene. "I would have expected worse, being hit by a train," he offered at last.

"That's just it."

The technician stood, wiping some gravel from his hands.

"The train didn't get him."

The detective's look revealed his confusion.

The tech pointed to a tree branch laying on the ground, about sixty feet further down the track. "We think that's what did it."

One end of the limb looked freshly broken, where it had snapped off against the train's ladder. The other end discolored with blood.

"We think it may have been sticking out from the train. Swiped the kid as it passed. Looks like his neck was snapped from the blow. At least it was probably quick. Chances are he didn't even have time to react."

Small consolation, Tuppelo mused.

"Any witnesses?" the detective asked.

"A couple."

14

The tech pointed to a man leaning casually against the side of an enclosed boxcar. The figure wore jeans and a flannel work shirt. A windbreaker – the letters CSX emblazoned on the front – hung at his side, as though he had gotten too hot wearing the jacket and had taken it off. He smoked a cigarette, taking quick puffs. He didn't seem to be enjoying the taste, but appeared too nervous to stop.

"Henry Cullins," the tech continued. "Works here in the train yard. He was up in the tower when it happened."

Tuppelo turned the indicated direction, taking in a three-story white-brick structure perched beside the track. A metal staircase clinging to the building led to the top floor. Lights glared from what must have been an office of some kind.

The tech continued his recitation. "Cullins says he saw four figures down here. Looked to be a bunch of kids. Didn't really get a good look at any of them."

"What happened to the others?"

"Two of them decided to vamoose after it happened. Probably scared shitless. Only one of them stayed behind."

"Where's he at?"

"She." The Tech pointed to a young girl sitting on the ground across from them, staring at hands that, even in the dim light of the yard, appeared to be stained in red. "Her name's Rosaletta. Rosaletta Guiterrez."

The Tech stopped to look back at the body on the ground. "She is – that is, she was   his sister."

Tuppelo sighed.

Sometimes he hated this job.

"I guess I better talk to her."

His steps took him past the railroad worker, who threw his half-lit cigarette to the ground and moved forward to approach the police detective. "Are you in charge here?"

Tuppelo answered with no hesitation. "Yes I am."

"Listen, I need to get back to work. Do I have to stick around here much longer?"

"I'll be with you in a few minutes, Mr. Cullins."

"You better be. The company don't pay me to stand around all night, you know."

"I'm sure you're a busy person."

"Damn straight. They told me I had to wait until someone in charge came here."

"That would be me."

"Good. Then I'm ready to tell you what I seen."

Tuppelo attempted to keep the irritation from his voice. "Like I told you, it will have to wait a few minutes, Sir. There's someone else I need to talk to first." The detective glanced once more at the teenage girl. She looked like an innocent child, lost and confused. Several police officers stood nearby, as though ready to pounce on her should the need arise. Their attention made her seem that much more vulnerable.

And, somehow, more alone.

The yardman caught Tuppelo's glance. "Who, her? Hell, she ain't going nowhere. She shouldn't of been here to begin with. None of them should a been here. This here's private property, you know."

"Is that so?"

The tone of the detective's response betrayed the fact that he held little interest in what Henry Cullins was saying. The yardman failed to notice.

"Them kids come in here all the time. Sneaking around where they don't belong. Hell, I'm surprised nothing like this has happened before. It serves them right, know what I mean?"

Tuppelo glanced back toward Thomas Guiterrez's body. "You mean that teenager deserved to be killed?"

"No. No. I don't mean that. It's a shame what happened to him. Of course it is. But he shouldn't a been here to begin with. Right?"

Tuppelo said nothing.

"Anyway, I'm ready to tell you what I seen tonight."

The detective studied the man for all of five seconds, the police officer's glance never wavering, an intense glow in his eyes.

"I'll be with you when I'm ready."

The matter obviously settled, Tuppelo turned and walked away, seemingly oblivious to the mutterings coming from behind him as he approached the young girl.

"Hello, Rosaletta."

Tuppelo waited several seconds, thinking she hadn't heard him, and was about to repeat his greeting when she looked up. Her mascara ran in streaks down her face, smudged from the tears she had shed. Her eyes held a pleading look, as though expecting to hear something that would ease her pain. But no such words were forthcoming.

"I'm Detective Benjamin Tuppelo," he continued. "I'd like to ask you a few questions, if that's all right?"

She nodded but continued her silence.

He towered over her, especially since the young girl sat on the ground. And though he was accustomed to controlling a situation, and under normal circumstances would be more than content to take advantage of his position, this seemed neither the time nor the place for a show of strength.

Tuppelo squatted down beside her, closing the gap between them.

"I'm sorry about your brother."

"Don't be." Her voice surprised him with it's harshness. "It was his own fault. His own stupid fault."

"Can you tell me what happened here tonight?"

"Not much to tell. Tommy was acting the big man. Like he always done. Trying to show off. I told him one day it would get him in trouble. I guess today was that day."

The detective made no reply, allowing Rosaletta time to collect her thoughts.

"Mickey was riding Tommy," she continued at last. "Like he always done."

"Who's Mickey?"

She nearly blurted something out, then apparently thought better of it. "It don't matter."

"If this other boy, Mickey, did something to your brother...."

"Mickey didn't do nothing."

She practically spat the answer out, as though she found the taste of the words awful but felt they had to be said.

"Tommy was just being stupid, that's all. Like he always done."

She looked past Tuppelo, toward the still form laying on the ground beside the train tracks.

"Guess he won't be doing that no more, will he?"

There was no need to answer the question.

"Do I need to stay here any longer?" she asked.

He was far from finished with her. Questions swirled though his head. But Tuppelo didn't need to be a seasoned detective to realize Rosaletta Guiterrez was reluctant to speak out about the night's events. It could have been grief concerning her brother. Or the fear many teenagers felt when confronted by authority.

Regardless, there would be time for questions later.

"Of course you don't need to stay here. I can take you home whenever you're ready."

She stood, slowly, as though uncertain how to face what was ahead of her. "That's okay," she managed. "I can find my own way home."

"I don't think that's a good idea, considering what you've been through."

She shrugged, displaying a lack of concern.

"Besides, I'm sure your parents are worried about you," Tuppelo suggested, fishing for information.

"That will be the day."

"Do they even know where you're at?"

"Mama wouldn't care none. She's with her boyfriend. That's all she cares about anymore."

"And your father?"

She looked toward her brother. The still form was being manhandled onto a gurney. He was covered up now, just a shapeless nonentity in the night.

"My father's with Tommy," she offered, before turning and walking away.

Chapter Three:

THE APARTMENT complex consisted of a series of two-story brick buildings, all of them a uniform dirty beige in color. Each building appeared to have five units, judging by the number of doors that opened onto the cracked and pitted sidewalks that fronted the apartments. Considering how late it was – or more correctly, how early, since it was approaching the dawn – it was hardly surprising that most of the buildings were dark. Through the uncurtained window of one ground-floor apartment a television could be seen, casting a flickering light onto the otherwise darkened room.

The police cruiser pulled into the parking lot and the headlights were extinguished. From behind the wheel stepped a woman in her mid twenties. Her short brown hair stuck out from beneath the cap she wore. Her uniform was crisp and neat, a testimony to her fastidiousness.

Officer Carolyn Shummer opened the rear door and Detective Tuppelo stepped out, giving the area a quick once-over. He took in at a glance the shattered windows in some of the buildings, the rusted screen doors hanging from broken hinges in several of the doorways, and the accumulation of trash that appeared everywhere. The few vehicles in the gravel parking lot were old and dingy looking, especially in the dim lights that graced the area. One car had a flat tire.

Tuppelo moved aside to allow the car's remaining occupant to vacate the vehicle. Rosaletta Guiterrez appeared to take no note of the surroundings as she stepped out. She had seen it all hundreds of times before and knew it looked no better during the daytime hours. To her the place was simply home.

She had calmed down some on the ride over, the tears having ceased, but had said little. Tuppelo wasn't certain if this was normal for the young girl or if her mind was still processing the events of the last few hours. She had answered questions in a straight-forward enough manner – about her mother and her home life – but had offered little in the way of details.

Her voice was quiet, barely a whisper, as she faced the detective. "Thanks for the ride."

She started to move away, but Tuppelo restrained her with a light touch on her shoulder.

"I think we should come with you, Rosaletta."

"You don't have to. I'll be okay."

"I'm thinking more of your mother. Someone needs to tell her about your brother."

She nodded, no doubt reflecting once again on what had happened to Tommy. "I suppose you're right."

As though that settled the matter she continued in her motion away from the cruiser.

Three long strides took the detective to the young girl's side, Officer Shummer several steps behind them. Tuppelo towered above Rosaletta, a formidable figure next to the teenager.

Yet, for all his seeming authority and confidence, he felt ill-at ease. He was uncomfortable enough around his own girls, Stacy and Stephanie. With all his experience reading people and assessing situations he seemed at a loss when dealing with teenage girls. Their world was something he didn't understand and couldn't relate to.

He attempted to mask his present inadequacy by starting a conversation.

"How long have you lived here, Rosaletta?"

The young girl took a quick glance around, as though aware of her surroundings for the first time. "In Paradise City?" She gave a halfhearted laugh to accompany the attempted joke. "'Bout three years now, I guess. I know the place sucks, but what the hell. You got to live somewhere. Right? It's about all Mama can afford."

"Does your mother work?"

"She used to. Waitressing. Until she hurt her back. Then she couldn't stand them long nights no more. That was a year or two before we moved here. She couldn't keep up the rent in the old place on her disability."

They came to a stop in front of a door that looked much the same as the others in the building. Rosaletta paused, as though uncertain what to do next.

"We can't stand out here all night," Tuppelo prompted, addressing her hesitation. "Your mother needs to know what happened."

"It's not that." She shrugged. "I don't have a key. Tommy had the key. He was supposed to be with me when we got home. To let me in after...."

She stopped abruptly, aware suddenly of what she was saying; perhaps, for the first time, appreciating the realization of what she had left behind in the train yard.

"It wasn't supposed to happen like this."

The tears had started once more, slurring her words; causing her body to shake with short convulsive sobs.

"We didn't mean nothing. We weren't there to hurt no one. Or do nothing wrong. We was just having a little fun. That's all. Is that so bad?"

She looked up, her gaze locking onto the firm expression on the police detective's face. If she was seeking sympathy there was none to be found.

"We didn't mean nothing," she repeated, as though trying to convince herself. She lowered her head, refusing to look the others in the eye. "But I see now we shouldn't have been there. It was stupid. How could we have been so dumb?"

Officer Shummer, who until then had remained silent, spoke up from behind them. "Don't be so hard on yourself. It's always easy to see your mistakes when you look back on them."

Rosie raised her head, a glare of defiance in her eyes. "Well, I won't let nothing like that happen to me again. If nothing else I learned that tonight. I'm not letting no one push me around no more. Nobody's ever gonna make me do something I don't want to do."

She swiped her sleeve across her eyes, wiping away the tears.

"I'm ready now," she announced. "Let's just get this over with."

Tuppelo leaned forward and rapped on the door.

Silence answered. Eventually – it was less than forty-five seconds later, but in the stillness of the night it felt much longer – a light turned on in the apartment. The shuffling sound of footsteps reached them from the other side of the door.

"Who's there?" a voice called out.

Rosie answered. "It's me, Nick. I forgot my key."

A chain could be heard on the other side of the door, which opened moments later. The greeting they received from the man within was less than cordial as he took one look at Tuppelo.

"Who the hell are you?"

The man had a coarse look to him, accented by a crop of uncombed hair and a growth of stubble on his chin. He glared at the detective, as though assessing a future rival of some sort. When he at last looked at Rosaletta his mood failed to change.

"What's going on here, Rosie?"

She turned away, as though embarrassed to continue. Or was there something else behind her reaction? The accusatory tone he used to address the young girl seemed to fit him, as though it was his normal deliverance.

Tuppelo pondered for a second only before addressing the man who had opened the door.

"I'm Detective Benjamin Tuppelo, with the Toledo Police." He held out his ID, turning the card to highlight his picture. The dim light from the outside fixture mounted beside the front door did little to illuminate the information. "I need to talk to Rosaletta's mother."

"Connie's asleep. She can't come to the door." He spoke the words as though it was the final say on the matter.

"Wake her up," Tuppelo suggested, with a trace of threat behind the suggestion.

The man in the doorway hesitated for several seconds before capitulating. "Come on in." He turned his back on them and walked away.

The door gave access to a cramped and messy kitchen area. Rosaletta entered. Tuppelo followed, leaving the door open behind them. Carolyn remained outside, a uniformed sentry, accustomed to the mundane tasks that often accompanied police work.

"That's Nick," the young girl offered as explanation, making a half-handed gesture toward the departing figure. "Mama's been seeing him for a few months now." She shrugged. "Sometimes he stays over."

The detective made no reply. Nick walked to the back of the apartment, pausing at the foot of the stairs. "Connie! You better get your ass down here!"

As though his work was done for the evening he sat on the couch, retrieving a pack of cigarettes from a nearby table before him and pulling out a light. He paid no further attention to the young girl and the police officers in the doorway as he leaned back to enjoy his smoke. He sat in the dark, the glow of the cigarette the only indication he was still in the room.

Rosaletta pulled a chair out from beside the kitchen table and slumped down.

Eventually the sound of footsteps shuffling down the stairs reached over to them.

Consuella Alegredo draped a well-worn robe around herself as she walked down the stairs. She looked tired, like she had just dragged herself out of bed. No doubt that was exactly what had happened. She paused at the foot of the stairs, glaring at her boyfriend sitting in the darkened room.

"What's so fucking important you had to wake me up?"

She took a quick glance out the window, as though noticing her surroundings for the first time. "Shit, the sun ain't even out yet. What the fuck's going on here?"

Nick waved his arm, the red glow from his cigarette pointing. "Ask them."

Consuella noticed the new arrivals then. Her gaze lingered on the uniformed officer just outside the door, standing sentry duty on the front walkway. She then returned her attention to Rosaletta, who eventually hung her head to avoid her mother's scathing look.

Consuella sighed, as though exasperated with a situation she had encountered before.

"So what kind of shit did you get into this time, Rosie?"

The young girl neglected to answer.

Tuppelo took a step closer. "Were you aware your daughter was out of the apartment tonight, Mrs. Alegredo?"

Though normally an intimidating figure, the detective's bearing failed to make any kind of impression on Rosaletta's mother. She shrugged off the query concerning her daughter's whereabouts, as though it was something she was totally unconcerned with.

"No." She was in the kitchen by now, which was beginning to feel crowded. "I didn't know Rosie was out tonight. But it don't surprise me none."

"Why is that?"

"She's done it before."

"Doesn't it bother you? Having a fifteen-year-old girl out wandering the streets at night?"

"What can you do? Kids do all sorts a stupid shit, don't they? It's part of growing up. I try to stop her, but what the fuck can I do? Besides, she usually ain't alone."

The woman paused, apparently having just become aware of something. "Where's Tommy?"

Rosaletta faced her mother once more. The young girl's hands, resting on the tabletop, shook slightly. Her eyes were wet with tears.

Tuppelo answered the question. "There was an accident this evening. I'm sorry, Mrs. Alegredo, but Tommy won't be coming home."

Panic rose in the woman's eyes. The reversal of emotion was an immediate change, as though a switch had been thrown in her head. She had exhibited a total lack of interest regarding her daughter, but now she exploded with concern about her son.

"Where is he?" She practically screamed the question. "Where's Tommy? I need to see my baby."

She turned toward the other room, staring into the darkness at the still figure in the chair. "Nick. We got to get going. Tommy needs me."

She jerked in surprise at the light touch of Detective Tuppelo's hand on her arm.

"I'm afraid it's not like that. Your son won't be coming back."

She froze in fear, the import of the words beginning to reach her.

"He's dead," Tuppelo announced with finality.

The silence that followed filled the apartment, every one present reluctant to disturb the mood. Nick stopped smoking, the cigarette inches from his lips, as though he was frozen. The police woman at the front door turned away from the scene.

Consuella Alegredo was the first to react. In a move that surprised the rest of the gathering the woman suddenly lurched forward, grabbing her daughter's shoulders and leaning in to within inches of Rosie's face. "How the fuck could you do this to me?"

"It wasn't my fault." The words stammered out between tears. "I didn't do nothing."

"You did enough. You were always no fucking good. Getting Tommy in trouble the way you do."

"No." The young girl shook her head in confusion. "No."

Her mother pulled away, straightening up and placing her hands defiantly on her hips. "I want you out of here. Out of this apartment. Out of my life. You get me? Take whatever shit you want with you now, 'cause I sure as shit ain't gonna let you back in once you walk out that fucking door."

Tuppello considered interjecting but before he could speak the distraught parent moved again. The slap sounded loud and clear. Rosaletta's head snapped to the side in reaction to the blow.

A moment later Rosie lurched to her feet. The tears she had displayed earlier were gone now, replaced by anger.

"I hate you!"

The fifteen-year-old stormed out the door, shoving her way past Officer Shummer on the front sidewalk.

"Stay with her, Carolyn," Tuppelo directed. "Contact Children's Services then wait in the cruiser for me." He flashed a look at Rosaletta's mother, the intensity in his glare displaying his opinion of the matter. "Looks like Mrs. Alegredo and I have a few things to discuss before we leave."

Chapter Four:

TO: ALL CASA volunteers

From: CASA Office Toledo Ohio

Subject: Can you help this child?

Young girl – age 15 yrs.

Teenager was traumatized after witnessing the accidental death of her seventeen-year-old brother. Following the brother's death police witnessed an act of Domestic Violence from the mother directed at the girl. Child was moved to protective custody and from there to a foster home.

Father deceased. No other relatives have come forward to help with the child.

If you can find it in your heart to be the CASA for this young girl please let us know. She is in need of someone who cares.

Thank you.

Rebecca Poole

Lucas County Juvenile Center

CASA – Court Appointed Special Advocates

Chapter Five:

THE SOUND of running water woke Melanie Cox from what had developed into a restless night's sleep. She snuggled under the covers, enjoying the warmth, and listened to the rhythmic cadence emanating from behind the closed door of the bathroom. She pictured in her mind her husband's form in the shower, the water droplets cascading over his shoulders and down his back. She was tempted to join him, relaxing beneath the warmth of the spray and feeling the comfort of his skin against hers.

But, as willing as the spirit was, the flesh was weak.

She glanced at the alarm clock. 7:13. The digital numbers seemed to glare at her, urging her to ignore slumber and step out of bed. But it was far too soon. She had worked until 11:30 the night before. By the time she had driven home, given herself some time to unwind, and gotten ready for bed, it was nearing one o'clock. Six hours just wasn't enough time. Especially not today!

Melanie knew she had no reason to be nervous about the afternoon. She had been to the Lucas County Juvenile Center several times during her CASA training, observing hearings and mediation sessions. She had also taken her lessons at the Center, though the classrooms were kept separate from the courts where the magistrates and judges resided. But – for the past few months – she had been an observer only, a spectator on the sidelines of events, not one of the participants.

Today that was about to change.

The water's cadence ceased. She heard the shower curtain being drawn back, the metal rings scraping against the bar with a volume that seemed unnaturally loud. She rolled over, facing the doorway, prepared to greet her husband when he stepped out of the bathroom.

She must have drifted back to sleep, because the next thing she knew Andy was fully dressed, rummaging in the dresser drawer for something while attempting not to rouse her.

"It's okay," she remarked. "I'm awake."

"I'm sorry." He found the necktie he had been looking for and closed the drawer, then wandered over toward the bed. "Late night?"

"No worse than usual. Just a lot going on, that's all."

"I thought you liked keeping busy at work?"

"I do," she admitted. "But last night was just one of those nights...."

She paused, reflecting on the events. Melanie had been a nurse for eight years now, the last five working the post-surgical wing at St. Vincent's Hospital. Things were usually fairly uneventful during second shift. The surgeries were for the most part done for the day, other than an occasional last minute emergency room patient, so she seldom had to deal with new arrivals. The evenings were the time when most visitors showed up as well, which kept the patients preoccupied with their own activities and less likely to bother the staff.

Of course there were always things that needed taken care of. Administering medications. Answering questions from concerned family members and friends. Updating charts with the latest patient information.

These were activities Melanie dealt with every day. She was good at her job, and handled herself with the easy grace of someone accustomed to her role. But last night she hadn't been at her best. Even the simple tasks had felt like chores to her.

And she was fairly certain she knew the reason why.

"I guess I'm just nervous," she finally admitted.

"About this afternoon?"

"Yeah."

"What's to be nervous about?"

"I don't know. I just feel there's so much I don't know yet. So many places where I could make a mistake."

"I don't see that happening."

"We all make mistakes."

Andy moved closer, sitting down on the edge of the bed beside her. He reached out to stroke her arm as he continued. "I know you, Mel. I know how determined you are to do what's right."

"That's just it. What if...?"

Her husband lifted his finger, pressing it gently against her lips, motioning her to silence as he continued. "I don't want to hear it. You're a great nurse, Mel. You're intelligent, and know what you're doing. You're sympathetic to people, aware of what they're going through and eager to help. You deal with things every day that a lot of people couldn't even dream of. I know I wouldn't want your job. But you're perfect for it."

She smiled, encouraged with his words.

Andy reached forward, giving her a quick hug as he whispered in her ear. "I know you'll make a great CASA volunteer. They're lucky to have you in the program."

He stepped back, took a quick glance at the clock, then hurried toward the door. "Listen, I got to run. See you after work. Love you."

"Love you more."

He smiled at her remark and then he was gone.

She rolled over, pulled the blankets up to her shoulders, and closed her eyes, looking forward to the opportunity to grab a bit more sleep. But it was no good. She was wide awake now, her mind too focused on the day ahead to even think about falling asleep again.

Melanie sat up in bed as she considered the program she had been training for during the last several months. She had known nothing about CASA until half a year ago, when she happened to pick up some extra shifts on the Pediatrics floor and met LaToya.

LaToya was three months old and weighed barely seven pounds. She had spent the majority of her life in the hospital, suffering from numerous conditions including pulmonary infections and heart palpitations. She was tethered to an apnea monitor twenty-four hours a day, a device to detect the infant's chest movement and heart rate. The child's life was a precarious existence; a struggle for survival.

Melanie fell in love with the baby at first sight, admiring the delicate features of the child and marveling at how precious life was when presented in such a tiny package. As a nurse she knew the child was too young to be aware of her surroundings, but she couldn't help thinking it made a difference to the little girl when other people were around. Melanie spent as much time as she could with the baby, holding the child and walking around the hospital room as far as the various cords and tubes attached to LaToya permitted.

One evening an elderly woman was present when Melanie arrived. The stranger sat in a chair beside the clear acrylic bassinet that held LaToya, apparently mesmerized, content to watch as the infant slept. She seemed unaware of Melanie's presence in the room until the nurse moved closer.

"I didn't mean to startle you," Melanie remarked, as the woman shifted position in her chair.

"I guess my mind must have been somewhere else."

Both of them paused, staring at the infant, taking in her features.

"She is a doll."

"She's a tiny one," the woman agreed.

"Are you a relative?"

"No. My name's Beverly Johnson. I'm LaToya's CASA guardian."

Melanie paused. "CASA? I'm not familiar with that."

The stranger sighed, taking a deep breath. "How much do you know about the baby's background?"

"Only what I've seen of her medical history. From the records here at the hospital. Poor thing. Life hasn't been very easy for her, has it?"

"Her mother...."

The woman paused, obviously considering how to proceed. She seemed to choose her words carefully.

"Her mother wasn't concerned with taking care of herself. Even after she found out she was pregnant. She drank heavily. Still does, I guess. LaToya was born premature, and with a lot going against her."

"That's a shame. It's bad enough people don't take care of themselves. But to do this to a baby...."

By this point Melanie held the little one in her arms, having checked LaToya's clothing and finding she needed a dry outfit. She held the infant in her lap as they talked. "I still don't understand your connection."

"I'm a CASA volunteer through Lucas County. A Court Appointed Special Advocate. Children's Services stepped in right after the baby was born. I was called in soon after that."

Melanie was still unclear on the situation "So you're, like, a foster mother to the baby?"

"Nothing like that. I'm empowered by the court to keep an eye on things and see that the baby is taken care of. I visit the children I'm working with on a regular basis. Talk to family members. And attend court hearings and meetings at Children's Services. My focus is on the child, and what's in the child's best interest."

Melanie smiled. "Sounds like it can be pretty satisfying."

"Yes, it can."

Beverly paused, her mind drifting back to a case that had ended recently, of a young mother who had struggled against heroin addiction and fought the odds to keep her family together. Ultimately the case hadn't ended as well as Beverly would have desired.

"They aren't all happy endings," Beverly admitted at last. "But even the sad ones can be rewarding, knowing that you've made a difference in the life of a child."

"CASA." Melanie considered the word. "I never heard of that before."

Beverly nodded. "A lot of people haven't. It's too bad, really. There's a definite need out there. Every day young children are subjected to abuse and neglect." Beverly smiled at LaToya, as the infant reflexively moved her arm as she slept. "Particularly tiny ones like her. And there's never enough people to help out."

She stopped abruptly, aware of an awkward silence in the room.

"I'm sorry," Beverly continued. "This isn't a sales pitch or anything. It's just when I stop to think of how hard some of these kids have it....."

Melanie nodded. She had seen enough as a nurse to realize what could happen. She often had to remind herself – or at least try to convince herself – that there weren't really bad people in the world. There were misguided people. People who didn't understand the ramifications of the poor choices they made in life. People who didn't realize the consequences of their actions, and the affect it had on those around them. Especially to the children in their care.

She looked again at Beverly, smiling at the woman who had taken it upon herself to get involved with a child in need.

Two weeks later, having considered the things the two women talked about that evening in the hospital, Melanie made up her mind. She contacted the CASA office and signed up to become a volunteer and advocate for children herself.

Chapter Six:

THE COURTROOM was bigger than she remembered.

Melanie had only been within the room once before, during one of her early training sessions, and while she had tried to pay attention and follow everything that was going on she had soon found herself overwhelmed with the thought of the entire prospect. The task she had set before herself – of advocating for children that needed someone on their side – seemed more and more formidable as she progressed further into the training. There was so much yet to learn.

Some of it was discouraging. And even frightening, to consider what some of these children had to go through. But Melanie refused to let it change her opinion of things. She still believed that people were inherently good. She had witnessed plenty of love and affection during her time as a nurse, watching as people struggled through an illness or a hardship. So often family members were amazing. They offered comfort. And guidance. Or even something as simple as a shoulder to lean on or an ear to listen with.

Even so, there was no denying there was another side of life. It was a side she tried to ignore but often confronted in her daily tasks as a nurse. Bad things did happen. Often it was due to an accident. Or a series of events that grew out of control, claiming victims along the way.

But many times – and this was a fact she was confronted with time and again during her training to become a Court Advocate – the very people that should care the most for the children in their care were the ones responsible for the bad things that happened.

She heard first-hand accounts of children severely neglected, left to fend for themselves in cockroach infested dwellings. Hunger was all too real for many of these kids, who viewed going to school not as an opportunity to learn, but rather as their chance to get at least one meal to eat that day.

There were accounts of children watching their parents succumb to the evils of alcohol or drugs. Or – impossible to believe but true nonetheless – children enlisted by adults to procure heroin and other opiates, sent with a handful of cash to the local pusher's to obtain what the parents didn't want to be caught in possession of. Money that could have been used for food was wasted on addictive habits that tore the struggling families apart.

Most heartbreaking of all were the horror stories of the abuse children suffered at home. These facts were graphically driven home during CASA training – observing pictures of children scalded with boiling water – images of broken bones and terrible bruises – accounts of children who never recovered from injuries received at the hands of their parents, spending their last moments alone and in pain until their suffering finally came to an end.

Melanie Cox was apprehensive of the future, wondering if she was prepared to do her part but willing to give it her all.

As she walked into the courtroom she was surprised at the number of people in the room. Several members of her class were already seated in the area set aside for the jury during trials.

She had grown to know them all during the last few months, not as friends or companions, but as dedicated men and women wanting to make a change.

Joan McKlurg waved at Melanie as she entered. Melanie smiled, returned the gesture, and observed the rest of the room as she approached her seat.

The back of the room held perhaps thirty people already, no doubt friends and family to the graduates of the training class. She felt suddenly alone, wishing Andy was there with her, but realized the commitments of his job didn't allow him to make an appearance. But that was okay, she told herself. She knew he'd be thinking of her.

As Melanie approached the seating area reserved for the CASA graduates Joan stood to greet her. They had met on the first night of CASA training and soon discovered they had similar opinions and ideas. The two were close in age to one another, perhaps another reason why Melanie found it so comfortable talking with Joan.

"Husband couldn't make it?" Joan asked, a look of disappointment on her face.

"Afraid not. His job keeps him pretty busy."

"I don't know. I'm beginning to think maybe you don't have a husband after all. Or maybe you just don't want anyone to meet him."

"Why wouldn't I want you to meet him?"

"Beats me." A mischievous grin spread across Joan's face. "Maybe you're afraid of some competition. You think I'm gonna steal him away from you."

"Just you try and see what it gets you."

A moment later they were sitting down, laughing over their interplay.

"So is your family here?" Melanie inquired of Joan.

"You bet." She pointed to a couple in the front corner of the seating area. The woman waved as she caught their eye. "That's my mother," Joan explained. "And that's Dad next to her."

"They look happy to be here."

"I think they're just glad to see me finish something for a change."

Melanie flashed a quizzical look, and Joan hurried to explain. "I have to admit, I'm not the best at completing things. I get bored too quick, I suppose. But not with this. I think this is something I'm going to enjoy doing. It must be pretty satisfying, knowing you can make a difference in a young person's life."

"I'm sure it is."

"But you already know that, don't you? I mean, being a nurse and all. You help people all the time."

"That's true. And it is satisfying. But I think this will be...." Melanie paused a moment, to organize her thoughts. "I don't know. Just different somehow."

"In what way?"

"Less of an obligation, I suppose. When I'm at the hospital it's a job. It's something I have to do. This is something I *want* to do."

"I think I know what you mean. Sitting in class, listening to the stories of what some of these kids have to go through, it's heartbreaking."

"I just hope I can do some good."

"You'll do great, Melanie. I'm sure of it."

By this point the room seemed to be filled. The chattering of conversations slowly abated as Christine Davis walked to the front of the courtroom. As she came to a stop Melanie noticed for the first time that Judge Carole Landers was seated at the bench at the front of the courtroom, dressed in her black robes. The judge seemed less formidable now than the last time Melanie had seen her.

Which was understandable. On that occasion the judge was presiding over Drug Court, shepherding a dozen young women through the difficult process of coming to terms with their addiction problems. One of the women had even been removed from the premises, having provoked the judge's ire.

Melanie's thoughts were interrupted as Christine Davis began to speak.

"I want to thank you all for attending today." She made a gesture toward the side of the room, where Melanie sat with the other graduates. "I have had the pleasure of working with these fine men and women as their instructor over the last six weeks and it is a pleasure to see them become Court Appointed Special Advocates.

"To you in the audience – the family members and friends that have come to show your support for these special people – I want to emphasize how proud you should be of them all. Because it does take a special person – with a lot of love – to volunteer for a program like this."

Christine turned to once again face Melanie and those gathered near her.

"We in the CASA office thank each and every one of you for the hard work you have put into your training. We know you have busy lives, and we know becoming a CASA is a big commitment. It's also an important commitment. The future of the children in our community is in your hands. What could be more important than that?"

She turned then to a distinguished looking man who had come up along beside her. "I would now like to introduce to you Malcolm McDougal, the Director of the Lucas County CASA program."

"Thank you, Christine." The man's voice was articulate and riveting, as though he was comfortable with speaking and accustomed to being listened to.

"As Christine has already indicated, you have each done a lot of work to get to this moment. I know the course assignments can be intimidating. Overwhelming, at times. You cover a great deal of material in an extremely short amount of time. And we certainly don't expect you to remember everything you went over in class.

"The doors of the CASA office are always open to you. If ever you have any questions, or concerns, or just need a sympathetic ear to turn to when you're not certain what to do next, don't ever hesitate to call or stop by the office. We – all of us here – appreciate the work you will be performing for the children of Lucas County, and if there is ever any way we can assist you then by all means let us know."

There was more to the speech, followed by words from Judge Landers, who also praised the CASA graduating class for the important duties they were embarking on. Then finally it was over, and Melanie found herself posing for pictures with Joan and the others – a group shot with Judge Landers, then individual portraits of each graduate next to the judge.

As she was preparing to leave Melanie was approached by a middle aged woman carrying half-a-dozen folders.

"Hi, Melanie. I'm Rebecca Poole. From the CASA office. And I have something for you."

"Oh?"

The woman leafed through the folders, finally selecting one that had the name Melanie Powers written on it. At the beginning of their training it had been suggested that the students select a CASA name, to preserve their identity. The name would be legally binding in court, and would serve as a protection for the CASA volunteer. CASA cases sometimes produced disgruntled families, with parents unhappy concerning the results. By protecting the true identities of the volunteers it offered them a certain amount of anonymity should a case ever go awry.

Melanie had chosen Powers as her CASA name, in homage to a teacher that had influenced her heavily in high school.

These thoughts flashed through her head as Rebecca Poole handed over the folder. "Your first case."

"Already?"

"Certainly. Didn't you expect to get a case?"

"I suppose. I just didn't think it would be this soon."

"We believe in getting your feet wet right away. Plus, considering the current workload, we can use all the help we can get."

Melanie opened the folder and leafed quickly through the

papers inside. The case apparently involved a young teenage girl, but before Melanie could delve too deeply into the information Rebecca continued.

"Everything should be there that you need to get started."

A worried expression crossed Melanie's face. "Anything in particular I should be concerned with?"

Rebecca paused. Melanie felt for a moment like the woman was reluctant to continue.

"Just proceed slowly."

"I don't understand."

"The young girl's name is Rosaletta Guiterrez. She's fifteen years old." The woman paused, took a deep breath. "Her brother was killed in a tragic accident four days ago."

"That's awful."

"That's not the worst of it. The poor thing was there when it happened. Saw everything."

"That must have been devastating to her."

"I'm sure it was. That's why I said take it slowly. She has a lot she's dealing with right now. Besides what happened to her brother."

Melanie's look of confusion obviously asked the question she had on her mind.

"Rosaletta's mother threw the girl out of the apartment after it happened. Actually slapped the girl with police officers at the scene. So besides losing her brother she's lost her home and any kind of family life she may have had. It sounds like she's got a tough road ahead of her."

"Sounds like she's had it pretty tough already. I hope I'm up to dealing with this."

Rebecca flashed a reassuring smile. "Just do your best. That's all we can ask for."

And then she was gone, moving on to the next graduate with another folder containing another case, and Melanie found herself wondering once more what she had gotten herself into.

Chapter Seven:

THE DAY was a dismal one. Gray skies threatened a downpour at any moment. A light mist filled the air, chilling the people lined up on the sidewalk outside the two-story white-brick structure. Green awnings arching over the grand entrance protected those in the front of the line. Those in back could only grumble and wait their turn as the queue slowly made its way into the building.

Once inside there was no denying the nature of the establishment. The odor of flowers assaulted everyone the instant they entered the foyer, the aroma managing to conceal, for the most part anyway, the lingering smell of antiseptic. Inspirational posters adorned the walls, speaking of love and spiritual well-being and the blessings of family and friends. Images of fluttering birds and soft-lit sunsets were interspersed with quotes from scripture.

It all failed to counteract the presence of death, and the reason for visiting the funeral home.

Thomas Guiterrez lay in a simple casket in a crowded room of whimpering and sobbing well-wishers. Death was difficult to confront at any time, but particularly when it struck down one so young. It forced everyone into an awareness of mortality, and how fleeting life could be.

Consuella Alegredo was dressed in black, hovering near the head of the casket, greeting all who approached. She was torn between glory and grief. Her son's death had hit her hard, and it was obvious how distraught she was. Her eyes were a perpetual shade of red, a testimony to the tears she had shed, her skin pale complexioned. Her hands shook as she greeted the turn-out, as though the limbs were no longer under her control and determined to embarrass her.

Yet, at the same time, she reveled in the attention thrown her way, relishing her position as the center of activity in the room. Yes, the well-wishers were here to say goodbye to Tommy. But their primary function was to console the grieving mother. This was only natural, and it was an activity Consuella accepted with pride.

The day was much different for Rosaletta Guiterrez, who sat alone and nearly forgotten on a chair near the exit. She was bookmarked with an empty seat on either side of her.

No one offered to join the grieving teenager. Visitors would pause a moment on their way out, offering some sort of lame words of sympathy, then depart, leaving her more and more alone in a room full of strangers.

Occasionally someone would linger.

Mickey and Jason arrived together. Having been present at Tommy's death – having experienced the sights and sensations Rosie had gone through that night – perhaps they alone appreciated the young girl's situation. They felt her pain, and longed to offer words of comfort, but they remained speechless. There was nothing they could say to change what had happened. It didn't make sense to even try.

They sat beside her for several minutes, fearful of deserting her but struggling for the proper words.

In the end they left in silence.

Rosaletta was alone once more.

It was still difficult for Rosaletta to grasp the fact that Tommy was gone. She had looked up to him in so many ways.

Her brother had always been there for her, offering words of understanding when needed. He was her pillar of strength, a protection against the evils of the world. She could always count on him to be there for his little sister.

In a household that was cold and empty – struggling to survive with a mother that offered no sympathy and demonstrated no love or compassion for her children – Tommy was the single best thing in Rosie's life. He was a constant the young girl could always depend on.

And now he was gone.

She felt like she had failed him somehow. Like the whole thing was her fault. And while she realized there was nothing she could do about it – no way she could ever make amends for the tragedy that had destroyed what little family she ever had – she still berated herself over what had happened.

It was something she would have to live with for the rest of her life.

"I'm sorry about Tommy."

Rosaletta, aware suddenly that someone was sitting beside her, turned to face the speaker. The young man was in his late teens or early twenties, dressed conservatively in slacks and a polo shirt. He offered neither a smile nor any sign of encouragement, just another empty face in the sea of strangers parading past her.

But then she noticed a look in his eyes, a show of understanding and sympathy that captured her on the instant. She felt suddenly less alone.

"Thank you," she mumbled, pulling away, afraid to confront him directly.

"Tommy was a good guy," he added.

She nodded.

For several moments nothing was said. A few isolated words reached them from others in the room, words Rosaletta paid no attention to.

He continued. "You're his sister, aren't you?"

She nodded. "Rosaletta. They call me Rosie."

"Okay, then. Rosie it is. You look a lot like him, you know that?"

She shrugged, as though she had never considered the point before. When she spoke again it was quietly, as though fearful to disturb the room, her eyes locked on the flowered carpeting at her feet.

"How did you know Tommy?" she asked.

"I met him a couple times. When he was over to my place visiting my brother Billy."

Rosaletta glanced up. "Is Billy here? I'd like to say hello. Thank him for coming today."

Now it was his turn to pull away. He faced the crowded room, staring into space as though looking into the distance at something that was no longer there.

"No. Billy isn't here today." His voice lacked any inflection, as though the life had been stolen from him.

He faced her once more.

"Billy died two years ago. In a car accident."

Rosaletta paused, wanting to withdraw from him, but found herself somehow mesmerized while looking into the stranger's eyes. "I'm sorry."

"No." He reached toward her, placed his hand gently on her arm. There was nothing uncomfortable with the gesture; no disturbance of personal space. It was merely a sign of comfort offered to someone in grief.

Rosaletta felt instantly closer to him.

"I didn't come here to talk about myself," he began. "I came here...."

He faced the front of the room a moment, as though inspecting the casket and contents barely revealed beyond the crowd of well-wishers.

"I came here for Tommy. To remember him, I guess."

Abruptly he shifted gears.

"It gets easier," he continued, facing her once more. "I know that's not what you want to hear right now. And you're certainly not going to believe it. Not the way you feel today. But it does get easier."

She sighed. "I just can't imagine what's it's gonna be like. Not having Tommy around. He was always there for me."

"And he always will be. There isn't a day goes by I don't think about my brother. Billy isn't gone. As long as I remember him he isn't gone."

Rosaletta felt the tears welling up in her eyes once more. "I wish I could believe that."

For perhaps a minute they sat there in silence. People passed by, nodding in recognition, offering meek platitudes before leaving the building.

"Your mother looks pretty torn up over everything."

"My mother...!"

Rosaletta stopped. She felt the anger welling up inside and urged it under control.

"I don't want to talk about my mother."

"I'm sorry. I didn't realize it was a problem."

"Problem?"

The sorrow was gone as she faced him, replaced by an anger that decorated her face.

"She threw me out! Can you imagine that? Actually threw me out of the house."

"No kidding? Why would she do that?"

"Who knows. I guess she figures it was my fault. What happened to Tommy."

"But that's not true."

"Isn't it? Maybe it is. Maybe we shouldn't of gone out that night. Maybe if I had been stronger...."

"Don't do this to yourself, Rosie. It doesn't help any. I know. When Billy was killed I had the same questions. The same doubts in my head. It didn't change anything. Just made it that much harder to move on."

"I don't think I can move on. It's like part of me is missing. I keep expecting to hear his voice." She looked around the room, surveying the people. "I keep thinking he's here, and he's gonna walk up to me like he always done."

She paused, as though searching the crowd for a glimpse of Tommy.

"But I know that won't happen."

She shook her head in confusion, studying the floor at her feet once more, her troubled thoughts disturbing anything else she had to say.

"So what happens now?" he asked, his reluctance to break her silence obvious. "You can't go home. So where are you staying?"

"They stuck me in a foster home."

"That's a shame you can't be with family."

She shrugged. "It's okay. There wasn't really no family to go to anyway. And the couple I'm with don't seem too bad. At least it's a place to stay."

"Probably screws everything up in your life. Going to school and all that."

"Not really. They don't live too far from Woodward. So I can walk to school."

"Woodward?" He voiced the word as though it held some significance to him. "That's where you go to school?"

She nodded.

"I don't live too far from there. Just a couple blocks away."

"Is that so?"

"Yeah. Maybe I'll see you around some time."

"Sure." Then, without really considering what she was saying, Rosaletta continued. "That would be nice."

He smiled. "Yes. It would be, wouldn't it?"

And, in spite of herself, especially considering the circumstances and her surroundings, Rosie actually found herself smiling.

They talked for several minutes longer, idle chatter that Rosie didn't pay attention to then and couldn't remember later. It felt good – almost normal – like a regular conversation between two people. And for a while, a few short minutes anyway, she nearly forgot where she was, and her reason for being there.

Everything came back to her as the young man stood to leave.

"It was nice meeting you, Rosie. I'm sorry it had to be under these conditions. But I'm glad we had the chance to talk for a while."

"Me too. It helped. Having someone listen to me. To take my mind off things, at least for a few minutes."

She glanced up front, toward her mother and the wooden box that held what was left of her brother, and quickly turned to face him again.

"Thank you."

"You're welcome."

He turned, took one step away, and only then did Rosaletta realize something.

She was on her feet a moment later.

"Wait a minute." She stopped him with a touch on his arm. "I don't even know your name."

"It's Todd. Todd Burkett."

"Todd." She stopped a moment, considering the sound of the name, and decided she liked it. "I hope I see you again, Todd."

"I do, too."

And then he was gone.

Rosaletta sat once more. She still had an ordeal to face, making it through the rest of the day, but things seemed a little easier now.

Chapter Eight:

MELANIE WAS nervous.

The sensation surprised her. She was generally comfortable dealing with people. She was accustomed to confronting difficult situations and coming to necessary resolutions. Melanie had seen much as a professional nurse, faced death on countless occasions, and had learned to control her emotions when needed.

Yet still here she was, nervous with the prospect of talking to a teenage girl.

One of Melanie's responsibilities as a CASA volunteer was to visit each child she represented at least once a month. This would give her the opportunity to become more familiar with the case, plus determine whether she felt the present living conditions were suitable for the child she represented. She had contacted the foster family and set up an afternoon appointment on her day off for the visit.

She found the house situated in an older section of town, a neighborhood that had weathered through some bad times but appeared to be on the mend. Several houses looked freshly painted; one appeared to be having replacement windows installed. She had driven through the area often – it was located several blocks from St. Vincent Hospital where she worked – but had never taken the time to notice much about it.

She gave it a silent appraisal now, as she slowed down while searching for the correct address, and decided that, while not necessarily prosperous, it seemed like a decent location for raising children.

Reaching her destination she pulled to the curb, and moments later was walking up the stairs to the front porch. She rang the doorbell and was soon greeted by a surprisingly youthful looking young man. He looked to be a few years younger than Melanie, and projected an enthusiasm and charm that set her at ease.

"I'm looking for Neal Daniels," she explained.

"I'm Neal," he informed her. "You must be Melanie?"

"That's right." She extended a hand to greet the one he proffered. "Melanie Powers. From the CASA office."

"Won't you come in?"

She followed him through the doorway, down a hallway, and arrived in a cheery looking family room. A woman, also about Melanie's age, stood to greet them.

"My wife, Sharon," Neal announced.

They sat down following the greeting, husband and wife sharing the couch together while Melanie occupied a plain wooden-backed chair across from them.

"So you're from the CASA office," Sharon Daniels began. "I'm embarrassed to say that we're still sort of new at this. I'm not familiar with CASA."

"A lot of people aren't," Melanie began, trying her best to project a professionalism she didn't truly feel confident with. "We're appointed by the court as guardians to the children in our cases."

"Sounds involved," Neal suggested.

"It can be. But, then again, the children are our entire focus. So we have time to concentrate on their needs. Their interests. I will be visiting with Rosaletta, at least once a month, to insure she's comfortable where she's at and there aren't any issues to be resolved before they develop into major problems."

Neal shifted slightly, as though suddenly ill at ease. "So

you'll be keeping an eye on us?" He said it with no malice, but rather with a slight smile in his eyes, as though he was testing her.

"I'm sure everything will be fine," Melanie confided. She made a sweeping motion with her hand, indicating the living space. "It's obvious you keep a nice house. I'm sure there won't be any problems."

She drew a notebook from her purse, prepared to jot down information as necessary. "How long have you been foster parents?"

"Actually, Rosaletta is our first foster child."

"Oh?"

Sharon leaned forward, taking over their end of the conversation. "To be honest, we were hoping to have a younger child as our first case. A toddler, maybe."

"Is that a problem? Rosaletta's age, I mean."

"Of course not. It's just...." She glanced at her husband, as though seeking support. "We're not really that much older than Rosie. And she's been through so much already. I'm just concerned whether she'll accept us. As authority figures, I mean. It sounds like she has a bit of a rebellious streak to her."

"Have you had any issues so far?"

"Oh, no," Neal quickly put in. "She's been good about everything. But I think she's still in a bit of a daze. What with her brother's death. The funeral was less than a week ago, after all. I think she's still recovering from the trauma of it all."

Sharon, hopeful optimism in her voice, continued. "I'm sure she'll be fine in no time."

"I hope so," Melanie added. "But you say things are going well so far?"

"Sure," Sharon began. "She hasn't really said much. Been keeping to herself a lot. We don't want to press her right away, after all she's been through."

"Is it okay if I talk to her?"

"Of course." Sharon stood. "I'll take you to her room."

A hallway off the living area led to the back of the house.

One door stood ajar, revealing a bathroom done in light pastel colors. Three other doors appeared to lead to bedrooms. Sharon knocked lightly on the second panel on the left side of the hall.

"Rosie?"

There was no answer.

"Rosie? There's someone here who would like to talk to you. Is it okay if we come in?"

A muffled voice answered at last. "The door's open."

The room was dimly lit and sparsely furnished – a bed with a simple bedspread, a folding chair in one corner, and a wooden three-drawer dresser. A small desk lamp on top of the dresser offered the only light in the room.

There was nothing to indicate the nature of the person residing in the room. No clothes could be seen. No personal objects were exhibited. It was cold and empty. Melanie felt apprehensive as she crossed the threshold, thinking this was a room she would not be comfortable in.

Rosaletta sat against the headboard, knees pulled up to her chest, arms wrapped around her legs. She neither looked their direction nor acknowledged their presence as the two women entered the room. Rather she stared straight ahead, her eyes dimly glazed, as though she saw nothing in the room, her attention focused on thoughts far removed from where she sat.

"This is Melanie Powers, Rosie. From the CASA office. She'd like to talk to you, if that's okay."

The young girl turned their direction.

Sharon Daniels seemed uncertain as to what she should do. A feeling of disappointment radiated from her, as though she felt Rosaletta was letting her down by being so unresponsive. Her fingers twisted together in nervousness.

Melanie placed a hand on the other woman's shoulder.

"I think I can take it from here. Rosaletta and I can just talk for a bit. I'll let you know if I need anything."

Sharon hesitated a moment then left the room, closing the door softly behind her.

"Hello, Rosaletta. My name's Melanie."

No response came from the still form on the bed.

"I understand they call you Rosie. That's a pretty name. Is it okay if I call you Rosie?"

Melanie stood in silence several moments, waiting for a reply that never came, then tentatively stepped further into the room. Grabbing the folding chair from the corner, she moved closer to the bed and sat down.

"I'm sorry, Rosie. For everything that's happened. If there's anything I can do to help...."

"What can you do?" The voice was deeper than Melanie had expected, choked with emotion. "Tommy's gone."

"Tommy was your brother?"

It took a while, but eventually a slight nod was the answer.

"I'm sure this isn't easy for you, Rosie. I can't imagine what you must be going through."

"Then what are you doing here?"

"To help you."

"How you gonna help me? You don't know what I gone through. What I seen. What can you do to help me?"

"I can listen. If there's anything you want to tell me....."

"No." The simple word spoke with a definite finality. "I don't want to talk about it."

"Okay. Then we don't have to."

Melanie paused, disturbed by the awkward silence lingering in the room and uncertain how to combat it. She knew Rosaletta had been through a lot. Of course she wasn't going to open up to a total stranger. But that didn't mean Melanie couldn't try to reach the teenager.

"Is there anything you need?"

The girl on the bed shook her head slowly back and forth.

"Any clothes? Something from home...."

"I don't need nothing from home!"

Anger flared in the words, as Rosaletta faced Melanie directly for the first time.

"I don't need nothing from my mother. I don't *want*

nothing from my mother. She don't want me. Well, I got news for her. I don't want her either."

"You don't mean that, do you Rosie?"

"How do you know what I mean?"

"Maybe you just need to stop and think what your mother's going through. It can't be easy for her. Losing Tommy that way."

"Tommy!" She practically spat the word out as she hugged her knees closer, drawing further into her protective position on the bed. "Tommy was all she ever cared about. She didn't never care about me. Always told me what a burden I was. And how I got in the way. Well, I won't be getting in her way no more.

"You tell her that! When you see my mother, you tell her she don't have to worry 'bout me no more."

Rosaletta turned away, the single lamp in the room casting a harsh light on the side of her face. Melanie wanted so much to comfort her in some way – a gentle hug, a soft touch on the shoulder – but felt reluctant to disturb her space. The young girl had issues to work through. Serious issues. Time alone, Melanie was certain, could heal what was bothering her.

For another minute they sat in silence. Finally Melanie opened her purse, removing a business card from within. The card glared at her with its newness. She had printed it at home several weeks ago, in anticipation of beginning her career as a CASA volunteer, proud of the fact that she was embarking on something new, looking forward to the opportunity to help children in need.

Now the bright white card in her hand just seemed a reminder of her inexperience.

The card listed her name – as Melanie Powers, of course – and the number and address of the CASA office. It also provided an email account Melanie had set up for her CASA cases. Other than that it was fairly generic. Nothing to indicate who Melanie really was.

Somehow it didn't seem like enough.

Melanie removed a pen from her purse and jotted her cellphone number down on the card.

She held the card out toward Rosaletta. "If you ever need to get hold of me. Just call me. Anytime. Okay?"

There was no reply; no show of response.

Melanie stood, walked over to the dresser, and slipped the card under the edge of the lamp on the desk.

"I do want to help you, Rosie. Please believe that. I don't know how. Or even if I can. But please believe that. If you need anything I'm here."

A moment later Melanie left the room, closing the door behind her and leaving Rosaletta Guiterrez in her self-imposed isolation.

Chapter Nine:

ROSALETTA, ON her way home from school, noticed the car while she was still a block away. She couldn't help but notice it. It was bright red in color, jacked-up with over-sized tires, and adorned with fancy wire sports rims. Dual hood scoops contributed to the sporty looks of the vehicle.

She didn't know cars, and had no idea the Pontiac Firebird was over fifteen years old. Its owner had kept the car immaculate. It looked like it had just driven off a lot somewhere, without a scratch or dent in evidence.

It wasn't the type of vehicle one would term inconspicuous. Whoever was driving had no qualms about being noticed. It stood out on the street, surrounded as it was by old wrecks and dilapidated models that had obviously seen better days.

Rosie was naturally curious about it, but fearful of being observed as she walked by. As unobtrusively as possible she stole a surreptitious look into the interior as she drew closer. She came to a halt beside the vehicle just as the window rolled down.

The young man inside leaned toward her, a ready smile on his face. "Hi, Rosie."

"Todd?"

Her surprise was obvious.

"I told you we'd be seeing each other again."

"Yeah, but...." She stumbled for the proper reply. "I guess I figured that was just empty words. You know. Something to say before you left the funeral home last week. I never expected to actually see you again."

His expression changed. Where before his face displayed enthusiasm, a glow of excitement almost, it now showed extremely serious.

"I wouldn't do that to you, Rosie. If I say something I mean it. Okay?"

She merely nodded, unsure how to respond. She wanted to say more but didn't know what.

Todd broke the silence. "So do you want to go for a spin?"

"Right now?"

"Why not?"

She looked around, as though fearful of being observed. Even though she detected no one around she couldn't help feeling like they stood out. She had never felt comfortable being the center of attention. She was more accustomed to being ignored.

Or totally forgotten.

"I don't know."

She considered the offer.

Todd Burkett was attractive, with a persona of confidence that set her mind at ease. It was a self-assured bearing, different from the confidence exhibited by the other boys she knew; boys like Mickey – and even her brother Tommy – who seemed to be constantly asserting themselves to prove something, as though they had to convince others of their value.

Todd didn't leave you with that kind of impression. He seemed to accept his worth, like it was merely a part of him and not something he had to constantly define. He wore his confidence with ease. Rosaletta felt comfortable around him, like she too could be herself, with no need to impress others and no desire to hide her feelings.

Part of her wanted to jump in his car and go wherever he

wanted to, to just forget her problems and enjoy Todd's company.

But at the same time it scared her, this heady feeling of self-abandon that was enveloping her. She had learned with time – in her dealings with the other girls her age, and especially with the young boys that seemed attracted to her and anxious to strut their stuff for her benefit – to be more reserved in her actions. Caution was her watchword when dealing with others.

Her words came slowly, portraying her indecision. "I really should be getting home."

The glow returned to his face, along with a mischievous glint in his eyes.

"Come on. Just a short ride. I'll take you home right afterward."

She still hesitated, reluctant to take the plunge.

Finally he leaned over, opening the door on her side.

"We don't have to go anywhere," he informed her at last, with a trace of resignation in his voice. "Let's just sit and talk for a few minutes. There isn't anything wrong with that. Is there?"

Rosaletta glanced around, carefully checking to see if anyone was observing them. As far as the rest of the world was concerned the two of them weren't even there.

Without a word she climbed into the car and closed the door behind her. Only then did she notice the car's engine was running, the sound of the motor a quiet backdrop to the noise of the city around them.

Todd shifted the Firebird into gear.

"I'm just gonna pull up a bit," he informed her. "I sort of feel like we're on display here."

The car traveled about half a block, turning into a parking area next to a diner down the street. Todd shut the car off after pulling in, shifting in his seat to more directly face her.

"You look better," he began, before she had the chance to say anything. "Than the last time I saw you."

She shrugged. "I wasn't at my best." Her hand drifted to

her hair, brushing back an errant strand that insisted on blocking her face. "I still look a sight."

He smiled. "You look great."

She accepted the compliment with a slight lift of her eyes, as though unconvinced of his sincerity.

"No I don't."

"Don't sell yourself short, Rosie. You're a very attractive young girl. You must know that."

She turned away, embarrassed, but managed a smile that she kept to herself.

"How are things working out for you? Are you still in a foster home?"

Rosie nodded.

"No chance of going back home again? You know. To your *real* home?"

She faced him again, her eyes tense with anger. "I'm not going back. I hate it there. I'll run away before I go back to my mother."

"That's a drastic step."

"I don't care. There's nothing left for me there. My mother don't want me. And her boyfriend...."

She stopped abruptly, as though she felt she had said too much.

"Is there a problem with the boyfriend?"

"I just don't like him. The way he looks at me sometimes. It just don't feel right. You know?"

"He sounds like an asshole."

She managed a weak laugh. "He is."

"But things are okay where you're at now? They're treating you okay?"

"Yeah. Thanks for asking. They sort of leave me alone. They don't ask too many questions and they don't get in my way none."

"That's good. And you have everything you need?"

She shrugged again. "I guess. Didn't get all my clothes when I left, but that's okay. I don't need them things."

Todd leaned closer. For a moment Rosaletta felt confused, wondering what he was up to. Then she realized he was reaching for the back seat, where he retrieved a plain plastic bag.

"Here." He handed the bag to her. "This is for you."

"What's this?"

"Look inside."

She hesitated, then looked within. Neatly folded in the bag were some clothes – a new pair of jeans, several tops, and a pullover sweater.

"What's this for?"

"I thought you might need something else to wear."

"I didn't expect this."

Now it was his turn to shrug.

"You didn't have to do this," she informed him. "I don't expect you to buy me things.

She started to give it back to him but he resisted, pushing the bag in her hands back toward her.

"Keep it. I want you to have it."

"But I hardly know you."

"Why does that matter? I just figured you might like it. That's all."

She still hesitated, unsure what to say.

"From one friend to another," he added.

"Thank you," she managed.

"I just hope they fit. You're about the same size as my sister so I asked her what size to get you."

"I didn't know you had a sister. What's her name?"

"Molly."

"So when am I gonna meet her?"

"One of these days. I'm sure of it."

Rosaletta looked at the clothes in the bag once more, then folded the top down to conceal the contents.

"That was real nice of you, to think of me like this."

He offered a smile as reply.

She looked outside, feeling suddenly uncomfortable to be

sitting in the car with him. "I really need to go home. Sharon will wonder where I am."

"I can drive you if you want."

"No. That's okay. I'm okay walking."

"Suit yourself."

She opened the door, stepped out of the car, then paused with her hand still on the handle.

"Thank you, Todd." She lifted the bag slightly, indicating the contents. "For this."

"Glad to do it. Hope you like what I picked out."

"I'm sure I will."

She closed the door, took a step away, then turned to face him once more. "It was nice seeing you again, Todd."

He offered a slight wave, turned the car on, and a moment later he was driving away.

Rosaletta watched his car as it came to a stop at the next intersection, halted by a traffic light. Her eyes remained focused on him until the light changed and he started once more. He turned right at the next street before disappearing from sight.

She turned, clasped the bag of clothes to her chest, and started walking.

The smile was still on her face ten minutes later when she arrived at the foster home.

Chapter Ten:

THE NEXT day when Rosaletta left school Todd was waiting for her once again, the same place as before. The situation seemed much less awkward for her this time. A smile graced the young girl's faced as she opened the door to greet the driver.

"You came back?"

"Of course." He made it sound like it was the most natural thing in the world.

Without waiting for an invitation she climbed into the car. It felt cool inside; the air conditioner hummed away, counteracting the heat generated from the sunlight pouring into the vehicle.

Rosaletta turned to face him, a look of concern on her face. "Don't you got some place better to be than stopping by here?" she asked, fearful of his answer but curious all the same.

"Not at the moment. Later tonight I need to be somewhere but there's nothing going on right now."

He seemed to notice suddenly what she was wearing. "That's one of the tops I gave you. Isn't it?"

She nodded, pulling down on the material to remove a wrinkle that blemished the appearance, doing her best to show off how well it conformed to her shape. "Fits pretty good, don't you think?"

"That it does."

He paused, admiring her for a moment.

Rosie felt self-conscious with the attention, as though she was on display for him to gawk at.

But, at the same time, it felt good to be noticed.

"Stop it," she managed at last.

"Stop what?"

"Looking at me that way."

"What way?"

"You know." She pulled away a moment, suppressing a smile, then turned to face him again. "Quit looking at me."

"Be that way."

Todd faced forward. For a moment a look crossed his face, as though he was offended with her words, but in an instant it was gone, replaced by a smile as he laughed over her situation. She joined him a moment later, surprised to find she could feel so at ease over anything considering all that had happened lately. But at that moment everything else was forgotten. Rosaletta was merely a young girl, without a care in the world and enjoying the moment life had given her.

"So where do you want to go?" Todd asked.

"I don't care. I don't really got much time, though. Sharon expects me home after school.

"Are you hungry?"

"Not really. A bit, I guess. Oh, I don't know."

"Let's get something to eat."

Without another word they pulled away.

Todd maneuvered the Firebird through downtown streets, slipping in and out of traffic with ease, and five minutes later they turned into the parking lot of a Greek Restaurant on Adams Street. It was a red-bricked structure, the bottom floor devoted to the restaurant. The windows on the second floor were shuttered tight, concealing whatever was behind.

"You ever been here?" Todd asked, as they walked toward the entrance.

"Are you kidding? If it ain't McDonald's then I ain't been

there. But I shouldn't really eat much. Sharon will have dinner ready when I get home."

They entered, Todd holding the door for her, and moments later were seated in a booth in a corner of the nearly deserted dining room.

"Sharon. Is that your foster mother?"

Rosie nodded.

"I hope she's taking good care of you."

"She tries," Rosie admitted. "But I don't think she knows how to handle what I'm going through. To be honest, I guess I really haven't made much of an effort, either."

"That's understandable. But you can't be stubborn about things, you know."

"You saying I'm stubborn?"

"Of course not. Let's face it. I don't really know you enough to say whether you're stubborn or not. But I know sometimes, when things happen in life, you just feel so alone. Like it's you against the world."

Todd stopped speaking, a faraway glint in his eyes, as though his words had reminded him of something long forgotten. It presented a more vulnerable image than Rosaletta had originally conjured up about the young man. Where previously he had seemed self-assured, and positive about things, she now realized that he too must have his doubts in life.

Rosie hesitated, wondering how to react. Without even realizing what she was doing she reached across the table, placing her hand on his. His hand felt warm, smoother than she had expected.

Her touch seemed to awaken him. He pulled away, as though embarrassed.

"All I'm saying," he continued, his words rushing forth as though he was anxious to have his say, "is that I know how hard it is to accept help from others. It makes you feel like you're weak. That you can't manage on your own.

"But you shouldn't feel that way, Rosie. If people are willing to help you, then you should let them."

"You mean people like you?"

"Sure." He smiled. "People like me."

The waiter, a swarthy young man with curly black hair, chose that moment to approach the table.

"Would you like to order now? We have a special on our Shish Kabobs...."

Todd waved the suggestion off. "Two Baklava sundaes." He turned toward Rosaletta. "Is that okay?"

"Sure."

"Very good, Sir. And to drink?"

"Just water."

Rosaletta, agreeing with the choice, nodded in reply, and the waiter left the table.

Rosie leaned back in her chair, taking a long look at the young man across from her.

"Why are we here, Todd?"

"For the baklava."

"No. That's not what I mean."

She leaned forward, stretching her hand across the table. She nearly touched his hand again – she wanted to touch his hand again – but at the last moment she decided against it.

"Why are you wasting time with someone like me?"

He shrugged. "Maybe I don't consider it a waste of time."

"Be serious." She leaned back in her chair once again. "My own mother don't even want nothing to do with me."

"Shame on her."

Rosie never heard his reply, as the words on her mind tumbled forth. "The kids at school avoid me. Even the ones I thought were my friends. Nobody wants nothing to do with me."

She wiped at her eyes, embarrassed with the tears.

"Why are you even here? Why are you the only one that seems to care?"

Now it was Todd's turn to lean across the table, bridging

the gap between them, but he made no attempt to touch her.

"That day I met you – at the funeral home – I didn't even know who you were at first. It was a long day for me, standing in that line. I can't imagine the day you must have had. But while I stood there I heard the people around me talking. About what happened to Tommy. About how you were there when it happened.

"And I remember thinking, that's something nobody should have to go through. Especially on their own. You've been through enough already.

"And then I saw the people looking at you. Uncertain how to react. Not sure what to do. But what they didn't see was what it was doing to you."

He paused to grab a paper napkin from the table, handing it to her. Rosaletta dabbed at her eyes as he continued.

"You just looked like someone who could use a friend."

She was still wiping her eyes when the Baklava sundaes showed up. The waiter, recognizing the tension at the table, left without a word.

Rosaletta, struggling to see through the tears, focused on the young man across from her. He flashed a smile, a genuine expression of friendship, and she felt for the first time since Tommy's death that maybe things could get better after all.

Chapter Eleven:

"TOMMY WAS always such a good boy."

Consuella Alegredo wrung her hands together while she spoke. It seemed a nervous habit – one she appeared unaware of. Melanie found herself watching the motion as the two of them talked. It was an irritating distraction the CASA volunteer attempted to ignore even as the grieving mother continued with the action.

"He never gave me any shit about anything," Tommy's mother was saying, in a tone of voice somewhere between praise and adoration. "He was always polite. And helpful around the house. He was a son a mother could be proud of."

"I'm sure you did a fine job raising him," Melanie added, feeling she needed to say something.

Consuella looked up. She stopped her fidgeting, her right hand finding its way to the cup of coffee on the table in front of her. She drew the mug closer, sliding the container along and leaving a trail of disrupted water rings in its wake, but made no attempt to pick it up.

"It wasn't easy. Not after...."

She stopped abruptly, as though hesitant to continue with what was on her mind. Her attention remained focused on the table in front of her.

"Tommy was only five when Josef...."

Once again the voice faltered.

As if her unspoken words explained everything she continued.

"After that it was just me and the two kids."

Melanie considered her options. She didn't want to pry – especially considering how difficult it obviously was for the woman to discuss the subject – but she couldn't help thinking that the missing information, the words that had gone unsaid, could explain a lot concerning Rosaletta's upbringing and the conflict between the mother and her child.

After a few seconds consideration the CASA volunteer elected not to pursue the matter further. When the time was right she would find out what she needed to know.

"That must have been hard for you. Raising two children on your own."

"It took some getting used to. I know things changed, after that. In so many ways. I had a hard time being strict with the kids."

She stopped to take a drink of her coffee, as though using the action to collect her thoughts.

"I guess I just didn't have it in me to get after Tommy and Rosie no more."

She spoke their names lovingly, as though recalling cherished incidents in her life. The memories seemed to allow her to live moments that were long gone to her.

"They were all I had left in the world. But I was on my own," she continued. "Trying to do it all. And we had been through so much already."

She sighed.

"I can see now that I should have been tougher with them. Especially Rosie. Once she hit her teen years there seemed to be no controlling her."

"In what way? I mean...."

Melanie paused, phrasing the words carefully in her mind before giving voice to her thoughts. "I met with Rosie the other day. She seemed out of sorts. Angry over recent events. But I didn't get the impression she was a troubled teenager. Confused, maybe. But not troubled."

"That's because you don't know Rosie. She can be manipulative about things."

"Oh? Why do you say that?"

"It's the way she uses people." She paused, a reflective expression on her face. "They way she used Tommy. She'd get him to do all sorts of shit they shouldn't be doing."

The woman's voice lowered with her next words. "Like the night at the train yard."

Melanie, her hand poised above a notebook where she was jotting down information, looked up. She had questions in her mind, concerns over what had happened that night. The information she had received from the CASA office was sketchy, at best. Melanie felt she needed to understand what had happened, to fully explain what the family was going through. But once again she couldn't help feeling she was invading the woman's privacy by pressing the issue.

It confused her, this hesitancy she felt. Wasn't that why she was here? How could she effectively help, both Rosaletta and the young girl's mother, without an adequate understanding of what they were going through?

"What did happen that night, Miss Alegredo?"

The elder woman shrugged. "Who can say? Kids do stupid shit. I think they were just showing off for each other. You know? The way kids do. Fucking around where they didn't belong."

She stood suddenly, walking away from the table. She approached the kitchen sink, leaning against the counter as though weak, her fingers white where she gripped the edge.

For several seconds the room was silent.

Nick, Consuella's boyfriend, was watching something on the television in the other room. It must have been a sporting event of some kind, because Melanie could pick up an occasional cheer of spectators and the staccato rhythm of the announcer's voice. The sound intruded, albeit softly, on the lingering silence in the kitchen.

"I really don't want to talk about it," Consuella said at last.

"I understand. We don't need to go into it further. I guess I'm just trying to understand your relationship with your daughter."

"Relationship?"

The woman turned around, a stern expression on her face.

"I'm her mother. What's to understand?"

"I'm told the police brought Rosaletta home that evening. And that there was an altercation between the two of you."

"What can you expect? What mother wants to see her teenage daughter brought home like that?"

"Did you hit her?"

There was no answer, the expression failing to change on the woman's face.

"I have to ask these things," Melanie was quick to explain. "I need to understand how things are between you and Rosie."

Consuella sat down, and once again the hand fidgeting began. "I might have. Shit, I don't know. I don't remember. I wasn't myself that night. It was a tough fucking night for me."

"It was a tough night for Rosie as well," Melanie pointed out.

"What do you want me to say?"

Anger resonated in the woman's voice. Her eyes portrayed no indication of remorse as she glared across the table at Melanie.

"What the fuck do you want me to say?" She repeated the question, as though to make certain she had Melanie's undivided attention. "You want me to say I'm sorry? That what I did was wrong? Well, whatever shit Rosie got, Rosie deserved."

Consuella stood again, pushing the chair back from the table as she rose. Her hands flew defiantly to her hips. "Who are you to be telling me how to raise my kids?"

Melanie felt suddenly on the defensive, the outburst

surprising her with its vehemence.

"I'm not trying to tell you how to raise your kids, Miss Alegredo."

"How old are you anyway? Twenty-five? Twenty-six?"

"I'm twenty-eight."

"Do you have any kids?"

"Not yet, but my husband and I are....."

"Twenty-eight, no kids, but you know all about what I should be doing with my fucking kids. You know all about what it's like to worry about putting shit on the table and keeping a roof over their heads. At the same time wondering what sort of fucking trouble they're getting into when they sneak out at night."

"I'm sure it hasn't been easy for you."

"Fuck right it ain't been easy. I do right by my kids. I always did. And I don't need someone from some highfalutin government agency that don't know shit coming into my house – MY HOUSE – and telling me what a lousy mother I am."

"I assure you, that wasn't my intention. I'm just concerned about what Rosie is going through. And how I can make things better for her."

"How about what I'm going through? How about the fact that I lost a son? Don't that mean anything to you?"

For several moments they stared at one another in silence. Melanie took several breaths, trying to calm herself down, before continuing.

"I can't begin to imagine what you're going through. I know there must be a lot of hurt. And anger. But you've already lost one child. Tommy isn't coming back to you. And there's nothing you can do about that.

"But are you prepared to lose another child? Are you ready to throw things away with Rosie?"

Melanie stood. She fought back the urge to shake, trying desperately to suppress the nervous energy that threatened to overwhelm her body. She had come today to talk to Rosie's mother, to get an idea of the situation and what the relationship between mother and daughter was like.

She had never expected such an explosive confrontation.

Finally, feeling herself under control enough to continue speaking, Melanie resumed.

"You have my deepest sympathy for what you're going through, Miss Alegredo. I know this isn't easy and I wish I could help you more. But my focus is on Rosaletta. That's why I'm here. That's why I'm talking to you now, and that's why I will continue to visit with Rosie and offer her my help and guidance until this whole issue is resolved."

She turned to leave as one more thought occurred to her.

"I just think you owe it to your daughter to have a greater appreciation of what she's going through here. Her life has been completely disrupted over all this. Your understanding and love could go a long way toward making things better for her.

"And for you."

Chapter Twelve:

FOR THE next two weeks Rosaletta followed the normal routines – going to school during the week, stopping at the Public Library several times to work on class projects, attempting to return her life to what it had been like before her brother's death – but there was nothing normal about what she was going through.

She felt completely isolated at school. Even in the past, before the accident in the train yard, she had been a loner, having no real friends and few people that even took the time to associate with her. The girls her own age tended to avoid her, as though she was competition they didn't need. The boys either shied away, as though afraid to approach her, or tended to the opposite extreme, presenting unwanted advances that only made her uncomfortable.

But now the circumstances were magnified. People turned away as she approached, uncertain how to treat her and reluctant to get involved. The student body was unprepared for dealing with Rosaletta's loss, and unaware how much their avoidance only intensified the young girl's loneliness.

Her isolation terrified her. She felt trapped, unable to resolve her situation and forced to anticipate a lifetime of emptiness ahead of her. Sometimes she found herself pausing to catch her breath, as though she was being smothered under an oppressiveness that controlled every aspect of her life. Even the simplest of tasks became ordeals to her.

Her grades had never been good. Achieving high marks wasn't a priority in Rosaletta's family. It was easier to just do the minimum work required, coasting along with the least amount of effort, than to apply yourself in the hopes that, maybe someday, it would all be worthwhile.

Somedays always seemed too far away, especially after what happened to Tommy.

A few of the teachers at school attempted to reach the troubled teenager, offering words of condolences. Mrs. Tripoli, Rosaletta's English instructor, pulled the young girl aside one day after class.

"I'm truly sorry about your loss, Rosie."

Uncertain how to reply, the teenager managed a meek reply. "Thank you."

"I understand what you're going through. How devastating something like this can be. But remember. There are people you can talk to. People who can help you through this. Don't be afraid to reach out to them."

For several moments they stared at one another in silence.

"If you need anything," Mrs. Tripoli continued, "please don't hesitate to ask. If I don't know the answer I promise to find someone who does. Okay?"

The words sounded sincere, and for a moment Rosie felt better having heard them, but it was a fleeting moment only. As Rosie walked away she realized there was nothing this woman could do for her. Her brother was gone. Nothing anyone could do or say could change that. This was a private matter, something Rosaletta knew she could only deal with on her own, and no well-meaning words from a stranger could change things.

She no longer saw Mickey and Jason. At first this hurt her deeply, another loss that reminded her of Tommy's departure. Rosie had felt close to the two boys for a long time, sharing in their activities or even just hanging out together with them and doing nothing. They had always accepted her; always made her feel like she belonged.

But they were Tommy's friends. They were his age, in his classes. She could see now that the only reason they had ever included her was because Tommy had demanded it. With Tommy gone there was no reason for Mickey and Jason to be involved with a girl so much younger than them.

It was just another loss she would have to adjust to.

School became more of an ordeal than ever before. Rosaletta managed somehow to make it through each day, anticipating the moment the final bell would ring and she could leave the stifling atmosphere of the classrooms behind her.

But returning home was only another obstacle to overcome.

Life at home, in the run-down apartment with her mother and whoever her mother's current boyfriend happened to be at the time, had never been good. There was the constant friction of too many people in too confined of a spot, leading ultimately to ongoing arguments that never resolved themselves and only increased the tension between the participants. It was no wonder Tommy and Rosaletta sought time away from the place, roaming the streets at night, seeking resolutions they never found but relishing the opportunity to be anywhere but home.

Rosie didn't miss the apartment. She certainly didn't miss her mother, and the constant bickering associated with the woman.

But as bad as it had been – an unloving household that neither nurtured nor protected the fifteen-year-old girl – at least there was a certain amount of familiarity to the place. Rosie had known what to expect with her life then. Even with the constantly changing drama that managed to surround the family she knew what she was walking into every day when she came home.

It was different with her foster family.

Neal and Sharon Daniels seemed uncertain how to deal with having a teenage girl under their roof. They were attentive to her needs. They made certain she had the basic necessities, anything she required for school or personal use. They insisted on a family meal together each evening, as though it was important to spend time together.

But there was a barricade between them, an unseen barrier that prevented closeness. Their lifestyle, their home, felt too unusual for Rosie to adapt to. It was as though their house was on display, a testimony to their willingness to help a child in need by providing the ideal living conditions.

It may not have even been a conscious desire on their part. Rosaletta felt like they were interested in her situation, and did want to be of assistance to her. But they seemed to lack the ability to relate to her. Rosie's background – her experiences in life – were foreign to Neal and Sharon. There was no common ground between them, nothing they could relate to that would bring them closer.

So each day after school Rosaletta Guiterrez would walk to her new home and make the best of the situation.

And each night she would cry herself to sleep, feeling alone and forgotten and wondering what the rest of her life had in store for her.

What made matters worse was that she hadn't seen Todd since the day they had shared desert at the Greek restaurant.

She missed him already. He seemed the one person in her life that accepted her and saw past the troubles she was going through. He spoke with her as though things were normal; like they were two friends visiting one another and neither had anything to hide. Something about his attitude, a carefree easiness that pervaded him, made her feel instantly comfortable around the young man.

And – Rosie admitted to herself, late at night when she laid in bed and thought about Todd – he was easy on the eyes.

Rosie knew she was making too much of the situation.

There was no way someone like him could be interested in somebody like her. She was just a kid, after all. And everything about him – the clothes he wore, the car he drove, the way he settled into conversations with an easy rhythm and total lack of airs – indicated to Rosaletta that he was somebody comfortable, not only with himself, but with his place in life.

She wanted to see him again. She knew that much. She wanted to spend time with him, and forget about the rest of her life.

She told herself next time he saw her she wouldn't hesitate. She would jump in his car and he could take her anywhere. As long as they were together.

It would be so nice to escape from everything else.

But two weeks stretched into three, and Rosaletta's life remained unchanged.

And each night she would cry herself to sleep.

Chapter Thirteen:

THE ADJUDICATION Hearing – the first step in bringing Rosaletta and her mother back together – was only three weeks away, yet Melanie felt like she still had so much to do before then.

She realized that a large portion of her concern was due to inexperience. This was her first case; the first time she would have to appear in court as one of the active participants instead of merely as a spectator. Her perfectionist tendencies came to the fore when she considered the role she played as a CASA volunteer. She wanted to be certain she didn't make any mistakes, so one day while Andy was at work and she had some time to herself she reviewed the case yet again in her mind.

Following the night Rosaletta's brother died – and the young girl was taken from her mother's home – Children's Services had held an Emergency Hearing at the Lucas County Juvenile Center. This was before Melanie was even involved in the matter, because at this point it was too early in the process for the office to assign a CASA to the case.

Annie Klume, a caseworker for Children's Services, was in charge of the investigation for Lucas County. Melanie hadn't met Annie yet, but they had corresponded through email. Melanie had also reviewed the case files the social worker had prepared both before and following the Emergency Hearing, which gave her much of the background concerning Rosaletta and her mother and the volatile relationship that existed between the two of them.

The next step in the process – from a legal point of view – was the Adjudication Hearing, which usually took place within six to eight weeks of the Emergency Hearing. At this point the principals would appear before Magistrate Elizabeth Jennings to review the pertinent facts of the case. Present would be the mother, Consuella Alegredo, along with her attorney. Typically the father would be there as well with his attorney, but this obviously wouldn't be the case with Rosaletta's hearing.

As Melanie understood it Lucas County would present the allegations against Miss Alegredo, asking for a ruling of child neglect and abuse against the mother. They would also review a case plan, a blueprint of services they wished to see established for the various family members. There would be an explanation of the classes and sessions Rosaletta and her mother would be expected to attend in an effort to resolve the dispute between them, dealing with such issues as good parenting techniques and anger management.

No doubt therapy sessions would also be suggested in Rosaletta's case, to help the young girl deal with the trauma associated with her brother Tommy's death.

Ultimately the goal of the court system was reunification; to bring the family back together. The willingness of Rosaletta and her mother to follow through on the treatments suggested by Children's Services in the months ahead would determine the final outcome of the case. The process often took a year – or longer – and Melanie would be involved every step of the way, monitoring activities and gauging the progress of events.

The day of the Adjudication Hearing – when all these details would be finalized and the court put its approval on everything – Consuella would have the opportunity to defend herself against the allegations of child neglect and child abuse. She would have her day in court.

The child involved – in this case Rosaletta Guiterrez – would be represented by the CASA volunteer. It was Melanie's responsibility to insure the child's wishes and desires were brought to light and the teenager wasn't overlooked by the court.

And there was something else.

Something Melanie knew she was forgetting, but couldn't put her finger on.

She pulled out a loose leaf binder, a large white folder that held the accumulated class reports and the notes she had taken during her training. Perhaps she would find what she was looking for by re-reading some of the material. With the hearing so close it seemed like a good idea to review things, anyway.

She delved into the information, surprised by how much she had forgotten already, and partway through she found the information she desired.

It was called the "Voices" Acknowledgment Form.

Every child over the age of ten was granted the right to speak with the magistrate at Juvenile Court. This was their opportunity to express themselves and let their wishes be known.

Reviewing her training notes, Melanie saw there were certain options available to the youth. Foremost was if they even wanted to have their say. If they chose not to attend the hearing that was their prerogative. The court had decided that youths aged ten and older were mature enough to make this kind of decision themselves.

Assuming they decided to go to court they still had other decisions to make. They could appear in front of everybody in the open courtroom and say what they wanted to say.

Melanie imagined this option wasn't taken advantage of very often, particularly in cases where a child could be fearful of repercussions from an angry parent.

More than likely, the child would talk to the magistrate ahead of time, in private chambers, without their parents or Children's Services being present. This would give the child the opportunity to speak their mind freely. If the child so chose they could have an adult present while talking to the magistrate – the social worker, a doctor or therapist, or even the CASA who represented the child. Once again, this was the child's decision to make.

After reviewing the details Melanie set the folder down. In the excitement of dealing with her first case, and considering the many new and unaccustomed details she was having to become adjusted to, she had neglected to speak with Rosaletta about this opportunity and the decision the young girl would have to make.

This was a mistake that would have to be rectified.

Melanie pulled out her cellphone, dialing the number for the foster parents who were caring for the young girl.

"Hello?"

She recognized the voice immediately. "Hello, Neal. This is Melanie Powers, from the CASA office."

"Hello, Melanie. What can I do for you?"

"While reviewing my notes I realized there was something I needed to talk to Rosaletta about. I was hoping to stop by to see her again."

"It was my understanding the CASA only visited the child once a month?"

"That's generally the case. But I need to discuss some things with Rosie, concerning the hearing, and since it's only a few weeks away I don't want to delay seeing her. It really is important."

Neal hesitated, as though mulling things over. "When did you want to stop by?"

"I know this is short notice, but I'm available any time this evening. I work the next three nights, then I'm not off again until Saturday. But anytime Saturday works for me as well. I don't want to put you and your wife out, so whatever fits your schedule I'll try to work around."

"I don't know what Sharon has planned for the weekend," he informed her. "But we don't have anything going on tonight. Would that be okay?"

"That would be great. What time works for you? I don't want to interrupt your dinner."

"Can you make it after 6:30?"

"Works for me. And I apologize again for the short notice. I'll see you tonight."

Melanie hung up, pleased that she would be able to see Rosaletta on such short notice, but embarrassed with herself for having been so ill-prepared on their initial meeting. She knew she had a lot to learn as a CASA volunteer. No doubt things would get easier with more time, and experience, under her belt, and she could avoid these types of situations.

She also hoped this didn't tarnish her professionalism in the eyes of the foster parents.

Or in Rosaletta's opinion, either. The young girl was going through a lot right now. She needed someone on her side, someone prepared to accept the challenges ahead and provide the proper advice and guidance the young girl would need.

Melanie found herself wondering, not for the first time, if she was indeed the right person for this job.

Chapter Fourteen:

"SO HOW are you doing, Rosaletta?"

The young girl shrugged, as though it was a question she hadn't ever considered before.

"Things are okay, I guess."

"Have you talked to your mother lately?" Melanie knew that, until the Adjudication Hearing, Consuella Alegredo was not permitted to spend time with her daughter. At the hearing times and lengths of visits would be determined, to allow the two family members the opportunity to interact while they worked on the reconciliation process.

Until then they were encouraged to keep in touch with one another. Most likely it would be through phone calls between the two of them. Social Media accounts, such as Facebook and Twitter, were often used for these purposes, especially among children Rosaletta's age. The stumbling block here was that these methods required computer access or the use of a smartphone. Melanie was pretty certain such services were not available to Rosaletta's mother, who seemed to be struggling just to keep her head above water.

"Me and Mama talked last week," Rosaletta replied, in answer to Melanie's query.

"Who initiated the conversation?"

"I did. But it weren't really much of a conversation. Mama didn't have much to say."

"Give her time. I'm sure she's still hurting. With everything that's been going on."

"So you're on her side now?" Rosaletta's voice betrayed her confusion. "I thought you was looking out for me?"

"I am looking out for you."

Melanie reached forward, to offer her hand in friendship, but the young girl pulled away without a word.

"There aren't any sides here, Rosie. It's just a family coming apart and people – people like me and the people at Children's Services – trying to keep things together."

"What if I don't want it to stay together? What if I'm tired of Mama and all her crap and don't want nothing to do with her no more?"

"Is that really how you feel?"

"I don't know. Sometimes, I guess. I'm just tired of fighting with her all the time. And being told how useless I am."

"Does she put you down a lot?"

The young girl nodded.

"I'm sorry to hear that. But maybe that's the only thing your mother knows. Maybe she just needs to learn how to be more encouraging."

"She never had no problem with Tommy!"

"Oh?"

"Tommy never did nothing wrong. His grades were always better than mine. He always kept his things cleaner than I done. No matter what it was, whenever my mother compared the two of use, Tommy was always the winner."

"She can't do that to you anymore, Rosie. It's just you and her now."

"Don't remind me. Sometimes I wish I could leave it all behind me and not have to deal with her no more."

"Where would you stay?"

Rosaletta looked around, at the plainly furnished room and the unadorned walls surrounding her.

"This place ain't so bad," she decided. "I could just stay

here."

"That may not be an option."

"Why not?"

"Because the courts will decide what happens if you and your mother can't patch things up."

"Don't I get no say in nothing?"

"As a matter of fact...."

Melanie opened the folder she had brought with her to the visit, withdrawing a single sheet of paper with some printed information on it. She stood, to take a few steps closer to the girl huddled against the head of the bed, and held out the form.

This time Rosaletta made no attempt to draw away. She took the paper – eagerly, almost – but made no attempt to look at it. Instead her attention was focused on the CASA volunteer.

"What's this?"

"You do have a say in things, Rosie. You're entitled to come to court and tell the magistrate exactly how you feel about the situation. You can say whatever you want."

"Yeah." Her skepticism was obvious. "I'm sure Mama's gonna like hearing that."

"She doesn't have to hear it. You can talk to the magistrate alone."

"Really?"

Melanie nodded. "Or, if you're uncomfortable with that, you can have someone go in with you. Maybe you'd like Annie Klume there. She's the caseworker from Children's Services."

"I don't think so," Rosaletta quickly replied. "Last time she was here she was telling me how hard it is for Mama. That I should be a good daughter and be there for her."

"I suppose there's a certain amount of truth to that."

"Why don't it work the other way around? Why can't she be there for me?"

Melanie hesitated, uncertain how to reply. She turned around, returning to her seat before responding. This gave her a few moments to collect her thoughts.

"It's a funny thing about mothers," Melanie began.

"When we're young we look up to our parents. We think they're the smartest people in the world. We think they have the answers to all life's problems."

"I never thought that about my parents."

"That's a shame. I'm sorry to hear that, Rosie. It sounds like your relationship has suffered all along."

"Blame that on Mama. She's the one always treated me so bad. She was always so wrapped up in her own crap that she never found time for me."

"Try to remember, Rosie, parents are people too. They were young once, just like you, and they grew up with the same doubts and questions you have. Maybe your mother didn't have anyone there for her, to teach her the things she needed to know. Maybe she just never learned how to give of herself."

It was obvious from her expression that the young girl remained unconvinced.

A new thought occurred to Melanie.

"Maybe you could be that someone, Rosie. Maybe you could help your mother grow to become a better person. It might be just what both of you need."

The teenager turned away for a moment. When she faced Melanie again she nearly said something, as though she was struggling with how to express herself and couldn't find the proper words. She finally gave up on the attempt.

Instead she bent her head down to examine the form Melanie had given her.

For several minutes nothing was said, as Rosaletta read the information and took the time to process what it meant to her.

"So I can really do this?" she asked at last. "I can go to court and tell them how I feel?"

"Yes you can. You have a say in what happens in your life. That's important to the courts."

Then, as an afterthought, Melanie continued. "It's important to me, too. That's why I'm here."

"And when it's time to talk to the.... What did you call

it?"

"The magistrate."

"Yeah. The magistrate. If I wanted you to come in with me you would do that?"

The question was an unexpected one, but it made Melanie pause to consider. Maybe she could make a difference in the young girl's life after all?

She resisted the urge to smile.

"Yes, Rosie. I could go in there with you. I'd be happy to go in there with you."

As though she had said too much, or revealed a side of her she was reluctant to expose, the teenager suddenly pulled away. She tossed the form carelessly onto the bed, an insignificant matter that she couldn't be bothered with.

"I guess I'll think about it."

"Just let me know, Rosie. That's all I ask."

Later, in the room by herself, Rosaletta Guiterrez picked up the form she had been given earlier and read it once again. She wasn't sure if she could go through with it – walk into the courtroom and tell the magistrate exactly how she felt about her mother and her life and all the things that had happened to her. But she liked the idea.

It was the first good thing that had happened to her since the accident that had taken her brother away from her.

No.

That wasn't quite true.

There was something else.

She remembered the first time she met Todd, at the funeral home, and how relaxed she had felt around him.

And later, talking together in his car, she had felt like here was somebody that was actually interested in her. Somebody that accepted her for who she was. It had felt great being with Todd, and forgetting – for a little while, at least – what was going on in her life.

But even that had passed. She hadn't seen Todd in over

three weeks now. By this point she was certain she wouldn't be seeing him again.

It had all been a trick.

It was as though life insisted on playing games with her. Promising something nice then yanking it away. She wasn't lucky enough to have anything good happen to her.

She looked again at the paper Melanie Cox had left behind.

It was just another con. It was just the grownups way of making her think she was being listened to. When it got right down to it nobody cared what happened to her.

They never had.

They never would.

In a fit of fury she wrinkled the paper, twisting it between her fingers into a little ball. She tossed it across the room. Without a sound it hit the wall and dropped to the floor, hidden now behind the dresser.

Rosaletta threw herself onto the bed and buried her face in the covers.

Chapter Fifteen:

THE FIREBIRD – Todd's Firebird – was parked once again in the familiar spot, on the side of the road partway between Woodward High and The Daniels' home.

Rosaletta nearly walked by without noticing it.

For the first few days Todd was gone – following the last time she'd seen him – Rosie had wondered what he was up to. It's not that she was concerned about his absence. After all, what did she really know about him? Maybe his job was keeping him busy? Or something with his family, some personal issue she knew nothing about, was occupying his time? He certainly didn't owe her any explanations. If he had something to do for a few days that was all right with her.

But with each passing day, each time she walked home from school expecting Todd to be there only to be disappointed, she became more and more convinced that she was never going to see him again.

The more she thought about it, that only made sense.

Why would anyone waste their time with someone like her? Rosie was a loser, a troubled teenage girl from a broken family who had nothing to offer to anyone. There was no reason for anyone to want to see her.

With time she accepted the fact and attempted to move on with her life. She tried to tell herself that if she threw herself into her school work, as an escape from everything else around her, then things would be better.

But she knew that wasn't true. School bored her. She had no friends there, no interest in the activities that took place in the classrooms. It was just a place to spend time, lingering each day away, longing for the opportunity to leave it all behind and move on with her life.

She had settled into a routine at the foster home as well. She was fairly certain Neal and Sharon Daniels meant well. They tried to be attentive to her needs. They tried to include her in their life.

But she knew she didn't fit in. Their middle class existence and family values were foreign to her way of thinking. Rosie understood it was an artificial existence only, a temporary fix while she waited for her life to get back on track. She saw no future with them.

So she struggled through each day, having abandoned all hope of ever seeing Todd Burkett again.

Yet there he was, parked once more in the familiar parking space.

She nearly turned and ran the other way. She had been hurt by his absence. His inattention to her, his apparent lack of concern for what she was going through, troubled her greatly.

But she missed him too much to turn away now. Catching her breath, straightening her hair, she moved toward his vehicle, hoping not to appear too anxious but excited with the prospect of seeing him again.

She walked to his car, opened the door, but made no attempt to get inside. Instead she merely stood there. She said nothing, content to wait for him to make the first move.

"You can sit down if you like," he finally offered.

So she sat, closing the door behind her, but still she said nothing. She stared ahead out the windshield. Several of her classmates passed by, girls she recognized but really had nothing to do with. They didn't notice the couple in the red sports car.

They were too intent with their own lives, and their own interests, to pay any attention to such matters. They seemed to have somewhere to go; as though they had someone waiting for them. No doubt they all had friends and families to go home to.

All of them but Rosaletta, she reflected. No one was waiting for her.

It was quiet in the car, the only sound the two of them breathing. Rosie wanted to face Todd, to see him again after all this time, but she was determined not to make the first move.

Finally he broke the stalemate.

"I'm sorry."

She faced him then, torn between anger and tears.

"You should be. I didn't think I'd ever see you again."

"Look, it couldn't be helped. I was called out of town. Some business I had to take care of."

"Business that was more important than me?"

"I said I was sorry. What more do you want? I wanted to let you know, but I had no way of telling you what was going on."

"You could have found a way. You *should* have found a way."

"Well, it won't happen again."

"I don't believe you." She turned away to stare out the window, reluctant to look his direction. "I want to believe you. But I don't."

"What if I promised you that it would never happen again?'

She faced him once more.

"Promises are cheap. I been getting promises all my life and what good did it ever do me?"

"But this is different."

"How do I know that? I want to believe you, Todd. But I don't think you can convince me."

Without a word he leaned closer, reaching out to her. He held something in his hand, though Rosie couldn't make out what.

"This is for you," he told her.

She opened her hand, to accept what he had to offer, and a moment later was holding a cellphone.

"My number's already been programmed into it," he explained.

"I don't understand."

"Like I told you, I didn't know how to get hold of you while I was gone. That won't be a problem anymore. And if you ever need to get hold of me...."

He tapped the phone with his finger to indicate the point he was making.

"All you have to do is call me."

For a few seconds she said nothing, staring at the device in her hand. It was a simple phone, small in size, a drab gray in color, but to Rosie it was something else. It was a sign of commitment on Todd's part. He had reached out to her, offering her the opportunity to be a part of his life.

Rosie felt her mood changing, her anger beginning to dissipate. Todd must have sensed it as well. He became more animated with his conversation, aware that he had softened her with the gift.

"It comes with prepaid minutes," he explained. "So you won't be able to use it a lot. But when you need more I can add to it any time."

He smiled, the smile she had missed so much in the last few weeks.

"Thank you."

She spoke the words softly, still surprised with the gift. It was so unexpected.

Todd continued. "Now don't go freaking out on me if you call and I don't answer right away. Sometimes I'm busy and can't get to my phone. Just leave a message and I'll get back to you. Okay?"

"Yeah. That's fine."

"So am I forgiven?"

It was her turn to smile now. "Of course you are. It's

just...."

She fumbled with the words. She knew she should stop talking. There was nothing to be gained by continuing. But she couldn't help it as the words came tumbling out.

"I didn't think I was gonna see you again. After losing Tommy. And my mother kicking me out of the house. Life's just been so crappy lately."

The tears started, the emotion she'd been struggling to contain washing over her.

"Why can't I ever get a break? Why do I have to be so miserable all the time? Is it too much to ask for me to get something nice once in a while?"

"Of course not." He reached over, placing his hand lightly on her arm. "Life gets tough sometimes, Rosie. It certainly has for you."

His hand felt nice against her skin, giving her strength and encouragement, though it failed to abate the rising sense of frustration she felt. Hopelessness washed over her when she considered what she had been through lately.

"I wish I could just run away from it all. Just take off and leave Toledo forever. Nobody would miss me anyway."

"Is that what you really want to do?"

"Yes."

"Then why don't you?"

She paused, examining his features, wondering if he was just making fun of her or if he was actually serious.

"You don't mean that, do you?" Rosie asked at last.

"Why not? There's a whole world out there, you know."

"It just seems such a big step. I don't know...."

"So you stay here, then." There was a note of finality in his tone. It was as though he was expressing an alternative that didn't make sense to him. "Then what happens?"

"I have court in a week and a half."

"And you think that's going to change things?"

She shrugged. "It might. My CASA worker says I can talk to the magistrate. Tell her how I feel about things."

"What good will that do?"

"If they know how I feel, maybe I can finally get what I want instead of being shoved around all the time."

He shook his head, obviously disagreeing with her line of reasoning.

"Wake up, Rosie. You really think some hotshot in a courtroom is going to give a crap about what a teenage girl wants? Grownups rule the world. Don't you know that?"

He continued, a trace of anger accenting his voice as he warmed to his topic.

"Sure, they talk real big. Like they want to be your friend. Like they're so concerned about what you're going through. But when it gets right down to it they don't care at all."

"How can you say that?"

"Because I've seen enough to know the way things work. The only thing you get out of life is what you put into it. I'm not about to let somebody tell me what to do with my life. And I don't think you should either."

"That's not gonna happen. I'll stand up for myself. You'll see."

"I hope so."

His voice grew calmer then, his emotions under control.

"It might not be easy, you know."

She shrugged. "My life ain't been easy so far. So what else is new?"

She tried to smile, but it was a hollow gesture only.

"Just don't forget. If you need a friend I'm here. If there's any way I can help just let me know."

"Thanks, Todd. That means a lot to me."

This time she reached out to him. Their fingers touched, and for a moment she found herself looking deeply into his eyes.

As though embarrassed, he suddenly turned away. He spoke quickly, as though to cover his feelings.

"So do you want to get something to eat before you head home?"

"I'd like that."

"Good. Because I'm hungry."

Chapter Sixteen:

Annie KLUME was a short woman. The top of her head barely reached Melanie's chin. She was older than Melanie expected as well. For some reason Melanie had pictured a young woman, full of spirit and energy, enthusiastic about the role she was playing in shaping people's lives.

Instead the woman had a haggard and worn look to her. From the top of her gray hair to the bottom of her well-worn loafers Annie presented the image of someone who had fought a long hard battle and ended up the loser. Where Melanie was hoping for encouragement, perhaps a mentor to guide her through the process that lay ahead, she found instead a government employee weary of the struggles and hardships she faced every day.

They met for the first time outside the courtroom the day of the Adjudication Hearing. No one else from the case was present yet so they sat down together to talk.

"Is Rosie here yet?" Melanie asked, after the introductions were complete.

"No," Annie replied. "Sharon will be dropping her off. Normally I would have brought her myself, but my caseload is getting pretty heavy lately. This is my second hearing today, and I have another one after lunch."

"Sounds like you keep busy."

"There's no absence of work, that's for certain. I wouldn't mind a slow week once in a while. But that never seems to happen."

"How long have you been a caseworker?"

Annie looked her over. "How old are you, dearie?"

"Twenty-eight."

Annie didn't roll her eyes, but somehow the expression she presented portrayed the same feeling. "Let's just put it this way. I've been doing this since before you were even a gleam in your daddy's eyes."

"It must be a good feeling, when you consider all the people you've helped over the years."

"Ahh. Enthusiasm." She nodded her head. "You're still pretty new at this, aren't you Melanie?"

"Yes I am. I just started. Actually, this is my first case."

"Then maybe I shouldn't even say anything."

The puzzled look on Melanie's face prompted the caseworker to continue.

"I don't want to give you the wrong impression, that's all. I was like you once. Young. Excited about helping others. But when you've seen some of the things I've seen...."

She paused, her hands twitching nervously. Melanie had the impression that, were she given the opportunity, Annie would like nothing better than to have a cigarette in her hand.

"Now, don't get me wrong. People like us, we can do a lot of good. There's children out there that need us. We can make their lives a whole lot better for them.

"But for every success story there's a failure waiting to happen. Some child that ends up abused and hurt, even after the system has done everything it can for them, and there's nothing you could have done to prevent it. Or else a decision comes down that you just aren't happy with. You know it's wrong. You know it's not in the best interest of the children involved. But all you can do is move on to the next case and hope for something better."

"So how do you deal with it?"

Annie smiled, and for a moment Melanie detected a spark of joy in her eyes.

"Because sometimes, when everything goes right, and you look back on all the hard work that got you to that point, you can tell yourself you made a difference. Because of you there's someone living a happier life. A well-adjusted, normal life."

She sighed, then. Not in annoyance. Or in despair. Somehow the gesture connoted a feeling of satisfaction.

"Yes, I get frustrated. But at the end of the day I'm glad I'm here."

As she finished her recitation a figure reached the top of the stairs across from them. Rosaletta smiled when she saw them, a meek display that revealed her indecision. She waved slightly and approached the two women.

Annie leaned closer to Melanie. She presented a final summation, quietly so only the CASA worker could hear her.

"Just remember, dearie. We don't do it for us." She motioned with her eyes toward the approaching teenager. "We do it for people like Rosie."

Annie was first to speak to the new arrival. "Where's Sharon?"

"Guess she didn't feel like coming in," Rosie explained. "Said it was too nice out and she was gonna just take a walk or something."

As she spoke the young girl glanced around, taking in the surroundings. A counter on one side of the floor was manned by several clerks, who checked in each new arrival. Plastic chairs, worn with age and use, filled the center of the room. They were arranged in groups of three or four, to at least allow a modicum of privacy to the people waiting for their hearings.

Down a hallway to the right was a series of doors, each labeled with the name of the magistrate who held sessions in the room beyond. Nothing was fancy or flashy. It was a working environment, a necessary component of the juvenile court system.

Rosie turned back toward the two women but said nothing.

"You look nervous," Annie suggested.

"I guess I am."

"Well, don't be. Everyone here is looking out for you. We're all on your side."

"Even the magistrate?" Rosie asked.

"*Especially* the magistrate," Annie assured her. "Magistrate Jennings has been around for a long time. She's seen it all. She understands how hard it is being a teenager."

Melanie spoke up. "Rosie has decided to speak to the magistrate today," she informed the caseworker.

"Good for you," Annie exclaimed.

Rosie shrugged, as if uncertain whether she was doing the right thing. "I guess. I don't know. Maybe this ain't such a good idea after all. What do I say to her?"

"Just tell her how you feel about things. Be honest. She can't help you if she doesn't know what you want."

Rosaletta turned toward Melanie.

"Can you go in with me?" Rosie asked.

"If that's what you want."

She paused, as though to consider, then nodded her head. "I'm pretty nervous. I think it will help if I don't have to face her alone."

"Then of course I'll go with you."

Eventually others arrived. The attorney for Lucas County was there, as well as another lawyer Annie identified as Lucy Lemly. Lucy was there to represent Rosaletta's mother, who hadn't shown up yet.

As they waited it became more obvious that Rosie was indeed ill-at-ease. She refused to sit down, while at the same time couldn't manage standing still. She moved around in tight little circles, hovering close to Melanie as though afraid to be on her own. At one point she stopped her pacing to ask a question.

"So when do I talk to the magistrate? How does this all

work?"

Melanie ran her upper teeth over her lower lip. It was a nervous tick she tried to suppress but, sometimes, it worked its way loose. "To be honest, Rosie, I've never done this before. I submitted the paperwork to the CASA office, so they know you want to have your say. I just don't know enough about the process to tell you what to expect."

Annie, the voice of authority in the room, spoke up. "You'll be called in before the hearing, Rosie. You'll approach the bench and introduce yourself to Magistrate Jennings. She'll ask you some questions, and if you want you can ask her questions as well. It shouldn't take more than a couple minutes."

"Then what?"

"Then you'll be excused from the room. You won't be there for the hearing itself."

The teenager nodded. "I guess it don't sound too bad."

"Just tell the truth," Annie encouraged. "That's the main thing. Don't try to pull anything over on the magistrate and you'll get along fine."

Rosie made to respond but stopped suddenly, detecting something out of the corner of her eye. Melanie noticed the glance and looked in the indicated direction. Consuella Alegredo, along with her boyfriend Nick, was approaching.

"Hello, Rosie."

There was nothing familiar in the mother's greeting; nothing that could be construed as an attempt to reach out to her daughter. There was a total lack of inflection, the type of greeting one would use on a total stranger. But at least, Melanie reflected, some of the anger she had witnessed in the woman during their previous meeting seemed to have evaporated.

"Hello, Mama." Rosie's tone was noncommittal as well.

A silence followed, as mother and child stared at one another. They both seemed embarrassed by the moment. It was as though something was expected of them, some sign of affection that was required to pass between them, but neither knew where to find it.

Those witness to the scene were spared further awkwardness when a young clerk approached them.

"Miss Guiterrez? Magistrate Jennings will see you now."

Rosie turned toward Melanie. "Are you coming in?"

"Right behind you."

They followed the clerk, and moments later it was just the two of them facing the high desk where the magistrate sat.

Magistrate Elizabeth Jennings was in her mid-fifties. Her hair was tied back in a severe bun, giving her a stern demeanor. She wore no jewelry – not even a wedding ring – and the black robe she wore concealed whatever clothes she had on beneath. Melanie couldn't help but think of the assorted schoolmarms she had seen portrayed on television and in the movies, dour spinsters who wore perpetual somber expressions.

But when the woman smiled her face lit up, breaking the tension in the room. She faced Rosie directly as she greeted them. "You must be Rosaletta Guiterrez?"

"Yes I am."

"I'm pleased to meet you, Miss Guiterrez. Though I'm sorry it had to be under these circumstances."

She turned then to face Melanie.

"And you are?"

"Melanie Powers, from the CASA office. I'm Rosie's guardian in the case."

"Very good." She faced Rosie again. "Miss Guiterrez. I want you to be aware that you may speak freely in front of me. If there is anything you don't want Miss Powers to hear she can be excused to wait outside."

"No." She turned slightly, offering a meek smile to the CASA volunteer. "I want Melanie to be here."

"Then let's continue. I have read the reports on this case, and I want to express my deep sympathy to you in regards to your brother. I'm certain the last few months have been a trying experience for you. Do you feel you have enough presence of mind to think things through clearly and answer any questions I may have?"

"Yes. I do."

"So what is it you want, Miss Guiterrez?"

The question seemed to surprise the young girl, who turned toward Melanie for support.

The CASA worker answered for the teenager. "I believe Rosaletta is confused concerning the hearing. She's uncertain what her options are, and what to expect in the future."

"Is that true, Miss Guiterrez?"

Rosie nodded.

"Then let me set your mind at ease. We're not here to force you to do anything you don't want to do. We want you to be safe. And we want you to be willing to abide by our decision in this case, realizing that we have your best interest in mind."

Rosaletta managed a smile.

"However," Magistrate Jennings continued, "this doesn't give you the right to do whatever you want. You are still a minor, and as such you aren't prepared to live on your own. We would like to see you return to your mother's care, if that is agreeable to all. If that doesn't work out – due to reluctance on either one of your parts or a failure to reconcile the differences you have between you – then suitable adult supervision will be provided for you, either through a foster family or adopted services."

A confused look crossed the teenager's face. "I thought I had a say in things?"

"You do. If you feel unsafe with your mother – if you feel it is an environment that could be dangerous to you – then we certainly won't return you to live with her. On the other hand...."

She shifted slightly in her seat. Melanie noticed the smile fading slightly.

"If you're just mad at your mother, and don't feel like obeying her rules, don't think we're going to go along with you. Parents have a responsibility to their children. To keep them safe. To provide for them. To nurture them. Sometimes there are tough decisions to be made along the way. But that's what parents do. Just keep that in mind."

She stopped, as though expecting a reply, but none came. Melanie, her attention riveted on Rosaletta, could see indecision on the young girl's face. It was obvious that the magistrate's words were not what the teenager had been expecting to hear.

Chapter Seventeen:

"**I** STILL can't get over how good it felt, being in court today. It felt like I was actually making a difference."

Melanie paused, the heady feeling of accomplishment that had enveloped her at the hearing still overwhelming her. She took a sip from her iced tea, swirling the glass afterward to chill the beverage, then faced her husband.

"I know my job at the hospital is rewarding. On a personal level, I mean. As a nurse, I get to help people all the time. But this was.... Different, somehow."

Andy, sitting across the table from her, smiled at his wife.

"Sounds like you had a pretty successful day."

"I did, if I do say so myself."

"And it wasn't as bad as you thought it would be?"

"No. Everything went pretty smoothly, actually. No flare-ups from the mother, which was good. I was afraid she'd make a big scene."

"I imagine people act differently when they're in front of a judge."

"Could be. Though I sort of got the impression, from the last time we talked, that she was pretty used to speaking her mind about things."

The conversation lagged for a moment, as Melanie took a bite of her lasagna. Meanwhile Andy swirled spaghetti onto his fork, using a piece of breadstick to hold the noodles in place.

They had met at The Olive Garden after Andy got off work, for what Melanie considered a celebratory dinner following her first appearance in a courtroom. The dinner was winding down now, the meal nearly over.

Melanie placed her fork on the plate, dabbing at her mouth with the napkin before continuing.

"Though, to be honest, this is a pretty easy case I'm dealing with."

"Why do you say that?"

"It just feels like it will be resolving itself soon. I don't really see any major issues here. The family's been though a lot. That's pretty much a given. I think they just need to work their way through things.

"It certainly isn't like some of the cases they talked about during my training, with the things some of these kids have to deal with. Parents that are all doped up – addicted to who knows what – neglecting their children while they ruin their own lives. Or parents who abuse their kids."

She shivered slightly with the thought, as though a chill had gone up her spine.

"I'm not sure how I would handle that."

"You'd handle it the way you do anything else," Andy replied. "With the skill and patience and understanding you bring to everything you do."

Melanie smiled, though whether it was a reaction to her husband's words or in remembrance of the day's events she couldn't say.

"I feel like I'm starting to reach her."

"You mean the daughter?"

"That's right. At first I thought it would never happen. It seemed she didn't want anything to do with me. Or anybody, I guess. But then when she asked me to talk to the magistrate with her...."

She paused, reflecting on the moment.

"It made you feel important," Andy offered.

Melanie paused, considering her husband's words. "I

suppose that was it. Because it did make me feel pretty good."

As soon as the words left her lips a worried expression came across her face. "Is that selfish of me?"

"Why would you say that?"

"Because I'm supposed to be helping children. I wanted to do this for them. It's not about making me feel good."

"Why can't it be both? There's nothing wrong with feeling a sense of satisfaction. You're doing a good thing here, Mel. You're making a difference in a young girl's life. A young – troubled – girl's life. And there is a lot of trouble a teenage girl can get into these days."

"You sound like my father, now. Those were the types of things he used to say to me."

She reached across the table for him, rubbing her fingers up and down his arm in a playful manner. "Seems to me it wasn't too long ago you and I were that age. And I seem to recall we didn't always do what our parents expected."

"But this is different, Mel." He grew suddenly serous. "You and I had a completely different upbringing than what these kids you're dealing with have to go through. Sometimes it scares me...."

He stopped abruptly, pulling away from her at the same time. It felt strangely quiet at the table, as though the restaurant had reacted to their interplay, the customers holding their collective breaths as they waited in anticipation for what would happen next.

"What's wrong?" she asked. "What scares you?"

"Nothing."

He bent down to look at his plate, his fork picking idly at the food in front of him.

"It wasn't nothing," Melanie responded. "What do you have to be afraid of?"

He hesitated several seconds, then forced himself to continue. "I just don't want to see you get hurt."

She laughed at the idea. "Now, Andy...."

He interrupted before she could say more.

"I'm serious, Mel. These people, they're not like you and me."

"You make it sound like they're lepers or something."

"That's not what I mean, and you know it. It's just that their lives are different than ours. Their values are different than ours. When I think about you getting involved with them...."

"Then why didn't you say something sooner?"

"Because I knew it was important to you. And I didn't want to stand in your way."

"I appreciate that. And I appreciate your concern. But I'm a big girl, Andy. I think I can take care of myself. Okay?"

"Sure. I know you can." He smiled again. "But that doesn't mean I won't stop worrying about you."

"You just go right ahead and worry. But I can't help feeling good about the way things went today. Anyway, I see her again next week. On Tuesday."

"Your CASA child?"

"That's right."

"I thought you only had to visit once a month?"

"That's the requirement."

"Then why are you visiting again so soon?"

She stopped to consider how best to express herself.

"I just think it's the right thing to do. I feel like I really made a connection with her today. Like we're starting to bond. I don't want to lose that. I don't want her to think that I'm ignoring her.

"She's gone through so much already, Andy. I think she needs some stability in her life. Someone she can count on."

"Then by all means do it. I just don't want to see you spending too much time on this case. It shouldn't take over your life, Mel."

"Oh, it won't. The courts are all about reunification of families. From what I can see, that's where this case is heading. I just want to make sure it gets there."

Chapter Eighteen:

"Y OU WERE right, Todd."

"About what?"

"About how things would go today."

"I don't understand, Rosie. Didn't you get the chance to talk to the magistrate? Like you told me you would?"

"Sure. I talked to her. But I could tell she weren't interested in nothing I had to say."

"Maybe you just got the wrong impression."

"I don't think so. It was pretty obvious she's on my mother's side."

"The magistrate came out and said that?"

"Not exactly. But she started getting real preachy like. Telling me how to run my life and how tough it is being a parent. About how kids don't understand what adults are going through. How about what I'm going through?"

"What did you say?"

"What could I say? I mean, I couldn't start yelling at her, could I? What good would that have done? And Melanie...."

"Who's Melanie?"

"She's a CASA worker. She's supposed to be looking out for me, I guess. Comes in telling me how she's gonna be my friend and make sure everything goes the way I want it to."

"But that's not what happened?"

"Hardly! She's no better than the rest of them."

"Well, you might as well get used to it. Some things will never change."

"What do you mean?"

"I've seen it before. I had a friend once. Larry. Now there's a kid who got a raw deal out of life. His mother was drunk all the time. And his father.... Well, his father was a nasty son-of-a-bitch. Used to beat Larry up all the time."

"That's horrible!"

"Yeah. It was bad. He showed me the scars one time. Nasty bruises all up and down his back."

"Couldn't something be done about it?"

"You'd think so, wouldn't you? Oh, Social Services got involved one time. Took Larry out of the house and placed him in a foster home. And for a while things were better."

"That's good."

"But it didn't last. He went through the whole dog and pony show, just like what you're going through. Going to hearings. Attending therapy. His old man even went to anger management classes, if you can imagine. What a joke that turned out to be."

"Why?"

"Because Larry ended up back with his parents. The courts insisted it was the best thing for him. That the family shouldn't be torn apart. Wasn't two weeks later his old man got mad about something. Only this time he was really pissed off, after being shoved through the courts and all.

"Larry never had a chance. Internal bruising, they called it. By the time the paramedics got there it was too late."

"But that's not right. That's not fair!"

"Who ever said life was fair? The cards are all stacked against you, Rosie. You're playing their game, so you have to follow their rules."

"I'm tired of their crappy game. I'm tired of the way Mama puts me down and criticizes me. Why don't they just leave me alone?"

"You might as well get that notion out of your head right

now. They're not going to leave you alone."

"I know. I know. But sometimes.... Sometimes...."

"Sometimes, what?"

"Sometimes I wish I could just take off and leave it all behind me. Just say goodbye to this crappy town and this crappy life and go out on my own."

"Then why don't you?"

"Be serious."

"I am being serious."

"But where would I go? I'd have to get me a job somewhere to start earning some money."

"There's jobs all over. That shouldn't be a problem. As long as you're willing to work."

"Of course I'm willing to work. How hard can it be? I just wish I knew somebody I could stay with for a while. Until I get on my feet."

"You do know someone."

"Who?"

"Me."

"Don't joke about this, Todd."

"I'm not joking Listen, I was going to mention something before I dropped you off, but I may as well tell you now. I have to leave Friday morning. I'll be out of town for a while."

"How long?"

"I don't know. A couple weeks maybe."

"Oh."

"Why don't you come with me?"

"What do you mean?"

"You say you want to get away from it all. Well, now's your chance. I'm leaving Friday morning. Pack some clothes and I'll pick you up in the morning."

"I don't know...."

"Listen, we'll be down by Columbus. It's only a couple of hours away. I have some friends down there we can stay with. Try it for a few days. If you don't like it we'll come back to Toledo. But at least you'll know you gave it a try."

"What would Mama say?"

"Who cares what your Mama says? Isn't she the reason you want out of here so bad?"

"Yeah."

"So what do you think? Friday morning. You and me. Starting our adventure together."

"It would be an adventure, wouldn't it?"

"Sure it would. Whatever you want."

"Still... I really need to think about this, Todd. It's just so sudden."

"I understand. It's a big decision. But I'm leaving Friday morning. With or without you."

"But you'll be back?"

"Who knows? Maybe I will. Maybe I won't."

"You'd do that to me? You'd leave me here all by myself?"

"Rosie, I can't help you if you're not willing to help yourself. It's your decision. I'm not going to force you to come along. Just let me know what you decide by Thursday night. Because after that...."

Chapter Nineteen:

"Y OU'RE UP early."

Rosaletta, rummaging through the cupboard for a bowl, hadn't heard Sharon enter the room. She turned at the sound of her foster mother's voice and offered a weak smile. She hoped she looked normal.

She didn't feel normal.

"I couldn't sleep," Rosie offered, as a response to the woman's remark.

In truth, she had been laying awake for most of the night. Especially after getting the text from Todd on her cellphone.

SEE YOU IN THE MORNING.

Five words. Five simple words.

But they meant a lot to Rosie.

Who could sleep after that? Excitement kept her awake, anticipating what the morning would bring. Yet she didn't feel tired. It was more like invigorated. She was excited and scared at the same time.

Rosaletta glanced at the clock on the stove. She had to leave in fifteen minutes to meet Todd. He was probably on his way already and she certainly didn't want to miss him. Not today.

By now she had found a bowl, and retrieved a box of cereal from the pantry closet. As she poured her breakfast the young girl looked up. Sharon was still watching, following

Rosie's movements with her eyes, as though the young girl's actions were the most interesting thing in the world.

Rosaletta sat down at the table, refusing to look up, hesitant to face the woman; fearful of revealing something with her appearance.

"Is there anything you want to do this weekend?" Sharon asked.

Rosie merely shrugged, concentrating on her breakfast and still refusing to look up.

"Would you like to go to the Art Museum? They have a special exhibit going on there."

"I don't know."

No reply came, which was all right with Rosie. She didn't feel much like talking to anyone this morning. Unless it was Todd. She couldn't wait to see him and discuss all the things they would be doing together. She felt like her whole future lay before her now.

The possibilities seemed endless. No more listening to her mother complaining about things. No more living in that dump of an apartment she used to call home. She'd be on her own. Able to do anything she wanted to do. Able to do *everything* she wanted to do.

The sound of a chair moving across the kitchen floor disturbed the young girl's thoughts. She didn't look up as Sharon moved closer, choosing to sit in the seat beside Rosie.

For several moments nothing was said, the only sound in the room the soft crackle of the cereal as Rosie played with her breakfast, stirring the contents of the bowl. She was really too excited to eat, she'd decided after fixing the cereal. So she toyed with her food, remaining silent, waiting for whatever it was that her foster mother wanted to say to her.

"I know this is hard for you," Sharon began at last. "I'm sure you feel like your whole life has simply fallen apart lately. But I can see you getting better already."

Rosaletta looked at her then. Her foster mother's words were unexpected. Rosie didn't see where anything had changed.

Nothing was better as far as she was concerned.

"It's true, Rosie. When you first got here all you did was sit in your bedroom. Now you at least get up and do things once in a while. That's an improvement, don't you think?"

"I suppose. If you say so."

"Of course it is. Things don't change overnight. Give it time. Neal and I.... Well, we want to be here for you. I don't know what's going to happen in the future. I don't even know how much longer you'll be staying with us. But you're always welcome here. We want you to think of this as your home now."

Rosaletta looked around, as though seeing the kitchen for the first time.

"This ain't my home. This is *your* home. I don't belong here."

"Of course you do."

"No."

Rosie stood suddenly. She felt a strange sensation, a rising sense of anxiety she didn't understand. She grudgingly admitted to herself that she *was* feeling more at ease in the foster home. The sensation scared her. She didn't want to be comfortable here. She didn't want to get attached to another place – to other people – and then lose it all again when her life was torn to pieces yet another time.

She needed to get out of there, and soon, before the decision became an even more difficult one to make.

She was glad she was leaving with Todd. It was the right thing to do. Only good things could come from moving on with her life. All she was leaving behind were bad memories of events she longed to forget.

Rosie glanced once more at the clock on the stove.

"I got to leave," she announced.

"Of course." There was a trace of disappointment in Sharon's voice. "But at least it's Friday. And tomorrow's the weekend."

"Yeah."

Rosie found herself smiling. She attempted to picture

what tomorrow would bring. She didn't know where she would be, and she didn't really care. Anything was better than where she was.

Rosie let the door slam behind her as she left the house. Her book bag felt unusual. It was jammed with clothes now, not school books, and had a different weight and feel to it than normal. She shifted the bag's position onto her shoulder and resisted the urge to run as she continued down the sidewalk.

Five minutes later she was nearly there. Only one turn separated her now from Todd. She stopped, feeling the tension rising in her chest, as anxiety overcame her. Breathing became more difficult. She leaned forward, struggling for air, taking in deep gulps that made her feel dizzy.

What if he wasn't there? What if he had just been leading her on, telling her stories that were never going to come true? After losing Tommy – after losing her home – she didn't think she could stand another loss.

Rosie nearly turned around. She wanted to run home. Even if it wasn't her home, even if it was just a house with a couple of strangers in it that she barely knew, it sounded safe and secure and a good place to be.

But somehow she forced herself onward. Her eyes were cloudy with tears, dreading the worst. She rounded the corner, her steps steady and slow, her eyes downcast. Coming to a stop the teenager lifted her head.

Moments later she was running toward Todd's car.

Rosie was breathless as she took her seat. She threw her bag in back, slammed the door behind her, and faced the driver. There was no denying the look of happiness on her face.

"You look like you're in a good mood," Todd prompted.

"Of course I'm in a good mood. Why wouldn't I be?"

"And you have everything you need?"

"Who cares if I don't? I'll worry about that later. I just want to get out of this place."

"Then what are we waiting for?"

The car pulled from the curb.

Traffic was light. Most of the businesses in the vicinity were still closed. It was too early for the office crowd, who wouldn't be hitting the downtown streets for another forty-five minutes or so. It was like they had the entire city to themselves.

Todd drove down Stickney Avenue, past Woodward High School. Rosie talked constantly, her excitement and nervousness manifesting themselves with a seemingly endless prattle of words. But when she passed the school she stopped talking.

For a moment her mind drifted back in time, recalling Tommy and the others. For years they seemed like the only friends she had. Now they were all gone to her. She couldn't help wondering if she would ever see Mickey and Jason again. Or, like her brother, were they a part of her life she could never return to?

She never stopped to think about her Mama. Consuella Alegredo was no longer a part of her life. She had no difficulty leaving that particular problem behind.

Rosaletta remained silent as the car turned onto Interstate 75, heading South. Todd seemed content with whatever her mood happened to be. If she felt like talking he would join in, contributing to the conversation. When she chose to remain silent he followed suit, keeping his thoughts to himself while he concentrated on his driving.

Occasionally he would turn her way. She seemed lost in a daze, resting her head against the window, staring out at the scenery they passed. They were away from Toledo, nearly to Bowling Green, before the young girl spoke again.

"Did you know I never been outside Toledo before?"

"I didn't know that."

She turned in her seat, to face him more directly.

"One time, when I was in fourth grade, they took us on a field trip. We went to a pumpkin farm. It was Halloween, and I suppose they figured we'd be excited about seeing all the pumpkins. I *was* excited, but only because they told us we would actually be going to another state. It sounded so exotic and foreign and.... Exciting, I guess."

"So what happened?"

"It was some dump of a place in Michigan. Right across the border from Toledo. You could have almost faced south and spit into Toledo, we were that close. That's the farthest I ever got from home."

"Well, you're further away than that now. And the day's just started."

A new thought seemed to occur to him.

"Are you getting hungry? Do you need something to eat?"

"No. Not yet. I'd like to drive some more before we stop anywhere."

"That's fine with me."

Forty-five minutes later they came to the city of Findlay. Todd maneuvered the car off the Interstate, onto a secondary road that headed east.

"Are we almost there?" Rosie asked.

"Not yet."

The young girl examined the scenery on either side, taking in the rolling hills and the sparsely located farms they were driving past. Bucolic vistas greeted them. There were cows strolling lazily through the fields, spending time in the mellow pace they greeted each day with. Massive tractors tilled the soil, leaving behind them voluminous clouds of brown that slowly dissipated as the dirt settled down once more in their wake. Silos – peculiar contraptions Rosie had never witnessed before except in pictures – dotted the landscape.

"I've never seen nothing like this," Rosie remarked.

"Like what?"

"All the open land. The emptiness. I'm used to cars and buses and buildings and people everywhere you look."

"It's a big country out there."

"I want to see it. All of it." Enthusiasm had control of

her voice. "We don't have to stay in just one place, do we? Can't we see it all?"

"We can do whatever you want to do, Rosie."

"Well, I want to see it all." Then, as an afterthought, she added words for his benefit. "With you, Todd. I want to see it all with you."

"Then that's what we'll do."

"How far away you been, Todd? I bet you've been all over."

"Nah. Not really."

"Why not?"

"I don't know. Guess I never had a reason to go most places." He took his eyes off the road long enough to look her direction. "Or maybe I never had no one to go anywhere with."

"Well, you do now."

Chapter Twenty:

ANNIE KLUME received the phone call at 10:30 that morning.

"Something happened to Rosie! She didn't make it to school today!"

The caseworker had initially failed to recognize the voice. But once the name Rosie was mentioned there was no problem identifying the distraught woman on the line.

"Slow down, Sharon. Tell me what happened."

"I don't know what happened. Rosie left here this morning, like she usually does. I assumed she made it to school all right. But I just got a call from the truant officer. She never showed up for class."

"Maybe there's been some kind of mistake."

"There's no mistake. Something happened to Rosie. I just know it."

"Calm down. I'm leaving my office now. It will only take me ten minutes to get to the school. I'll call you as soon as I find out anything."

"What should I do?"

"There's really nothing you *can* do right now. Except stop worrying. I'm sure we'll have this all sorted out in no time."

"What about Neal? Should I call him at work? Does he need to be here?"

"I don't think so. Let's not jump the gun on things. I'll get back to you as soon as I can."

"I hope she's okay. I keep thinking this is all my fault. If I had only...."

"It's not your fault, Sharon. Whatever is happening, I'm sure it's not your fault."

Annie replaced the receiver, staring at the device for several seconds after hanging up.

"Damn."

Two minutes later her coat was on and she was out the door.

Chapter Twenty-One:

B Y THE time they were on the outskirts of Mansfield, Ohio, Todd announced he had to stop for gas.

The afternoon was a pleasant one, and the car sat with all the windows down. As the self-service pump administered fuel to the vehicle Todd meandered over to Rosie's side. He leaned against the door, his face nearly inside the car.

"What say we walk around a bit?"

She looked around. The service station seemed to be in the middle of nowhere.

"Here?"

"No, not here. But there's a shopping mall just down the road a bit. Be a good place to stretch our legs."

"Don't you need to be somewhere?"

"We have time. Besides, this will give us a chance to do some shopping."

"What kind of shopping we got to do?"

He reached behind her, grabbing her book bag from the back seat. He shook it several times, as though judging its weight.

"I can't imagine you have too many clothes in here."

She turned away, embarrassed. "I don't."

"It's settled, then. It's time to get you a new wardrobe."

"I don't like you buying me stuff all the time, Todd. It just don't seem right."

"Why not? It's not as though you're making me do it."

"Still...."

"Besides," he continued, not giving her the opportunity to say more, "this is just until you get on your feet. I'm sure you'll have a job in no time. But until then, I can't let you walk around in rags."

She shot him an indignant look. "They're not rags."

"Maybe not now. But they will be if you keep wearing them every day. So what do you say?"

She smiled, inwardly pleased with his attention, and nodded her head.

Fifteen minutes later they arrived at the shopping center. It was small, not nearly the size of Franklin Park Mall in Toledo, but there were still plenty of stores to shop in.

At first Rosie was hesitant. As comfortable as she was around Todd, it just felt funny to be picking out clothes with him. She felt bad – making him wait while she tried things on – but he insisted she should be certain everything fit properly. So each time she'd come out of the dressing room he'd be sitting there, patiently waiting for her, like he had all the time in the world to spend while she picked out clothes.

The third time she tried something on she decided to model it for him. She walked out of the changing area and did a simple twirl in front of him, showing off the selection. He clapped, and she laughed, and after that it became sort of a game with them.

The three hours they spent at the mall flew by. They were preparing to leave, each of them loaded down with shopping bags, when Todd came to a stop in front of a particular store.

Rosie took one look and shook her head. "Oh no you don't. Not Victoria's Secret."

"Why not? You need underclothes, right?"

"Yeah, but...."

She turned to look at the scantily clad manikins in the

display window. She had to admit, at least to herself, that she would love to be able to try some of the things on. But she was too embarrassed to even consider doing so.

Rosie leaned closer toward Todd, keeping her voice just above a whisper.

"I couldn't. I mean, I'd love to. But I just couldn't. Especially with you here."

Without a word he set his bags down on the ground and retrieved his wallet. He pulled out a couple bills and presented them to Rosie.

"What's this for?" she asked.

"Take this and go get something. I'll wait outside. I'll even wait out in the car if it makes you feel more comfortable."

"I don't know...."

"Why not? You deserve something nice. Go for it."

She noticed then the denominations of the bills he had handed her.

"There's a hundred dollars here!"

"So?"

"So? It's too much."

"Believe me, it's not too much. Have you seen the prices in there?"

Rosie hesitated. Part of her still felt embarrassed. But part of her – and this was the portion that seemed to be winning the argument – was dying to find out how it felt to wear some of the things she saw on display.

Twenty minutes later Todd awoke with a start. He had fallen asleep waiting in the car, only to be disturbed by the sound of Rosie opening the door. He looked her way – saw the Victoria's Secret bag in her hand – and smiled.

"So did you get something nice?"

She smiled – a mischievous grin – but said nothing.

"Do I get to see it?"

"I don't think so."

As soon as she said the words she felt it was a mistake.

Todd had been so nice to her all day. She didn't want to upset him.

The smile on his face reassured her.

"It's your choice," he told her. "Now get in. We have another hour or so to go."

"And then we'll be in Columbus?"

"Actually, we'll be in Dublin. It's sort of a suburb of Columbus."

"So what's in Dublin?"

"Some friends of mine. And some business I have to attend to."

And then they were off.

Todd offered no further explanations, nor did Rosie ask for any. The day had been perfect so far. She didn't want to screw things up by asking too many questions. If he wanted to tell her he would. If he didn't want to, well, that was okay too.

Rosie settled back in her seat to enjoy the rest of the ride.

Chapter Twenty-Two:

THE SCHOOL secretary's name was Agnes. The name brought to Annie's mind a wrinkled old crow of a woman, which couldn't have been further from the truth. Agnes was young and vibrant and eager to help. Her concern showed on her face.

"This is just awful," the young woman remarked. "I can't understand what could have happened."

"And you're certain Rosaletta Guiterrez never showed up this morning?" Annie asked.

Agnes hesitated. "I can't say we're *certain*. We checked with all of her instructors, and none of them have seen Rosaletta today, but we haven't had the opportunity to look any further into this. That's all I know for sure."

"So she *isn't* here, then?" The caseworker shook her head, her confusion obvious. "Isn't that what I just asked you?"

"I'm just saying we don't know for *certain* that Rosaletta didn't come to school this morning. Maybe she came and left at some point."

"Does that happen very often around here? Children come and then unexpectedly leave during the school day?"

"No. Of course not. It's just that...." She paused, a look of hesitancy on her face.

Annie leaned closer. "A young girl is missing. I need to find her. The more you waste my time the harder it is for me to do my job."

A new voice answered.

"Then let us do *our* job."

He strode into the room as though he owned the place. In some respects that wasn't far from the truth.

"I'm Dean Shallot. I'm the principal here at Woodward." He turned toward the secretary. "You may leave us, Agnes." His crisp note of dismissal allowed for no refusal.

Shallot still stood in the doorway. The young woman had to squirm past him to make her way out of the office. She stopped to face Annie once more before departing.

"I hope Rosaletta's okay, Miss Klume."

"As do I, Agnes."

Once she was gone the principal closed the door behind the secretary. The motion was deliberate on his part, performed slowly so not a sound was made, as though he was in fear of disturbing someone. He then headed for the desk that occupied the majority of the room.

He was barely seated before Annie began again.

"I don't think you understand the seriousness of what's going on here."

"It's Annie Klume, correct?"

"Yes it is."

"And you're from Children's Services?"

"That's right."

"I see." He steepled his fingers together, held them to his chin for a moment, then resumed. "I think it is you, Miss Klume, who fails to see the seriousness of the situation."

"I beg your pardon?"

"We have students accused of truancy every day here. It's obviously something were not proud of, but it happens. And, in most instances, there is a logical explanation behind what's going on."

"But this time is different."

"How do you know that?"

"Because I know Rosie. I know what she's gone through.

I'm concerned about her state of mind, and what she may be up to."

"I appreciate your concern, Miss Klume. All of us here at Woodward were devastated when we heard what happened to Thomas. A horrible thing. I can't imagine how it must have affected his sister."

"Exactly. So you understand my concern."

"I understand you are concerned with Rosaletta's welfare. And I understand that you are involved with her recovery. But what you don't understand is the panic we could have on our hands if this gets blown out of proportion."

"Blown out of proportion? A child is missing!"

Shallot sighed. He gave the impression of someone dealing with an incorrigible learner; that no matter how hard he explained things he knew there was no way he could make his point of view known.

"I can't turn the school upside down searching for Rosaletta."

Annie nearly said something, but the man behind the desk held up his finger, motioning her to silence.

"Not yet," he continued. "We're very concerned about Rosaletta. But she isn't the only child at this school. If we go jumping to conclusions, throwing the school into a tizzy over this, we're liable to start a panic. The children – and their parents – will be imagining the worst happened. I don't need a score of angry mothers and fathers telling me how unsafe my school is."

"No one's blaming the school here."

"That's just the point, Miss Klume. They will be."

"So you're not going to do anything?"

"I didn't say that. We want to get to the bottom of this the same as you. But there's no reason to panic. I suggest you check back with the girl's parents. Maybe there was some kind of problem – a misunderstanding, perhaps – that simply needs to resolve itself."

"Rosaletta is in a foster home right now," Annie admitted.

"All the more reason we shouldn't jump to false conclusions. After all the young girl's been through, she obviously isn't thinking properly. I have the feeling this whole issue will resolve itself in a day or two."

"And if it doesn't?"

"Then by all means come back here. We'll set up a room you can work from. You're welcome to interview anyone here at the school – teachers, students, whatever. We'll do everything we can to help."

Annie nearly said more, then considered the futility of the act. It was obvious there would be no movement on Principal Shallot's part concerning his decision.

Annie left, determined to follow up on the matter with Sharon and Neal Daniels.

She also planned on visiting Consuella Alegredo as well.

Chapter Twenty-Three:

THE MAJESTIC Hotel hadn't lived up to its name in years. It had obviously seen better days. It was no doubt a product of the 50's, that booming era when Americans took to the highways and strip malls and hotels sprung up, seemingly overnight, to litter the countryside. There was lots of concrete and lots of glass, all designed to evoke a space-age look to the place. The Majestic was two stories tall, with outside entrances to each room that opened onto a hallway that encircled each floor. It may have been state of the art at the time it was built – perhaps even cutting edge – but now it stood as a symbol epitomizing how far things had deteriorated over the last sixty years.

The red Firebird pulled into a parking place near the front, joining the half-dozen cars in the lot. Todd shut off the engine then turned toward Rosaletta.

"I'll see about getting us some rooms."

"Here? It don't look like much."

He laughed halfheartedly at her remark. "Well, I can't argue with you about that. But I've stayed here before." He glanced out the window, surveying the establishment, then returned his attention to Rosie. "It's not as bad as it looks. It's clean, and it won't cost us an arm and a leg to stay here."

He patted her arm in a show of reassurance and stepped out of the vehicle.

Rosie watched as Todd entered the office at the front of the hotel. She could see him inside, just barely, as he approached the front desk. A long discussion ensued with the desk clerk. It seemed pretty lengthy, Rosie thought, a lot of talking just to procure a couple of rooms. But what did she know about such things?

Eventually Todd returned, a look of satisfaction on his face. "Here's something I hadn't expected. There's someone I know staying here."

"Really?"

"Yeah. Listen. Let's get your stuff to your room. You can freshen up if you want. I'm going to stop in and say hi to my friend."

Rosie didn't want him to leave her. Everything was so unfamiliar to her; so strange. She knew she'd feel better having Todd with her.

But she didn't want to complain about anything, either. Especially since he'd been so nice to her all day long. She'd still be stuck in Toledo if it wasn't for Todd looking out for her. No sense rocking the boat by saying anything that might upset him. Besides, he'd only be gone a couple of minutes.

"Okay," she replied at last, in answer to his remark. "Then what will we do?"

"No plans. What do you have in mind?"

"Oh, nothing really. Just spending time with you, I guess."

"Well, you can count on that."

By this point he had opened her car door, a gesture Rosie still wasn't quite used to. She realized he did it to be polite, but it made her feel awkward; like she was helpless, and unable to fend for herself. Todd grabbed her bag from the back seat, along with several of the bags from their shopping excursion, and they approached the flight of stairs at the front of the hotel.

"You're on the second floor. I hope you don't mind."

"No. That's okay."

She followed him up the worn steps, then down a

concrete hallway bordered by a flimsy metal railing. Paint flecks lined the hallway, some falling from the railing while others appeared to have precipitated from the ceiling above them. An empty pop can rested partway down the walkway, leaking it's contents onto the gray floor and attracting several honey bees.

Eventually they arrived at Rosie's room. Todd opened the door, threw on the light switch, and they entered together.

A large bed occupied most of the available space. A worn dresser along one wall held a television. A doorway in back obviously led to a bathroom.

Rosie had never seen the inside of a hotel room before. She had always expected something more grand. Like she had seen on TV. But this was reality, she told herself. At least Todd was right about something. It did appear to be clean. So it had that going for it.

Todd placed her bag on the bed.

"So what do you think?" he asked.

"It's okay. I guess."

"Listen, I know it's not the Ritz. But it's only for one night. Two at the most. Then we'll find something better. Okay?"

She nodded her head.

"Great. Anyway, make yourself at home. Watch TV if you want. I'll be back in just a couple of minutes."

He paused in the doorway, his hand on the knob. "You gonna be okay?"

"Sure. I'm fine" A waving motion with her hand dismissed his concern. "Go see your friend. But hurry back. Okay?"

He flashed a smile and then he was gone.

Rosie sat down on the bed, bouncing several times to see how it felt. A little firm, but it would probably do. Especially since it would only be for the one night.

She got up to wander around, though the place was too small to do much roaming. The bathroom seemed adequate, the fixtures old and worn but apparently functional. A steady drip from the spout in the sink had left a discolored ring, while the fluorescent light hummed unusually loud.

For a moment she stood in the doorway and her mind drifted. Actually, when she stopped to think about it, it wasn't much smaller than the bathroom at her mother's place. And there had been four of them sharing that bathroom. At least this one she would have to herself.

Moving over to the television, she picked up the remote control and went back to the bed. She turned on the TV, at the same time settling against the headboard while she kicked off her shoes.

The television came on louder than she had expected. But that wasn't the thing that surprised her the most.

As the set warmed up the picture came into focus, the image zooming in on the naked breasts of an overly-developed young woman. She seemed to be on her knees. As the camera moved back on the scene a man came into view. He sat on the edge of a bed, his pants pulled down to his ankles.

Rosie barely had time to notice the man's privates before the woman's head blocked the sight as she bent down in front of him. A look of satisfaction crossed the man's face.

A moment later the television was turned off.

Rosie threw the remote down onto the bed beside her and stared at the blank screen.

The young girl was aware that such things went on. She had never been intimate with a boy before, though many had attempted to coerce her into doing things. But she had never felt ready.

And, to be honest, it sort of scared her.

She had overheard the other girls talking about sex – snippets of conversations in the locker rooms and hallways of the school. They talked freely about the things they did to please the boys they were with.

But this was the first time Rosie had ever been exposed to sex in such a raw manner.

She was curious, and was tempted to turn the program back on. But then her better sense took over.

What would Todd think if he came back to the room and found her watching something like that? How would she explain it to him? How could she even look him in the eye?

No. It was better to just leave the television off. Todd would be back soon, and then there would be plenty for the two of them to do together.

Chapter Twenty-Four:

T HERE WERE five people crowded together in the room. The four girls occupied various positions on the two beds, relaxing like they had nowhere else to be.

One of the girls, wearing a flimsy nightie, lay partway under the covers reading a paperback, a tawdry romance novel if the picture on the cover was any indication. She seemed oblivious to what was going on around her, even ignoring the sounds from the television that blasted away in the corner.

The three others conversed together in loud terms, saying little of interest. It was idle chit-chat only, just words to pass the time.

They were all scantily clothed. One wore short shorts and a torn t-shirt tied at the bottom, exposing her midriff and revealing the piercing in her navel. A colorful tattoo encircled the piercing. Other tattoos adorned her arms and legs. Her hair was a bright blue in color, cut short and contributing to the punker look.

Another of the girls wore tight fitting slacks that revealed everything, including the fact that she wore no panties beneath. Likewise she was bra-less, her ample breasts threatening to burst from their confinement out of the tight top she wore.

The last girl in the room wore bra and panties only, lacy things in matching shades of purple. She was doing her toenails, her right leg propped up on the bed, painting them a scarlet red. Her fingernails already featured the same color. From time-to-time her long blonde hair would drape in front of her eyes, blocking the view of the procedure she was involved in. She barely noticed, reflexively brushing the errant strands away to continue with her toenails.

Besides their apparel, the girls had something else in common. They were all attractive, but in a crude sort of way. There was a harshness to them they didn't bother to conceal, a look that told you they had seen things – and done things – that had hardened them.

The lone man in the room was big. He looked like he should have been a lineman for a professional football team. The short-sleeved shirt he wore revealed arms that would have put Dwayne Johnson to shame. The top of his head was cleanly shaven; it glared from the harsh light in the room. He sat at a table by himself, playing a game of solitaire, paying no attention to his four roommates.

Cigarette smoke filled the air. Empty beer bottles lay forgotten on the floor. No one seemed to care. A half-empty bottle of scotch sat on the night stand. A glass of the brown liquid was in easy reach of the man playing cards, who occasionally halted his game long enough to take a sip of the whiskey.

The scene hadn't changed much for over an hour, and no doubt would have continued the same for at least that much longer, if the knock hadn't come on the door.

All conversation immediately ceased.

The large man at the table paused, a card still in his hand. Three of the girls looked his way, questioning expressions on their faces. The fourth girl remained too preoccupied with her book to react in any way.

"See who it is, Vi," the man at the table instructed. His voice was every bit as large as he was.

Vi, who wore the shorts and tank top and sported the blue coiffure, answered with a whine. "Why do I have to see who it is?"

"Because I told you to. Now see who the fuck it is."

She walked to the front window, using a purposely slow gait to express her displeasure, then drew back the curtains ever-so-slightly to take a peek outside.

"Shit. It's only Slick."

She went to the door, drew back the chain, and turned the knob. She never offered a word of greeting. By the time Slick was in the room Vi was back on the bed with the other girls, continuing their prattle.

Slick paid no notice to the girls in the room as he approached the card player.

"How's it going, Motorman?"

"Fucking slow, that's how it's going." He set the card in his hand onto the discard pile. "How the fuck you doin', Slick?"

"Just got in."

"You got the new recruit with ya?"

"Yep."

Placing his cards down, Motorman grasped between his legs with his right hand in a lewd gesture. "Great, man. When the fuck do I get to take her for a spin?"

"Keep your fucking dick in your pants," Slick suggested, the tone in his voice a lighthearted one. "There'll be plenty of time for that shit later."

"Well, don't keep me waiting too long."

Slick, apparently feeling the conversation with the big man was over, turned toward the girl doing her nails.

"Get dressed, Shasha. You're coming with me."

Without a word she put down the nail polish and walked toward the single dresser in the room. Opening the bottom drawer, she pulled out a blue dress that had been neatly folded within.

"Not that one," Slick told her. "I don't want you looking slutty right now. Pick out something that makes you look less...."

Motorman finished the sentence for him. "...like a fucking whore!" He laughed uproariously at himself.

Shasha gave him a scathing look. "Stick it up your ass."

"I'll stick it up *your* ass, you fucking bitch."

Having had his say, the big man returned to his card game, ignoring the others in the room, chuckling under his breath.

"Just put on something decent," Slick suggested.

She selected a beige-colored pair of slacks and a lime-green top, casually slipping them on. She then held her hands out, presenting herself for inspection. "Do I look okay?"

"You'll do. Now come with me."

Without questioning his demands she followed him out the door. As they walked across the parking lot together he leaned closer, keeping his voice low.

"Now don't go saying nothing to fuck this up. She's got no idea what the fuck's going on here and I want it to stay that way for now. Understand?"

"Sure, Slick."

"You're just a friend of mine, that's all. Tell her we went to school together. And you're down here on business."

"What kind a business?"

"I don't know. What the fuck do I care what you say? Tell her you work for Staples."

"Okay."

"Just keep her busy for a couple hours. I don't want her wandering off on me."

He pulled out his cellphone, took a look at the time.

"It's nearly 4:30 now. I'll be back by 6:00."

"I got a client comin' at 6:00."

"I'll be back by quarter to, then."

By this point they had reached a flight of stairs. Shasha followed Slick up to the second floor.

"What's the girl's name?" Shasha asked.

"Rosaletta," he answered, knocking on the door. "But she goes by Rosie."

"Then Rosie it is."

By this point the door had been opened and a youthful

voice greeted them.

"Todd! I'm glad you're back."

"Rosie, this is my friend Shasha."

The two entered the hotel room, closing the door behind them and shutting out the rest of the conversation.

Chapter Twenty-Five:

THE THREE adults sat at the kitchen table. Anxiety painted their faces; particularly Sharon's.

"She was sitting right there." The distraught woman indicated the sole vacant chair in the room. "Eating her cereal, just like any morning. We talked for a while, then she said she had to go. That's the last I saw of her."

"How did she seem?" Annie asked. "Nervous? Like something was bothering her?"

Sharon considered a moment, then slowly shook her head. "I couldn't really say. It's so hard to tell with Rosie."

"What do you mean?"

Neal took over the conversation. "We just don't know Rosie that well. Not yet, anyway. She's been quiet ever since she came here, which we assumed was normal under the circumstances."

"We didn't want to come on too strong," Sharon added. "We wanted her to think of us as friends. As someone she could talk to if she ever had a problem."

"And did she?" Annie asked. "Talk to you, I mean. About anything in particular?"

"No. Even when we asked her direct questions – about school and stuff – she was evasive with her answers."

"We didn't want to push too hard," Neal added, reinforcing his wife's earlier comment.

"Of course. But how about friends?" the caseworker asked. "Was there anyone at school she saw on a regular basis?"

"No one she ever mentioned," Sharon confided. "We got the impression she wasn't very popular at school."

"So you don't think she could have gone to someone's house without telling you?"

Sharon and Neal exchanged glances before each shook their heads.

Neal stood, walked over toward the sink, then turned around. "So what do you think happened to her, Annie?"

"It's hard to hazard a guess until we know more. But let's try to remain optimistic. It's not uncommon for a child placed in a foster home to run away. Sometimes they just can't handle the regimen of a new home, which can be radically different from what they are used to.

"Or sometimes it's just a way to get noticed. A lot of these kids are starving for attention. They're desperate for the one-on-one time they've always been denied at home. They hope for it in the foster home, and will do everything they can to get it."

"We tried to be there for her," Sharon commented, taking over their share of the conversation. "Sure, we gave Rosie her space. But we didn't ignore her. We were there for her. We gave her attention. Saw to her needs."

"I'm sure you did. But sometimes it still isn't enough. Children in these situations are confused. Adolescence is tough enough on kids without throwing a family crisis into the mix. And for Rosie...."

Annie paused, reviewing in her mind the particulars of the case.

"Rosie's had it worse than most kids. Her brother's death is something she's still dealing with. She's hurting inside but doesn't know how to handle it. She wants something in her life, some sort of stability, and doesn't know how to achieve it. Unable to articulate what she needs she's apt to be spontaneous, irrational, doing things that ultimately could be harmful to her."

"Including running away?" Neal asked.

"Exactly."

"I guess we should have done more," Sharon resumed. "We were afraid of pushing too hard so we held back on our affection. Maybe things would have been different if we had worked harder at getting closer to Rosie."

"We don't know that's true," Annie said. "Believe it or not, some children actually run because they get *too* much attention in their foster home."

The concept seemed unusual to Sharon. "How can they have *too* much attention? Isn't that what most of these children need? Someone to look out for them? Someone to give them the love and affection they didn't get from their parents?"

"You would think so. And, in the long run, that's the very thing they need the most. But you have to understand their situation. Many of these children have never had the opportunity to bond with an adult. In a very real sense they have had to fend for themselves for most of their lives. So when they do finally get some attention – attention they so dearly need – they don't know how to react to it. They get scared. And they run."

"So no matter what we did," Neal summarized, "it could have been the wrong thing? We're damned if we do and damned if we don't."

"It's sad to say, but there is some truth to that. Though there's probably more truth in the fact that if a child decides to run they are going to run. Regardless of what you did or didn't do. Very often a child will run, not to get away from the foster home, but rather to be with family. She may have returned to her mother."

"Why would she do that? Her mother kicked her out."

"That's true. But it's still the only family she's ever known. Now that her brother is out of the picture, Consuella is all she has left.

"I hate to speculate at this point, given we don't have

much information to go on. But we know Rosie's in a vulnerable position. That's a given. She has been ever since her brother died. She's not thinking clearly, and she feels like she has no one to turn to."

"She has us," Sharon answered. Tears were in her eyes by now.

Annie shook her head. "It's not the same. You're just strangers to her. But it's not your fault," she added quickly. "Trauma can affect people in a lot of ways. It's hard to say what Rosie is thinking right now."

Neal spoke from his position across the room. "So what happens now?"

"The first thing I'll do is visit with Rosie's mother. Just to rule out whether she did go home or not. I'll follow that up with some phone calls. Check up on some leads. Hopefully we'll have this all resolved before the day's out."

"And if we don't?"

"Then we'll need to call the police."

"We never meant for this to happen." Sharon's words were slurred, distorted from crying. "We wanted so much to do right by Rosie."

"It's not your fault, Sharon." Annie offered a smile of encouragement as she stood up. "I'll keep in touch. And let you know the minute I hear anything."

Sharon offered a meek "Thank you" as her husband walked Annie to the front door.

Neal paused, his hand on the doorknob, a worried look on his face. "How will this affect us?"

"What do you mean?"

"We're new at this. Being foster parents, I mean. Rosie was the first child we took in. And now this happens. How does this make us look?"

"Whatever happened to Rosie, Neal, it's not your fault. I'm sure you and Sharon did everything right."

He looked toward the kitchen. They could just barely

make out the crying from the woman in the other room.

"We never expected anything like this."

"These are troubled children we're dealing with, Neal. You can't expect their lives to be easy."

"I know. But this...." He shook his head, concern clouding his features. "I don't know if we can go through this again."

"Don't give up. Not on the foster program. And certainly not on Rosie. Hope for the best and we'll see what happens."

"If you say so."

He opened the door and Annie stepped outside. She paused a moment, then turned back to face him.

"One more thing. It wouldn't hurt to say an extra prayer tonight."

Chapter Twenty-Six:

SHASHA WAS simply gorgeous!

The thought kept floating through Rosie's mind as she sat there, watching the girl across the room. It wasn't as though Shasha was showing off, or flaunting her looks. She was dressed conservatively in a beige pair of slacks and a lime-green top, simple clothes that fit her well and accented the figure beneath. Her long blonde hair seemed radiant to Rosie, even in the unflattering light of the hotel room, while her blue eyes sparkled – at least from the teenager's point of view – with a hypnotic quality she was certain no man could resist.

And there she was, sitting beside Todd, the two of them talking so casual and relaxed, as though it was the most natural thing in the world for them to be spending time together.

It wasn't fair.

Todd must have been attracted to her. How could he not be? And how could Rosie expect to compete with someone as glamorous as Shasha?

In the past plenty of boys had told Rosie she was attractive. She almost believed it – sometimes – when she looked at herself in the mirror, yet she lacked the confidence to fully appreciate the compliments she had been given over the last few years. And while puberty had brought substantial changes to the teenager it had also brought questions regarding what she was experiencing.

She tended to focus on her flaws. Like the fact that her eyebrows were too bushy. Or the way she tended to slump sometimes when she walked. So many things told her there were other girls more attractive out there.

The fact that her mother constantly reminded Rosie of this very fact – constantly putting the teenager down and offering nothing in the way of encouragement – didn't help her self-esteem. Instead she became more withdrawn, ill-at-ease around others her own age, afraid to even consider making friends with her classmates.

So she kept to herself. This provided a certain amount of security. It did seem safer, not having to worry about saying the wrong thing at the wrong time.

But it also brought an intense loneliness.

It had always bothered Rosie that the other girls at school perceived her as some sort of competition because of her appearance. Rosie could never understand what it was that made them feel threatened. She certainly went out of her way not to antagonize them.

Looking now at Shasha it all made sense to Rosie. She couldn't compete with the gorgeous girl sitting across from her, with the long blonde hair and the brightly painted fingernails. If this was what Todd was comparing her to, then what chance did she have?

The trio exchanged pleasantries for a few more minutes until Todd stood up. "I have to leave for a bit."

"Do you got to?" Disappointment was obvious in Rosie's tone.

"Afraid so. But I won't be gone for long."

"But there's nothing to do here." She looked around the cramped little room, taking in the drab appearance of the hotel furniture and the plain white walls surrounding her. "I don't want to sit here all by myself."

She tried not to look toward the television. That would only remind her of the show she had glimpsed earlier on the set. As curious as she was, that was a temptation Rosie chose not to consider.

"I'm not doing anything tonight," Shasha spoke up. "I wouldn't mind hanging out with you for a while."

"No. I couldn't ask you to do that."

"I don't mind. Really. I was getting pretty lonely myself."

"Then it's settled," Todd remarked. "I'll try not to be too long."

As he opened the door to leave a sudden thought seemed to occur to him.

"Rosie. Do you still have the cellphone I gave you?"

"Of course I do. Why would you even ask? I got it in my purse."

"Can you get it for me?"

"Why?"

"I'm just thinking it's probably getting low on minutes. I thought I'd renew the time for you."

"It probably ain't that low yet."

"I just don't want to take a chance with it. Okay?"

Seeing the look of sincerity on his face how could she refuse him?

"Sure. I'll get it for you."

Rosaletta retrieved her purse from the bathroom, where she had left it earlier, and rummaged through until she found the phone. She then handed it to Todd.

"Great. I'll take care of this. And I'll be seeing you, Rosie. Real soon."

After Todd left Rosie realized how awkward it was, spending time with this girl she knew nothing about. She sat there in silence, wondering what to say.

Shasha seemed equally at a loss for words, sitting on the edge of the bed, moving her left leg up and down, dangling her sandal from her foot. Or maybe she was just content to sit there and say nothing?

"So how long have you known Todd?" Rosie asked at

last.

For a few seconds Shasha paused, as though uncertain what Rosaletta was talking about. Then a smile – as if she was in on a private joke – graced her face. "Oh. You mean Slick?"

"Slick?"

Shasha nodded.

"You call him Slick?"

"Everyone does."

"I didn't know that. He never told me."

Shasha shrugged, as though the matter was unimportant. "Maybe it just never came up."

"I suppose that's probably it," Rosie agreed. "So how long have you known...." She paused, wondering whether she should do it, then decided to try out the name. "Slick. How long have you known Slick?"

"Six years, I guess. Maybe longer. We met in school." She said the last sentence in a rush, as though it was important to get it out.

"He seems like a nice guy," the teenager commented.

Shasha smiled, the same knowing expression she had exhibited earlier. "Oh, yeah. Slick can be real nice."

Todd reached his car. He still held the cellphone he had retrieved from Rosie. He stared at it for a moment, as though not sure what he wanted to do, then he noticed the garbage can near where he had parked.

He threw the phone to the ground. The screen cracked instantly on contact with the pavement, though the plastic case remained intact. Todd brought his foot down, smashing his heel against the device.

Shards of plastic scattered about. Electronic components spilled out, the lifeblood of the phone exposed, attesting to the fact that it had made its last call. Todd picked up the biggest pieces and threw them into the garbage can.

Turning away from his car, Slick headed back toward the room Motorman occupied with the three other girls. He had been out of town for nearly a week. It was time to check on what profits had accumulated in his absence.

It was time as well to verify that each of the girls was bringing in their share of the take. Violet had been slacking off lately, claiming the guys didn't seem interested anymore. Slick couldn't believe that. She was a girl. She had tits, and an ass, and a cute little pussy. What else did guys want?

If she didn't start bringing in more money soon Slick would find a way to motivate her.

He knew lots of ways to motivate the girls.

And he wasn't afraid to use them.

Chapter Twenty-Seven:

Consuella Alegredo opened the door slowly. She squinted as she peered outside; the harsh light apparently hurt her eyes. With her hand to her forehead she shielded the worst of the glare. A puzzled look crossed her face as she identified her visitor.

"Did we have a meeting scheduled today?"

"No, we didn't," Annie answered. She generally made appointments with her clients, but it wasn't unusual to stop in unannounced. Often this was a useful way to find out what the people she worked with were actually up to. You could learn a lot by catching them in an unguarded moment.

Annie continued. "Something came up that I need to talk to you about."

For a moment both women stood there, staring at one another, until Consuella relented and backed into her kitchen.

"Come on in, then" she offered.

The kitchen was a disaster area. Things had deteriorated since the last time Annie had visited. Dirty dishes were everywhere. Pots and pans on the counter were grimy with cooked-on food. An ashtray on the table overflowed with cigarettes, the stubs lingering on the table, ignored and overlooked. The garbage can in the corner of the room mimicked the scene. Soiled paper towels hung on the edge, dripping onto the filthy linoleum floor beneath.

Consuella seemed to notice the appearance of the room for the first time. "We can go in the other room," she suggested. She made no attempt to explain the condition of the place, choosing instead to ignore the disruption around them.

Nick sat in the living room, watching television and smoking a cigarette. He paid no attention to the two women, nor did he offer any word of greeting as they entered. The living area was cleaner than the kitchen, but that was only because the kitchen was such a mess it would have been difficult to surpass it.

Consuella made no attempt to sit down. Considering the looks of the place, Annie decided to stand as well.

"Sorry about the way things look," Rosaletta's mother began, in a half-hearted apology. "Guess I'm a bit behind on my housework."

Nick, his eyes intent on the show he was watching, chose to make a remark. "You're always behind in your housework. I don't know what you do all day, but it sure as shit ain't cleaning this place."

His tone left Annie with the impression the remark was a running diatribe between the two of them. Tension filled the room. It occurred to the caseworker that she had interrupted something. Or perhaps this was merely what their relationship consisted of?

Consuella shot Nick a scathing look but had no comeback for her boyfriend. Instead she turned back toward Annie, a tired and depressed woman seeking sympathy wherever she could find it.

"It just ain't that easy no more. What with Tommy gone and all."

"What about Rosie?" Annie asked.

She paused, as though considering the question. "Yeah. Rosie too."

Annie had hoped the woman would say more; perhaps revealing something about her daughter's whereabouts. But when nothing else seemed forthcoming the caseworker continued.

"When's the last time you saw your daughter, Consuella?"

"I haven't seen her since the hearing. We been trying to work something out. To get together, you know. Some time what works good for both of us." She shrugged. "Just haven't got around to it, I guess."

"When's the last time you spoke to Rosaletta?"

"I don't know. Three, maybe four days ago."

"How did she seem?"

"Same as always. Didn't say much, except reminding me what an awful mother she thinks I am. Same old shit I always get from her."

"She didn't seem apprehensive? Or nervous about anything?"

"No. Nothing like that."

Consuella answered the questions as though they were a matter of routine, giving little regard to what she was actually saying.

Nick, on the other hand, seemed to be taking an interest in things. Using the remote by his side he muted the television, then leaned forward in his chair.

"Why are you asking all these questions? Has something happened to Rosie?"

Annie hesitated. Nick seemed concerned, an attitude she hadn't expected, and as his interest grew Consuella, too, became aware of where the conversation was leading.

"What happened to Rosie? Did something happen to my daughter?"

"We don't know for certain that *anything* happened to her."

"Then why the fuck are you here?" The woman seemed to be reviving. The apathy she had initially exhibited was gone now, replaced with the belligerent attitude she had expressed on earlier visits. "What's going on?"

"All we know for certain is that Rosie didn't show up at

school today. We're checking into things. Seeing if maybe she went to a friend's house."

"Or here?"

The woman's voice sounded incredulous. She glanced around, taking a quick survey of the room, as though looking for someone lurking in the shadows.

"You think Rosie might have come here?"

"We thought it might be a possibility."

"Honey, you got another think coming. The last thing Rosie's gonna do is come home to Mama. She's not wanted here and she knows it."

"Surely you don't mean that, Consuella?"

"Fuck yes I mean that."

"Aren't you concerned about her safety? About what may have happened to her?"

"Why the fuck should I care what happens to her? She never gave a fuck about me. When she was out running around at night, did she ever care about me? No."

"Rosie's just a teenager...."

"That's no fucking excuse. My Tommy was a teenager. But he treated me right. Never talked back. Always done what he was supposed to. Tommy was a good boy. Not like his bitch of a sister."

It occurred to Annie that Tommy had been out running around nights the same as his sister; possibly more, considering he was older than Rosie. Tommy's tragic death would have been avoided had the boy been more the son his mother seemed to have imagined he was.

But there was no sense pointing that out to Consuella. She viewed the world in a certain way. Any attempt to dissuade her otherwise would be wasted effort.

Annie continued. "So you have no idea where your daughter is?"

"I don't fucking know and I don't fucking care."

The caseworker nearly said more but, considering the futility of it all, decided against it. There was obviously no getting through to the woman.

"Please let me know if you hear anything from Rosie," Annie concluded.

Without another word she turned to leave, making her way through the ramshackle house. No one followed her, so she let herself out. She considered slamming the door behind her – it was what she felt like doing – but there was no sense in antagonizing things further.

She would have to pursue her search for Rosaletta Guiterrez elsewhere.

Annie sat in her car, staring at the door to the apartment she had just left. She tried to imagine what it had been like for Rosaletta, living in a home with so little love. It must have been a constant sense of disappointment to the young girl, a struggle to maintain her self-esteem living with a parent who had so little regard for her.

The caseworker then considered Rosie's placement in the foster home with Sharon and Neal Daniels. Though they were inexperienced as parents their concern for Rosie was obvious. Rosie had finally found a place where she could be nurtured and cared for.

Yet, after suffering with her mother for fifteen years, she apparently had chosen to run from her foster home after less than two months.

Annie had enough experience with troubled youth to realize that sometimes, no matter what you did, children ran away. Often you could see the signs ahead of time; the restlessness, the withdrawal, the reluctance to become attached to their new living situation. She had seen some of that with Rosie, though not enough to be concerned that something drastic was imminent. What signs she had detected Annie had put down as the reaction following Tommy's death.

No doubt the trauma of losing her brother still weighed heavily on the young girl's mind. People in pain don't think clearly. And, as any parent could tell you, teenagers are apt to make rash decisions with little regard for the consequences.

But the more Annie considered the situation, the more convinced she was that Rosaletta wasn't running *away* from something. She felt, instead, that the teenager was running *to* something.

Annie couldn't help but feel worried over what that something could be.

There was one more thing she could do before contacting the authorities. She withdrew her cellphone and made a call. A cheery voice answered almost immediately.

"Hello. Melanie Powers speaking."

"Good evening, Melanie. This is Annie Klume. I hope I'm not catching you at a bad time."

"Not at all. My husband's still at work and I had some shopping to do. Just leaving Target now. What's up? I assume this concerns Rosie?"

"Yes it does. Have you seen her lately? Or talked to her?"

"Not since the hearing. I was planning on stopping in next week some time to visit. Why?"

"Rosie didn't show up at school today."

Silence answered, a lingering pause as Melanie digested the information. "What does that mean?" the CASA volunteer asked at last.

"I don't know. I checked at the school, and with the foster parents. No one has any idea where she is."

"How about the mother? Maybe Consuella has been in contact with her daughter?"

"No. I'm just leaving there now."

"This is just awful. So what do you do now?"

"Now I contact the authorities."

"The police?"

"That's right."

"I want to help. What can I do?"

"Not much, I'm afraid. I just called you on the chance that Rosie might have reached out to you. But since she hasn't...."

"I'll meet you at the police station."

"That's not necessary. I appreciate your concern, Melanie. But there's really no need for you to go to the police with me."

"But I want to. Maybe there's something I can tell them that will help. I feel like I need to do something."

"Very well. I'm heading to the downtown station on Erie Street. Do you know where it is?"

"Yes. I had to stop there to be fingerprinted when I signed up for the CASA program. I'll be there in ten minutes."

Chapter Twenty-Eight:

THE EVENING dragged on. Rosaletta soon came to the conclusion that she and Shasha had little in common. The woman seemed reluctant to share anything about her past. Rosie couldn't help thinking there was something she was keeping hidden. At times the conversation screeched to a halt, while the two of them stared at one another, deliberating what they should talk about next.

The ordeal ended when Todd eventually returned. Rosaletta sighed as he walked in the door, grateful for his arrival.

Shasha, too, seemed relieved by his return. As soon as Todd entered Shasha stood, obviously anxious to leave. She grabbed her purse and headed for the door.

"Time for me to go."

She was nearly outside when she turned back to face the room. "Nice meeting you, Rosie." The comment seemed artificial, as though presented because she was obliged to and not with any true meaning behind the words.

Rosie's reply was equally lackluster. "You too. Thanks for keeping me company."

Shasha stepped outside and Todd followed, though he remained standing partly in the doorway. "Everything go okay?" he asked.

"Sure." When she spoke next it was in a whisper, so the words didn't reach the teenage girl in the hotel room behind them. "I can see where she'll be bringing in plenty in no time. Them fucking guys will be lining up for the chance to get a crack at that sweet little ass of hers. When you plan on sending her out?"

"Won't be long now. Another day or two, maybe." A trace of frustration colored his voice. "I've wasted enough time with her as it is. It's about time Rosie started pulling her weight around here."

"Motorman will be glad to hear that. He's been getting restless. Maybe with little Rosie here to play with he'll be chasing her around with that big black dick of his instead of waving it around at me all the time."

"You tell Motorman he'll get his chance soon."

She smiled at the thought. "I'm sure he'll like that."

"Now get going," he commanded. "I don't want you missing your appointment."

She glanced at her watch. "I'm not worried. Besides, I like to keep them waiting. It gets them more excited. And the more excited they are the more..."

She smiled again, a glow of avarice in her eyes.

"The more generous they tend to be."

She turned and walked away.

He watched her as she crossed the parking lot, his attention focused on the creases in her pants as Shasha strutted toward her room. From the expression on his face it was obvious he was pleased with what he saw.

"So what do you want to do?"

Rosie's voice from behind him broke the moment. By the time he turned his expression had altered. He continued to smile, but it wasn't the leer he had exhibited with Shasha. His features now personified friendship. It was the type of look one would use to greet an old friend.

"I thought we'd grab something to eat," he responded. "Are you hungry?"

"You bet."

"There's this nice Italian place down the road. How's that sound?"

"Sounds good."

She followed Todd down the stairs, then the two of them walked side-by-side across the parking lot.

The sun was sinking in the sky, casting shadows over the vicinity, while the red tint of the clouds imparted a warm glow to the surroundings. Somehow the hotel seemed less decrepit when deprived of the harsh light of day. The decay that lingered over the establishment, the garbage that littered the environs, could almost be forgotten as nighttime approached.

Todd led Rosaletta to his car, stopping on the passenger's side to open the door for her. But before she could get in he halted her with a hand on her side.

"I'm glad you're here, Rosie."

The words surprised her. She made no reply, uncertain what was expected.

"I was afraid you might not come," he continued. "That maybe you'd decide against it. Or maybe I wouldn't see you again. But here we are."

As he spoke he leaned closer. His arms wrapped around her – gently – his hands rubbing her sides and then making their way to her back. He pulled her near. She offered no resistance. Their lips met.

Rosie shut her eyes, overwhelmed with the sensation, a feeling of ecstasy pervading her as the moment lingered.

Then it was over as he moved away.

She opened her eyes and Todd stood there, smiling at her, a look of happiness on his face. She was quite certain her expression matched his.

The restaurant was more than Rosie had expected. It was fancier than any place she had ever experienced. The wait staff wore suits, linen cloths adorned the tables, while candles in empty wine bottles dripping with melted wax served as centerpieces. A grill lined one side of the establishment, with a wood-burning fire lending light – and an unexpected air of sophistication and charm – to the establishment.

Rosaletta felt immediately uncomfortable.

She moved closer toward Todd, leaning in his ear. "I can't eat here."

"Why not?"

"It's too fancy. I've never been to a place like this before."

She glimpsed a reflection of herself in a window at the front of the restaurant, aware suddenly of how drab she looked in the clothes she was wearing. And she caught herself slouching. She realized she did that, from time to time, and it had never bothered her in the past. But now it served as a reminder that she didn't belong here.

"I'm not dressed right," she finally admitted, hoping he wouldn't demand a further explanation.

"Nonsense. You look fine." He smiled. "And you're the prettiest girl here. So why don't you give me the chance to show you off?"

She tried to believe him, tried to believe she was as attractive as he implied, but an image returned to her mind.

"I'm not as pretty as Shasha."

"Why would you say that?"

"Because it's true. I can't compare to her." She looked down, afraid to face him. "I bet you wish you was with her right now. Instead of someone like me."

His hand went to her chin, slowly tilting her head back to force the young girl to look at him.

"I'm not here with Shasha, am I?"

She shook her head back and forth.

"I'm here with you. That's because you're the one I want to be with. Okay? Now let's forget all this nonsense and enjoy our dinner."

They were led to their table, a booth in the corner that suited Rosie just fine. She felt less conspicuous there, like she could hide in the shadows and no one would even notice her. She still felt ill-at-ease, like she had no right to be visiting such a place, but watching Todd sitting across the table from her and listening to the steady stream of conversation he initiated soon made her forget everything else.

The meal was delicious, Todd was a joy to be with, and the evening ended all too quickly.

Chapter Twenty-Nine:

MELANIE ARRIVED at the Toledo Police Department to find Annie Klume sitting on a wooden bench near the entrance. The caseworker looked exhausted; like she was ready to fall asleep. She held some papers in her hand, some work she had no doubt been catching up on, but the information was largely ignored. Instead she stared straight ahead into the empty room, as though her thoughts were lightyears away.

"Are you okay?" Melanie asked, as she wondered over and sat down beside the older woman.

"Just tired. Been a long day."

"I can only imagine. Does this come up often? Children turning up missing?"

"Unfortunately it does. There are a lot of mixed up kids out there. Growing up in a lot of mixed up families. And no matter how much of it you see it never gets easier."

"How do you do it? I mean, after all these years, doesn't it get to you?"

"Of course it does. But you try not to dwell on the failures. You consider the successes. The kids you've helped over the years. The ones that have moved on to better lives because of the work you do."

She offered a smile, then reached over and patted Melanie on the knee.

"No matter what happens, Melanie, just remember this. It's not your fault. That's something I keep telling myself. You do what you can to help them out. Some you reach. Some you don't. It's all part of the job."

"I suppose." Melanie glanced at a large plain clock on the wall. "So what do we do now?"

"We wait. I gave them some basic information concerning Rosie. They're finding someone to talk to us about it right now. It shouldn't be much longer."

Ten minutes later a uniformed officer ushered them from the waiting room. They walked through a series of hallways, and up a flight of stairs, then into a vast open area with desks and file cabinets scattered throughout. As they entered a man stood from a desk to greet them.

"I'm Detective Benjamin Tuppelo," he announced. "Won't you sit down?"

The detective was big. Not bulky, but large in stature and filled out, to the point where he was an intimidating presence. But his face portrayed something else, a sympathy and understanding that gave the impression he was a man to be trusted. He never smiled, nor did he frown. Rather he wore a dour expression, like he had a job to do and do it he would, regardless of the consequences.

Tuppelo examined some paperwork in front of him. "Which one of you is filing the missing person notice?"

"I am."

"And you're Annie Klume?"

"That's right. I'm a caseworker with Lucas County Children's Services."

"And you are?"

"Melanie Cox. I'm the CASA, the guardian assigned to the child." A thought suddenly occurred to Melanie. "But if you need to contact the CASA office for anything use the name

Melanie Powers. That's how I'm registered through the Juvenile Court."

The detective added the names on the paper in front of him, then perused the rest of the information. "Rosaletta Guiterrez. Fifteen years old. And the fact that the two of you are involved tells me there's something going on in the young girl's life. Why don't you give me a rundown on things? Might help me determine what I'm dealing with here."

"Rosie's been through a lot lately," the caseworker began. "Her brother Thomas was killed about six weeks ago. A tragic accident."

She meant to elaborate, but before she could the detective spoke up.

"I remember."

Tuppelo leaned back, a pensive look on his face. "An accident. In the CSX train yards." He voiced it, not as a question, but as a statement of fact.

"That's right," Annie said, startled that Tuppelo would so readily be aware of the particulars concerning Tommy's death. "But how'd you know about it?"

"I was on duty that night and called to the scene. I remember it well. It's a pretty hard thing to forget."

Melanie spoke up. "I'm sure Rosie will never forget it."

The detective continued. "I seem to recall there was an incident at the apartment with the mother."

"That's correct. That's when Children's Services was called in. We transferred Rosaletta to a foster home."

He referred to the paperwork. "That's the address listed here on Bronson Avenue?"

She nodded. "Neal and Sharon Daniels are the foster parents."

"And you spoke with them?"

"Yes I did. Sharon said Rosie left for school this morning, the same as any other day. But she never made it there."

"And you talked with the school officials as well?"

It was Annie's turn now to consult her notes. "Dean Shallot. That's the principal at Woodward High School, where Rosie attends. They have no idea what might have happened to her."

"Do you have a recent photo of Rosaletta?" Tuppelo asked. "Something we can circulate throughout the precinct?"

Annie dug through her folder to retrieve a few images. "These are some pictures I obtained at the beginning of my investigation. They aren't the most recent, but I hope they'll do."

The large man behind the desk gave the photos a quick look-over. "Do the foster parents have any newer pictures?"

"No. I asked and they said they hadn't taken any of Rosie."

"That seems a bit odd," Tuppelo commented.

"Not really, when you stop to consider. Rosie's been through a lot. The Daniels are trying to give her space, not invade her privacy. Rosie hasn't done well at acclimating to her new surroundings. So they figured, given time...."

She paused, realizing that, with Rosie gone, the time they had been waiting for may never show up.

An awkward silence followed, as each of those present considered the implication of Annie's words.

"Maybe the school has something," the caseworker suggested.

"Wait a minute," Melanie exclaimed, as she dug into her purse. She retrieved her cellphone and started scrolling through the pictures. A look of satisfaction came to her face as she found what she sought.

"Part of my CASA investigation included writing a court report," Melanie informed them. "We always include a picture of the children we're working with, in an effort to more humanize the report. I have several here on my phone that I took of Rosie the first day I met her."

She held up the device, revealing an image of the dark-haired, troubled young girl. Rosie looked sad in the picture.

Her body clearly portrayed the feeling of hopelessness and desperation that had enveloped her following Tommy's death.

"If you give me a number," Melanie suggested, "I can forward these pictures to you."

Tuppelo provided the information for the exchange. He then set his paperwork down and leaned back in his chair. The springs groaned, as though protesting the man's weight.

"I have to be honest with you, Miss Klume. Children run away all the time. We'll send out a bulletin, and start an investigation. But there's not much here to work with. Do you have any idea where she may have gone?"

"No. I spoke to the mother, and she claims to have no knowledge of her daughter's whereabouts."

"Do you believe her?"

"Yes I do. There's not a lot of love between Rosie and her mother. I don't see the child returning home."

Melanie leaned closer. "So what do you think, Detective Tuppelo? What happened to Rosie?"

"It's a tough life out there, Miss Cox. And as bad as life on the streets seem to us, some kids are just drawn to it. They feel security with others their own age. They love the freedom of being able to do what they want. Of course, they never stop to think about the consequences of their actions."

"They're just kids," Melanie reminded. "What do they know?"

"More than you can imagine," he replied. "Just because they haven't had a normal upbringing doesn't mean they're dumb. These kids are smart. Street smart. They know the ins and outs of things. They know how to manipulate the system. They know how to get what they need. By stealing. Or whatever they have to do."

"It's just all so unbelievable," Melanie commented. "Rosie seems like such an innocent young thing. Sure, she's gotten into some trouble. But she's only a kid."

"Some of these kids grow up pretty quickly, Miss Cox. They have to. It's the only way for them to survive."

Chapter Thirty:

Rosie FELT awkward on the return to the hotel, as they drove through the darkened streets of the city. It was such a strange environment, so far from anything she knew or anything she had ever encountered before. Everything she looked at – every building they passed, each street they traveled down – was strange to her. There was no familiarity to be found in the sights surrounding them. There was nothing she could refer to as a landmark, no links to her former life or the people and places she had once known.

She didn't even have any idea what city she was in, just that Toledo was somewhere behind her.

She wondered, for the first time since leaving in the morning, if this was such a good idea. What had she gotten herself into?

Rosie turned in her seat, to look more fully at Todd, and all her doubts disappeared. She felt strengthened by his presence. Just knowing he was close, knowing that he was looking out for her, made all the worries seem inconsequential.

The only thing that mattered, the only thing she even stopped to consider, was being with Todd. As long as he was there everything was okay.

By the time they reached The Majestic Hotel it was getting late. It surprised her to see how many cars were in the parking lot of the place. Business seemed to be thriving, but she couldn't begin to imagine why. She saw several men standing by their cars, drinking beer and smoking cigarettes.

Several turned her way as she got out of Todd's car. The looks they gave her Rosie had seen before, from boys at the schoolyard or late at night, while roaming the streets with Tommy and Mickey and Jason. She had learned to ignore the stares, and tonight was no different. She didn't want anything to do with them.

Rosie followed Todd as they headed up the flight of stairs to the second floor. He opened the door for her – she never stopped to consider that he had maintained control of her hotel room key ever since their arrival – and the two of them entered.

It felt cold in the room. Deserted.

Night had descended, and the glow from the parking lot lights invaded the room. The illumination failed to relieve the cold within.

Without a word Todd switched on the lights. Moving to the window he drew the curtains closed, isolating them further from the outside world.

"There." He turned toward Rosie. "Maybe that will keep out some of the chill."

Rosie shivered but said nothing.

"Are you cold?" he asked.

"A bit."

"Well, we can't have that."

He reached for her, rubbing her arms with his hands. It was a gentle motion. It should have comforted her. But suddenly, as if awakening from a daze, Rosie became aware of her situation.

She had a pretty good idea now what the evening had been leading up to.

She had never been alone with a boy before; never had the opportunity to experience what it would be like. She had always imagined it to be a special event, the two of them discovering one another and learning together the joys of intimacy.

Now here she was in a hotel room with a man she hardly knew.

She trusted Todd. There was no doubt in her mind on that point. He had been good to her already, and she could think of no reason that should ever change. But she couldn't help feeling vulnerable.

And inexperienced.

Todd must have been with other girls before. He probably even knew Shasha better than he was letting on. How could Rosie compare with someone like that? What if she failed to please him?

She wanted to please him. It was important that he keep liking her. She didn't want to lose that. She didn't want to let him down.

He drew closer, until their bodies were touching one another. His arms reached around and, like a repeat performance of their encounter earlier in the parking lot, his lips found hers. The young girl closed her eyes, once more enraptured with the experience.

She felt movement, then his hands reaching under her shirt from the bottom. His fingers strayed to her bra and, with an ease that surprised her, Todd undid the clasp.

Moments later they were on the bed together.

Rosaletta lay under the covers. The warmth of the blankets comforted her, but it wasn't that alone which appealed to the young girl. She felt the need to hide. It was as though she had exposed herself too much, having yielded to a craving she never even recognized in herself before. Part of her felt ashamed of what she had done, giving in to such desires and succumbing to such personal sensations.

But another part of her, the part she struggled against, felt a newfound freedom and exhilaration in what the two of them had done. They had performed an intimate dance together, having shared a connection that was as old as time itself – a primal juxtaposition of the sexes that was as fresh and new as the experience of a young girl on her first night as a woman.

Torn between emotions, uncertain how she should respond to what had just occurred, she sat on the bed in silence, watching Todd as he dressed. He would stop occasionally to take a drag from the cigarette he had lit-up shortly after the event. Then he would continue his task, silently occupied with the activity.

"What are you thinking?" she asked at last, disturbing the silence of the room.

"Nothing."

He answered quickly, as though in a hurry to conceal what was on his mind.

Rosaletta sat up straighter in bed, grasping the blankets to her in a bid to cover her nakedness. "What is it?"

He stopped smoking, placing the cigarette in an ashtray, then reluctantly sat down on the edge of the bed. His hand found hers, squeezing it gently, as he looked in her eyes.

"It's nothing you need to worry about."

"Then something *is* bothering you."

He shrugged, his discomfort obvious. "I can take care of it. It doesn't concern you."

"But it does." She pulled him closer. He resisted at first but eventually relented, sitting closer to her on the bed. "You mean so much to me, Todd. I don't want to see you like this. If there's something bothering you I want to know about it."

"Why? There's nothing you can do about it."

"How do you know that? After all you've done for me...."

She dropped the blanket. Rosie inched closer, her nakedness temporarily forgotten. "If there's something I can do for you all you got to do is ask."

"If only it was that simple."

"But it is that simple. I want to be here for you. Please. Tell me what to do and I'll do it."

He lowered his head, as though considering the proposition. "No. I'll find a way. I don't want to involve you in this."

"But I *am* involved, Todd. I *want* to be involved. I want to be involved with *you*."

He stood up, turning away.

"Let me think about it."

She nodded her head, satisfied that he would at least consider what she had said.

"Anyway," he said, "I should be going."

The announcement surprised her.

"You're not staying here tonight?"

A smile lit his features. "I really shouldn't. It's been a long day and we can both use some rest. But I'll be here first thing in the morning. Okay?"

He leaned closer, kissing her on the cheek. "See you tomorrow then."

Rosie lay in bed, thinking about the things Todd had said. She considered as well the words that had gone unspoken. It made no sense to her, what was going on. She wanted to be there for him, especially after all he had done for her, but she didn't know how.

It was a puzzle she couldn't solve, as she lacked the information to fill in the missing pieces. Eventually the night got the better of her and she gave up trying to find answers to anything.

Todd had been right.

It had been a long day.

Even though they had spent most of the day driving, which could hardly be called a strenuous activity, Rosie found that she was tired. She huddled under the covers, enjoying the warmth, but sleep still eluded her.

So much had changed in a single day.

She had awakened a confused little girl in a house full of strangers, uncertain of her future and anxious to leave her past behind. Now she was a woman, on her own with the man she loved, ready to take on the world and whatever it chose to throw her way. Rosie couldn't recall ever feeling so alive before. The world was full of possibilities. There were new worlds to explore. New experiences to discover and savor. And she and Todd would discover them together.

Todd puffed on another cigarette as he strolled across the parking lot.

It was all too easy anymore, he considered. He had the dumb kid eating out of his hand.

Shasha was right. Rosaletta was a sweet young thing, a magnet that would attract the guys to her in no time. True, she lacked experience. She had been clumsy in bed, nervousness prohibiting her from truly exploring and appreciating what the future had in store for her.

That would change.

And soon.

He looked at all the cars around him. At the far end of the lot a young man stepped from a pickup truck, glancing around in apprehension. He headed to one of the rooms and knocked lightly on the door. Violet greeted him in a blue negligee that was a shade darker than the color of her hair. She presented the visitor her typical "come-fuck-me" look, a look the client was no doubt admiring as he closed the door behind him.

Todd shook his head, considering the day's events.

It was too bad they had gotten such a late start on things. Friday nights were always jumping, and Rosie could have turned quite a few tricks tonight. Oh, well. She'd just have to work that much harder tomorrow.

Slick threw the cigarette on the ground, grinding the discarded butt into the pavement with his shoe, then resumed his journey. He knew Motorman would be up, unobtrusively keeping an eye on things like he always did. He also knew the other girls were, like Vi, entertaining in various rooms throughout the hotel.

His stable of girls was steadily increasing, which meant

that much more money coming in every week. The overhead was small – the arrangement he had with the hotel was working out well. There was no reason his business wouldn't continue to thrive.

The thought brought a genuine smile to his face, a smile more sincere than anything Rosaletta Guiterrez had yet seen from the man.

Chapter Thirty-One:

"SO HOW can I make things better?"

Melanie smiled at her husband following his question to her.

"I don't think you can," she responded.

She was grateful for his concern, thankful that she had somebody in her life to share things with. But she realized, in this situation, there really wasn't anything Andy could do to help.

"You're a dear for trying," she continued, stroking his hand. "But there's nothing you can do. There's nothing *I* can do either."

"So you're giving up?"

"What choice do I have? It's out of my hands now, anyway."

They were sitting beside each other on the couch, the room darkened save for a table lamp in the corner. The remains of their dinner rested on the table in the kitchen. Melanie's food had gone mostly untouched. She had lost her appetite, her concerns for Rosaletta the only thing on her mind.

She shifted in her seat, to face Andy more directly.

"The police are looking into things," she continued. "But they weren't overly optimistic when we talked to them."

"You'd think they could do something."

"Oh, I'm sure they *are* doing *something*. I know they got some pictures from me, to circulate. So I imagine they're canvassing the neighborhood, to see if anyone saw her this morning. But it's sort of like looking for a needle in a haystack, don't you think?"

"Why would you say that?" Andy asked.

"Because there are a lot of places where a young girl can lose herself. If she's running, and doesn't want to be found, it's going to be tough to locate her."

"Is that what they think? That the girl is running away?"

"No. That's what *I* think. Or, at least, that's what I'm telling myself."

"I don't understand."

She stood then, her nervous energy propelling Melanie to her feet. She paced about the room. It made things easier to think when she was in motion.

"I just don't want to think of what *could* have happened. It's such a crazy world we live in. With so many crazy people. I just hope, wherever Rosie is, it's where she wants to be."

"So what happens now?" Andy asked. "With the case?"

Melanie shrugged. "I don't know, really. This is all so new to me. Even in a normal situation, where everything goes as expected, I'm still unsure of myself. Yet now...."

She stopped her pacing.

"It wasn't supposed to happen like this. I was supposed to be helping her. I was supposed to be making a difference."

"It sounded like you were," Andy pointed out. "From what you told me things were looking great at the hearing."

"But that's just it. I was fooling myself."

"Why would you say that?"

"Isn't it pretty obvious? If things were going great Rosie wouldn't be gone right now."

"You don't know that for sure."

"What does it matter?"

Her pacing had taken her to a position in front of their recliner. As if collapsing she fell backwards, slumping into the chair. She felt defeated. Beaten after just a few months in the program.

"I'm a failure. I never should have gotten into this to begin with."

"That doesn't sound like you, Mel. You're always the one that's so enthusiastic about things. The one that radiates positive energy."

She looked up at him, smiling at his choice of words. It was a phrase he had used before, to describe his wife and the way she approached life. Without a word Andy stood and walked across the room. He knelt on the carpeting beside the chair, reaching for her hand.

"You can't give up, Mel. Not after all the work you've put into it."

"I thought you didn't like the idea of me being involved with CASA?"

"I never said that, Mel. I don't like the idea of you going, alone, into some of the neighborhoods you need to visit. I don't like the thought of some of the people you'll be associating with.

"But I love the fact that you want to make a difference. I love the fact that you care enough to help others. And I love the fact that you never.... Ever.... Give up on something once you get started."

Their hands were still clasped together. She pulled his arm closer, kissing his fingertips.

"You always do know how to say the right thing."

"Hey. That's what husbands are for."

She laughed, a short little chuckle of a sound. "I guess I was wrong again."

"About what?"

"When I said you couldn't do anything to help. Just having someone to talk to and confide in is a help."

"You know I'll always be here for you."

"I know. And thank you. I do feel better now. And I know I'll get through this. It's just.... I feel so bad for Rosie. I just wish there was more I could do for her."

"You've done all you can, Mel. It's out of your hands now. All you can do is remind yourself you did everything you could for her."

She nodded in agreement, realizing that what Andy was saying made sense.

But that still didn't make her feel any better about the situation.

Chapter Thirty-Two:

THE SOUND of the door opening woke Rosaletta the next morning. She rolled over in bed, caught sight of Todd entering the hotel room, and smiled, thinking he was a wonderful thing to wake up to. He closed the door behind him. Two steps took him to the side of the bed. He sat on the edge, reaching over to caress the young girl's side.

"Good morning."

He sounded tired. He even looked tired, as though he'd been up all night and hadn't gotten much rest. Rosie wondered for a moment why, but the thought escaped her mind a moment later with his next words.

"I've been thinking about what we talked about last night."

She sat up in bed, rubbing the sleep from her eyes, uncertain what he was referring to.

"I don't understand."

"You said you wanted to help me. That you were willing to do anything."

"And I meant it," she answered. "I still do. If there's something I can do just name it."

His hand still rubbed against her body through the flimsy hotel blankets. It drifted now to the side of her face, touching lightly against her cheek. His fingers explored further, rubbing against her hair, twisting the long black strands playfully. A smile of satisfaction lit his face.

His voice turned suddenly serious. "You have to understand, Rosie. Everything in life comes at a price. Nothing in this world is free. Not for me. And certainly not for you."

"What do you mean?"

She felt a growing apprehension, as though something wasn't quite right. But she couldn't put her finger on the cause of her concern.

He made no reply. Instead he grasped the edge of the blanket and folded the material down, exposing Rosaletta to the cool air of the hotel room. She wore a simple t-shirt and panties, her limited wardrobe denying her more elaborate bed clothes. Her breasts seemed to attract his attention. He stared blatantly. It was obvious from his expression he was pleased with what he saw.

Rosie wanted to be excited. She had looked forward to Todd's arrival this morning, anticipating how things would transpire between them. But this was not what she had expected. His eyes looked at her with a coldness she had never noticed in him before, as though she was a decoration on display for his amusement.

She attempted to withdraw, to move away from him, but with her back up against the headboard she had nowhere to go.

"It's time you started earning some money around here," he remarked. "Which means you need some more training."

Before she could reply Todd stood, grabbed the bed coverings, and flung them to the floor. She felt cold, and vulnerable, exposed in a way so very different from the night before. Rosie tucked her legs further beneath her, assuming a protective stance.

She expected Todd to draw nearer, but instead he moved away.

It took only two steps for him to reach the door, which he flung open to reveal a large man standing just outside. A look of satisfaction – and eagerness – stared back at Rosie from the stranger's face.

Rosaletta pulled her t-shirt down, in an attempt to conceal herself further, but the maneuver did little but to stretch the fabric over her breasts and accent her attributes, exactly the opposite of what she had anticipated. She felt more exposed than ever, the two of them leering at her in a way that was far worse than anything she had ever experienced from the boys in the schoolyard.

"Damn, Slick." The stranger was in the room now, moving closer, an evil smirk on his face. "You done good with this one. She's fucking smoking."

"What's going on, Todd?"

Panic was in her voice. She wanted to jump up, and run away, but there was nowhere to go.

"I don't understand." Tears were beginning to form in her eyes.

Todd remained silent, oblivious to the girl's rising panic, and closed the door. Motorman drew closer.

Rosie moved away, to get off the bed, but before she could complete the motion a hand reached out to restrain her. Motorman's grip on her arm offered no resistance, preventing any chance of escape. His fingers pinched into her.

"Now don't go struggling, girlie." His voice betrayed a lilting quality, as though he found the situation comical. "I intend to see what you're fucking made of. What Slick gave you last night weren't nothing. Let me show you what a real man's got in his pants."

She started to scream. Motorman's free hand moved forward with practiced ease. The slap caught her left cheek, spinning her head to the side. The suddenness of the motion halted any further sound the young girl could make. The side of her face burnt from the blow.

Todd spoke from his position by the door. "No sense putting up a fight, Rosie. Motorman likes it rough. The more you resist, the more excited he's gonna get."

"Ain't that the fucking truth," the big man replied, an expression of utter delight on his face as he leaned closer. "It's about time me and you got to know each other better."

He had hold of both her arms now. As though she was merely a doll, a plaything he could control with ease, he yanked her away from the wall, at the same time spinning her around. She ended up flung on the bed, laying on her stomach, her face buried in the mattress. She felt a tug against her panties, heard the material rip, then the cold air of the room was against her exposed flesh. A moment later the bed groaned as Motorman straddled her.

Rosie turned her head to face the door, tears clouding her vision. Todd stood calmly leaning against the panel, lighting a cigarette. He looked upon the scene as though it was the most natural thing in the world.

"Please." She barely managed more than a whisper, fear stifling her voice. "Please, Todd."

He stepped closer. His voice, as he spoke, was cold and distant. "I already told you, Rosie. Everything has a price. And this is the fee you must pay."

Rosie felt an abrupt pain as a jolt shot through her, the man above forcing himself on her with an utter lack of regard for her comfort.

"You owe me, Rosie," Todd continued, unaffected by what the young girl was going through. "I rescued you from your old life. Welcome to your new one."

Rosie felt the pain increase as Motorman continued his exertions. She cried out in agony, but the sound was stifled as a hand pushed against the back of her head, forcing her face into the mattress. She could barely breathe now. Even with opening her mouth and gasping for air her lungs felt starved.

But that discomfort paled when compared with the other.

The bed began to heave in a rhythmic motion, the ancient springs groaning in protest. The sound intermingled with heavy breathing and moans of delight as Motorman's frenzy increased. His hands groped her, forcing her t-shirt up, reaching beneath her and mauling at her breasts as his excitement mounted.

A wave of nausea washed over the young girl. Rosaletta

felt sick to her stomach, but managed to squash the urge to wretch. She bit her lip, fighting back the pain that increased with each forward motion of the stranger's body. She was shaking now – from pain, from fear, from the shear physical ordeal of what she was subjected to – and as a reaction to the unbelievable situation she found herself in.

And then, suddenly, it was over.

Motorman sighed, taking a deep breath following his exertions.

"Damn, girl. You're a fucking expert at this. I can see me and you gonna be getting along just fine together."

The bed squealed once more as he stepped off. She heard the sound of him pulling his pants up.

"I'm heading back to the other room, Slick," the big man announced, his voice casual, as though what had just occurred was nothing out of the ordinary.

"That's fine. Tell Jasmine to come on over."

"Sure thing."

Rosie heard the door open. A blast of cool air entered from outside to wash against her nakedness, and then he was gone.

She lifted her head, struggling to see through the tears. Slick faced away from her, holding her purse in his hands. He upended the bag, spilling the contents onto the top of the dresser, and began rifling through the contents. She couldn't see too clearly what he was up to, though a few items he selected caught her eye – her photo ID from school, some homework papers with her name on it. He paused, a photo in his hand, and turned toward her.

"You won't be needing this any more."

She watched as Slick tore Tommy's picture into four pieces, dropping the scraps onto the accumulated pile of articles he had removed from her bag. He collected them all, just completing the task as a knock came on the door.

Without a word, ignoring the young girl on the bed who

had just been ravaged, he took what he had accumulated with him as he greeted the visitor. Anything that could identify Rosaletta, or point to her former life, was gone to her now.

The girl outside entered the room, her manner nonchalant. She seemed unaffected by the sight of Rosaletta laying exposed and naked on the bed.

Slick turned, taking one last look at Rosie, then addressed the newcomer.

"Get her cleaned up, Jasmine. I want her ready for tonight."

And then the two girls were alone in the room.

Chapter Thirty-Three:

ROSIE SAT naked on the edge of the bed, oblivious to everything around her. She stared into space, paying little heed to her environment. She heard the water running in the other room but, still in a daze, didn't comprehend what was happening.

Moments later Jasmine returned, damp washcloth in her hand.

Jasmine was a petite thing, with small features and a delicate face. Her breasts were tiny, barely visible beneath her shirt, as though she had yet to develop. From a distance she appeared to be merely a child. But as she drew closer her age became more evident, the wrinkles in her face attesting to the years of hard living she had already seen. She wore glasses, a condition perhaps accelerated from her constant reading, which was her sole means of solace during slow times.

With practiced ease, as though she had performed the maneuver countless times in the past, she knelt down in front of Rosaletta. Jasmine dabbed at the young girl's eyes, wiping away the dried tears that had streaked across her face. Rosie offered no resistance as Jasmine continued with the ablutions.

Rosie's arms were limp, her limbs lifeless, as though her entire body had shut down following her ordeal. She allowed herself to be washed, exhibiting no reaction to the attention she was receiving. She said nothing, refusing to look the other girl

183

in the eyes.

Eventually Jasmine was content with her work. She stood back, surveying the handiwork.

"There you go, Sugar. You look better already. Come on. Let's pick something out for you to wear."

Rosie faced the other girl directly for the first time. There was no disguising the sorrow in her eyes, the pain she made no effort to conceal. But there were no tears. After what she had just been through there were none remaining.

"How could he do this to me?" The words stuck in Rosie's throat as she said them, as though it was difficult to force them out. "How could he just stand there like that? And watch that other man...?"

She stumbled over the next words, too shocked to continue.

Jasmine shrugged. "That's just Slick."

That seemed to be all the explanation required, but the stunned look on Rosie's face revealed her lack of acceptance.

Jasmine sat down on the bed, but made no attempt to touch the teenager as she continued.

"Men are no fucking good, Sugar. You need to just get that through your head right now or you'll never get through what's in store for you. And as for Slick...."

She paused to collect her thoughts.

"Slick don't think of us as people."

Jasmine looked around the room, as though searching for something, then bounced up and down on the bed a few times before continuing.

"Shit, we're like this here bed. Or that dresser. They're just things. That's how Slick thinks of us. As things. Fucking things to be used whenever the mood strikes him."

"I don't think I can do this," Rosie admitted, shaking her head back and forth.

"Oh, it ain't so bad. At least we got a roof over our heads. A place to sleep at night. And Slick makes sure we get something to eat every day. So you don't ever have ta worry about going hungry.

"Shit, before I met Slick I spent eight months on the streets. Eight fucking months. You think this is hard? Shit, this ain't nothing. Sleeping with the rats. In the rain and the cold. Your stomach growling 'cause you're so hungry but there ain't no shit to eat and you ain't got no fucking money to get yourself something.

"And if you think the guys out there treat you any better than the fucking guys that visit us here you're wrong. You don't know the meaning of low-lifes till you seen the shit out on the street."

"So what happens next?" Rosie's voice was quiet. She was afraid to voice the question but needed to know the answer. "What does he want me to do?"

"Ain't that obvious, Sugar? Slick expects you to earn your keep. By making the fucking men that come to this shit hole of a place happy."

Rosie shook her head. "I don't think I can do this," she repeated.

"Don't worry You'll get used to it. We all been through what you're going through. Believe me, it gets easier once you don't fight things so much. The guys who show up here are just looking to shoot their wad off. Sometimes it's all over in no time. Show them your titties. Give 'em a quick hand job. Fuck, once they've had their happy ending they'll be ready to leave."

"I've never done these things before," Rosie admitted. "It's all so new to me."

"It ain't rocket science, Sugar. All you got to do is spread them legs of yours. Believe me, these guys know how to take it from there."

On hearing the words Rosie glanced down. It was as though she noticed her nakedness for the first time. She clasped her legs together then reached over for a pillow to hold in front of her.

"I don't know how," Rosie exclaimed, as though that settled the issue.

"Shit, that ain't what Motorman was saying, Sugar. He claims you're the best piece a ass he's had in a long time."

"I don't belong here. I want to go home."

Rosie never saw the hand coming. When Jasmine slapped her it took the teenager completely by surprise. Then Jasmine grabbed Rosie's head with both hands, forcing her attention.

"Now you listen to me. You'd best stop talking like that. You'd best stop even *thinking* about that. If Slick hears you saying that..."

She shook her head, as though hesitant to consider the consequences.

"You don't want to cross Slick And you for sure don't want to get on the bad side a Motorman. He can be one nasty nigger when he wants to be."

Jasmine released her grip on Rosie's head, walked across the room, and started rummaging through the bags on the floor by the dresser. She pulled a lacy brassier with matching panties from the Victoria's Secret bag.

"Well, this should get you some attention." Jasmine faced the bed once more. Her eyes roved over Rosie, a look of satisfaction on her face. "Not that you need these to get noticed. With them titties of yours you won't have no problem at all."

Jasmine grasped her own breasts.

"Shit, look at me. I wish I had half what you got going for you, Sugar." She smiled then, a provocative smile, as though she knew a secret that was hers alone. "But I make up for it in other ways. Ain't never heard any of the guys complaining, that's for sure."

Jasmine flung the undergarments over to the bed, then continued to rummage through the clothes. She finally decided on a selection.

"Why ain't you getting dressed?" she asked, noticing Rosie hadn't changed position any.

"How do you do it? How do you let all them guys see you?" Rosie flung the pillow away, spreading her legs slightly to indicate her point. "Like this?"

"Listen here, Sugar. It ain't really that bad. You just got to learn not to take no shit from any of them fuckers. You got to let them know you're in charge."

Jasmine advanced closer to make her next point. "You got something they're willing to pay for. Take advantage of that. Shit, men are so fucking stupid anyway. Just do what you have to ta earn your money and then you're out a there."

She grabbed the underclothes off the bed.

"Now come on. Slick don't like to be kept waiting."

Chapter Thirty-Four:

DETECTIVE BENJAMIN Tuppelo was familiar with the routine. He had been through it enough times in the past to know what to expect.

Rosaletta Guiterrez's picture had been circulated throughout the station. The precinct patrolmen had been informed to be on the lookout for the teenager. Several officers had gone door to door, in the neighborhoods that the young girl would have walked through between school and her foster parents' home, in an effort to discover information. By all accounts no one knew who the girl was. No one had seen anything suspicious on the day of her disappearance.

It was a phenomenon Tuppelo had encountered before in his investigative work, but it never ceased to amaze him. How could someone go about their routines – day after day, week after week – yet remain invisible to those around them? Were people so wrapped up in their own lives that they didn't notice those around them? Were their powers of observation so poor they failed to take note of anything? Or were there just too many distractions, from cellphones and text messages and the over-abundance of information that barraged people everyday, that there was no room for anything else?

Another explanation, one that always had to be considered, was that people were reluctant to get involved.

He hoped this wasn't the reason, but the policeman in him realized this was often the case. People tended to live in isolation from those around them. What did it matter to the rest of the world if a teenage girl turned up missing? Their lives continued regardless.

For several days Tuppelo explored possibilities. He visited the foster parents, heard once again the story of how Rosaletta had left for school in the morning and hadn't been seen since. He talked to the mother, but elicited nothing worthwhile from that source.

The detective took to the streets, walking the path the young girl must have followed the morning she disappeared, hoping to come across something of meaning. He realized the beginning of an investigation was often the most important portion of the hunt. This was when the clues were the most fresh; when the memories of witnesses were the most reliable.

In this he was hampered somewhat by the timing of events. Since Rosaletta had disappeared on a Friday morning, it was logical to consider the daily morning routine of the neighborhood a reasonable place to find answers. Maybe someone on their way to work, or a student walking to school, had seen something out of the ordinary.

Unfortunately, weekday routines and weekend activities were generally two different things. The sidewalks were nearly empty of pedestrians Saturday morning. Sunday morning was even worse. Tuppelo had the sidewalks to himself. And while that allowed him time to muse on the matter, it served no purpose in advancing the investigation.

Nothing was discovered by Sunday afternoon, which meant two days had been lost already.

Monday morning the detective visited Woodward High School.

Principal Dean Shallot, though willing to cooperate, seemed oddly unsympathetic. Tuppelo questioned the principal in the man's office.

"Aren't you concerned about what happened to Rosaletta Guiterrez?"

"Of course I'm concerned. But I have a school full of students to contend with. As much as we try to control things we have a multitude of issues to deal with in our hallways. Drugs. Gang activities. Young girls getting pregnant and dropping out of school.

"It's a tough life for a lot of these kids. Many of these children come to school just so they can get something to eat. Child hunger is a very real thing, detective, when parents are more concerned about purchasing heroin than providing food for their kids."

"I'm aware of the issues you face, Mr. Shallot. But I face a different issue. Which is to determine the whereabouts of a missing teenager."

"And you have the school's complete cooperation in the matter. I'll arrange to make a room available to you. And we'll provide a list of teachers and students you can talk to that may have known Rosaletta. If there is anything else you require just let me know."

And so began the tedious task of questioning and probing, hoping someone could provide a glimmer of information as to what had happened to the missing girl.

For the most part it was wasted effort.

Tuppelo questioned the students first, on the assumption the young girl would be more apt to confide in someone her own age and may have revealed what her plans were for the previous Friday. The responses were as varied as the faces of the children who walked in the room.

"I don't really know Rosie that well. Sorry."

"She never said much. Kinda quiet."

"It's a shame what happened to her. With her brother and all. She was hard to talk to after that. Kept to herself, you know?"

"Is she the dark-haired girl that sits behind me in Peterson's class? I think that's who she is. Or maybe that's

Laura. I don't remember now."

"She didn't hang out with us. Didn't hang out with anybody, that I know of."

"Don't know her."

When it was all said and done the detective had accumulated a lot of names, of the students he had spoken with, but no useful information.

He questioned the teachers next, with a similar lack of success, though they seemed more openly sympathetic to what the young girl had been going through.

"It was tough for Rosie," Mrs. Tripoli announced. "I don't think she knew how to move on following her brother's death."

"Why do you say that?"

"Because I tried to help. I talked to her. On several occasions. To let her know she could come see me if she needed anyone. But she just seemed so distant. She made no attempt to fit in. Though, to be honest, she never tried that hard before all this happened, either. She was a lot like her brother in that respect."

"So you knew her brother?"

"Oh, yeah. I had Tommy in class three years ago. You see a lot of siblings going through here, you know. And a lot of them seem to have the same kinds of problems."

"What kinds of problems did Rosie have?"

"She was detached. She and Tommy. It was like they never learned how to relate to other people. They kept to themselves all the time. Withdrawn. Know what I mean?"

Tuppelo nodded.

"And you could tell they were hurting inside. You'd see them walking down the hall. So alone. So removed from everyone else. It made you want to go up and hug them."

The teacher sighed, no doubt recalling the two children.

"Of course I couldn't do that. And I really couldn't help them, either. There are just so many troubled kids out there. You see them come to school with cuts and bruises on them they didn't have the day before. And you know – you just *know* – that something is going on at home. But you feel so helpless about it. Like there's nothing you can do to save them."

"Was that the case with Rosie and her brother?" he asked. "Did you suspect abuse at home?"

She stopped to consider, giving the matter some thought. "No. I never suspected abuse. Neglect. That's what I saw a lot of with Tommy and Rosie. Notes sent home to their parents that went unanswered. That sort of thing."

"I thought the father was deceased?"

"You may be right. After all these years, all these children, it's hard to keep things straight. I do know I never saw anyone from home here at school, for parent/teacher conferences, or after-school activities, or anything the kids were involved with. Rosie and her brother seemed so much as though they were on their own."

"Maybe Rosaletta is *still* on her own," the detective suggested.

The teacher nodded.

"And there's nothing else you can tell me? No indication that the girl was involved with anything?"

"No. Sorry. I wish I could help you more."

Tuppelo saw a few more of the girl's teachers, and was about to call an end to this portion of the investigation, when one of the ladies from the school office approached, chaperoning a student who appeared to be in his late teens.

"Detective Tuppelo?"

"Yes?"

"I have a young man here who says he'd like to talk to you. His name's Michael Lentz."

"Hello, Michael." The detective offered his hand, which seemed to surprise the boy. Eventually the student lifted his own arm, shaking the big man's hand.

"What can I do for you, Michael?"

The teenager hesitated, reluctant to continue. He glanced

at his escort; the woman seemed oblivious to the implication of the look.

Tuppelo spoke up. "I think you can leave now," he addressed the woman, "while we have our talk."

The suggestion seemed to surprise her, but then she realized the futility of resisting. "Very well."

She turned and left, walking perhaps a bit more quickly than was necessary, her heels clicking loudly through the hallway.

"Come on in, Michael."

Tuppelo ushered the boy into the room, then closed the door behind them for privacy. He re-positioned one of the wooden chairs in the room, indicating to the boy to have a seat, then sat down himself in another chair.

"What's on your mind, son?"

"What do you think happened to Rosie?"

"I don't know at this point." The detective stopped, expecting a reply, but none was forthcoming. "Do you know what happened to Rosie, Michael?"

"No." He answered without looking up, shaking his head, with his attention devoted to the floor between the two of them.

Tuppelo remained silent, to give the youth time to collect his thoughts. The boy apparently had something to say, or he wouldn't have sought out an interview with the policeman. He was older that Rosaletta Guiterrez, by a couple of years at least. It made Tuppelo wonder what the connection was between the two students.

The boy lifted his head at last. His eyes sparkled with moisture. "I'm sorry."

The words barely reached the detective.

"About what, Michael?"

"About Rosie. And what's she's had to go through." He turned away for his next words. "And I'm sorry about Tommy."

"You knew Tommy?"

A nod was his only answer.

"You were friends?"

"Yeah. We used to hang out all the time. Before...."

He stopped abruptly, as though he had said too much.

Tuppelo said nothing. Sometimes it was better to remain quiet.

"I was there," Michael continued at last. "With Rosie. The night.... ....at the train yard."

"You were there when Rosaletta's brother was killed?"

"We were just having some fun." His voice raised, as though by speaking louder he could convince the detective of the truth in what he was saying. "Nobody was supposed to get hurt."

"Nobody ever expects somebody to get hurt," Tuppelo pointed out. There was no malice in his voice. No anger following the boy's confession Rather it was a tone of sadness, as though he had seen these scenarios too many times in the past and knew how they were bound to end up.

Michael continued. "I think a part of Rosie died that night, too. You could see it in her face. Her and Tommy were so close. So close."

"Tragedy affects people in different ways. But it's never easy on anyone."

"I wanted to be there for Rosie." He faced Tuppelo once again. "I really did. I tried so hard to be strong. For her sake. But I couldn't do it. It was too hard."

"Do you know what happened to Rosie, Michael?"

"No. I would tell you if I knew," he was quick to add.

"So why are you here, then?"

"I just felt I had to tell somebody. About that night. And how sorry I was about the way things turned out."

"You should have told Rosie."

"I know."

He sat there in silence for another thirty seconds, then slowly rose to his feet. Without a word he approached the door. He opened the panel, was about to step out into the hallway, when he spoke up again.

"When you see Rosie.... Will you tell her I'm sorry? Tell her Mickey's sorry?"

"Yeah. I can do that."

And then the boy was gone.

And Detective Benjamin Tuppelo of the Toledo Police Department sat there in silence, wondering if that was a message he would ever be able to deliver.

Chapter Thirty-Five:

SHE PACED about the room, smoking her cigarette, leaving a pungent trail of white behind her. Nervousness propelled her. She couldn't sit still. Inactivity made her consider her situation that much more, which only further disturbed her. She found she couldn't even watch television anymore. The programs failed to catch her interest, their mundane story-lines lost on her.

She surveyed the cramped apartment as she roamed, taking in the disheveled appearance of her home, and knew she should do something about it. But what was the point? What did any of it matter anymore?

Nick, lounging on the couch, faced her.

"Does that pacing really do any good, Connie?"

Consuella Alegredo paused, for a moment only, to glare at her boyfriend, then continued her ambulations. "What the fuck do you expect me to do? Just tell myself everything's fucking fine and not to worry about anything?"

"I know things are bothering you," Nick conceded. "But you're killing yourself. I know you ain't sleeping at night. You hardly eat. It's not good for you, Connie."

"I can't help it. First Tommy. And now this." She stopped to take another drag from her cigarette. "Rosie's been gone three weeks now."

Nick stood then, walking over to her side. He intercepted her pacing, halting her movement by placing his hands on her shoulders. He looked into her eyes. "You can't keep doing this."

"You think I want to be like this?"

She pulled away from him and began once more her random steps about the room. Her voice cracked when she continued, the pain within distorting her words.

"You think I like waking up in the middle of the night? Wondering where Rosie is? Wondering what happened to her?"

"I thought you wanted her out of your hair?" Sarcasm tinted his words.

She glared at him. "Not like this. I never wanted this."

"Well, you sure took a long enough time getting your shit together, didn't you?"

"What do you mean?" She approached him. "What the fuck are you trying to say?"

"Who are you kidding, Connie? You treated Rosie like crap. Ever since I known you that's all you ever done. Putting her down. Criticizing her. Hell, you threw her out after Tommy's death, when she was hurting and needed you most. What kind of mother does that?"

"She was hurting? What about me? What about what I was going through?"

"All I'm saying, if you'd treated Rosie better maybe she wouldn't be gone right now."

"So this is all my fault?"

"I'm not saying that."

"Yes you are. You're saying I'm no fucking good as a mother."

"I'm saying you should have thought about your kids once in a while. Considered what they were going through. That's what parents do."

"How the fuck would you know? What kind of fucking father are you? You got two kids out there you don't ever see. You don't even know where the fuck they are. Who are you to be telling me what a good parent is?"

"I just think if you stopped being so selfish all the time...."

Nick never completed what he had to say. Consuella slapped him, hard, across the face.

"You get out of my house." Anger controlled her words. "Just get the fuck out of my house!"

For several long seconds they stared at one another. Consuella's eyes glared at him, daring a confrontation.

Nick said nothing. His face seemed to relax, as though he'd been through an ordeal and the worst was over. His voice, when he spoke next, lacked any kind of inflection. It was calm; annoyingly so.

"I can't help you no more, Connie."

"Who says I need your help? I don't need you. I don't need nobody."

For a moment it looked as though he might respond. Then, without a word, he walked from the room. Consuella followed him with her eyes, watching him depart through the kitchen. The door made hardly a sound as he left, his exit a silent epilogue to the excitement of the last few minutes.

Consuella stubbed out her cigarette and slumped onto the couch. She looked about the room, examining the empty and forgotten place that had become her life.

Burying her face in her hands she began to cry, deep sobs of pain that shook her body.

Chapter Thirty-Six:

"**I** THINK I'm reayy for another case."

Melanie Cox found the words difficult to say. It had been over a month since Rosaletta's disappearance. There had been no sign of the teenager in that time, no indication as to what might have happened to her.

For the first two weeks Melanie had greeted each day with optimism. Today's the day, she would tell herself. Rosie will be back today, and we'll return to the process of helping the young girl bring some normalcy to her life.

And each night she would go to bed disappointed. Each night she would say a silent prayer for the teenager's safe return.

With time Melanie grew to accept the reality of the situation. Either Rosaletta didn't want to be found or, what frightened her even more, she couldn't be found.

So Melanie considered what to do next. She had become a CASA volunteer to help children in need. She had enjoyed working with Rosie, doing her part to assist the troubled teenager.

Her enthusiasm for the project – her enthusiasm for the entire CASA program – had crashed when she heard Rosie was gone.

Maybe there was just no helping some people, she considered. As important as the program was, and as well-meaning as the people were who worked at helping kids in need, maybe none of it did any good. Maybe there was no helping some children. Maybe some youths were so troubled that there was no repairing the damage created by years of neglect.

Melanie struggled with the concept, tottering on the brink of despair, prepared to throw the entire program aside as a useless endeavor. It was a lesson in futility. No good could come from it. She may as well accept the fact and move on with her life.

As the days passed, and Melanie found herself more distanced from the problems of Rosaletta Guiterrez, the CASA worker came to the realization that her attitude – her sense of defeat – wasn't appropriate. There were still children out there who needed help. There were still children who suffered every day and needed a friend to rely on.

Which was why Melanie Powers, CASA volunteer, marched into the CASA office, approached Rebecca Poole where the woman sat at her desk, and made her announcement.

"I think I'm ready for another case."

Rebecca smiled at her visitor. "I'm glad to hear that, Melanie. I'm sure this hasn't been easy for you."

"No. It hasn't," Melanie admitted. "Dealing with Rosie.... With what happened and all.... This isn't anything like what I expected when I signed up for the program."

"Every case is different," Rebecca pointed out.

"But are they all this hard?"

"Of course not. But sometimes it's the most difficult ones that are the most rewarding."

"Well, I'm ready for a simple case now."

"None of them are simple, Melanie. Because you never know what you're getting into at the start. I had a case a while ago where the father was totally detached from the child. The mother was having issues, but was working hard to get her life turned around. I was certain things would work out for her."

Melanie had a good idea where the story was heading. "But things didn't work out?"

Rebecca shook her head. "Sad to say, no. The father has custody of the child now, which I would have never thought possible. And the mother is still struggling with her problems."

"That's too bad."

"Yes it is. But the main thing, what you can't lose track of, is that the child is in a better situation now. And that's what we're here for. To help the children."

Rebecca retrieved a pile of folders from a shelf behind her and opened the first one.

"Let's see what we have," she announced, leafing through the information. She read for a few seconds, then closed the folder. "No. Not this one."

She started to set it aside when Melanie interrupted.

"What's wrong with that one?"

"I just thought...." She paused, then opened the file to the information. "It concerns a thirteen-year-old girl. Her mother was involved in a domestic violence altercation after drinking."

"So why do you think I shouldn't take it?"

"Since it's a teenage girl, I just thought...."

Melanie completed the sentence. "...that it would be too similar to Rosie's case?"

"That's right. I thought it might be hard for you. That you'd rather do something different. With a newborn, perhaps?"

The CASA volunteer considered for several seconds.

"No. It's okay. I want to help these kids. Whatever their problems, and whatever their age. It doesn't do me any good to sit at home wondering what happened to Rosie. Or if she's all right. It doesn't change the fact that there are other kids out there that need help."

Melanie reached over and tapped the folder on Rebecca Poole's desk.

"I'll take the case."

"Good for you." Rebecca handed over the folder. "If you have any problems, or if you find you change your mind and don't feel comfortable working on this...."

"No," Melanie interrupted, determinedly shaking her

head. "I want to do this. I can't be letting another child down."

"You didn't let anyone down Melanie. Rosie is dealing with the trauma of losing her brother, and being estranged from her mother. She's obviously not thinking clearly. You can't change that. Whatever she did had nothing to do with you. Just continue to do what you can and hope for the best. At the end of the day that's all any of us can do."

Chapter Thirty-Seven:

T HEY CALLED her Raven now.

Slick had insisted on a different name for the new arrival. He didn't want anything tying Rosaletta to her past life. That was why he had removed her ID card and personal effects from her purse. That life had been left behind, along with Toledo and Woodward High and Tommy Guiterrez and Consuella Alegredo. All the things that had formerly been part of her life were lost to her now.

Her name was Raven.

Which was all the same to the teenager from Toledo. She was too embarrassed by what she was going through, too ashamed with what she had become, to admit who she really was.

The first two weeks had been the worst. She felt violated and abused each time a man touched her. A part of her life, a part of her spirit, died whenever she was called upon to perform a sexual act with a stranger in the cheap hotel room she now called home. She was fearful of the way they looked at her, anticipating what was to happen next. She had nightmares constantly, of men not just using her but brutally abusing her as well.

By the third week she was beginning to be numbed by the entire process. She had seen so many naked men by then, had opened her legs to so many different strangers, that she no longer cared. How could life possibly get any worse than this?

Raven began to slip into the lifestyle, learning the ropes of the trade from the other girls under Slick's control.

Rosie, it would seem, was gone forever.

Shasha was Slick's favorite. Raven had no idea how long the attractive blonde had been selling her body. She seemed to have no problems with the lifestyle. She enjoyed the attention she received from the men, and was willing to experiment with any deviant suggestion they brought to the table. Or, in this case, to the bedroom.

Shasha was regarded by Slick as a trusted confidante, someone he could rely on to keep the other girls in line. In the vernacular of sex trafficking she was the bottom girl, the one called upon to police Slick's stable of prostitutes. She watched them all like a hawk, exploiting their weaknesses to her own benefit. Raven still regarded the woman as gorgeous, but now realized the beauty was truly only skin deep. Inside Shasha lurked a bitter and vindictive soul.

Violet – or Vi, as they referred to her – looked every part the punker but, strangely enough, failed to act the part when around the other girls. She was the one the others confided in, always there to lend a shoulder to cry on when things got out of hand. Raven made use of that shoulder on many opportunities those first few weeks.

The young woman known as Diamond, though not as attractive as Shasha, had no qualms about flaunting her good looks. She dressed provocatively, even when the girls were by themselves. She boasted constantly of the things she did with the men that came to see her, as though she was proud of her behavior and couldn't get enough of it. To her sex was just a game, a game she played to win.

The girls were thrown together out of necessity. It was easier for Motorman to keep an eye on them that way. When they weren't in their own rooms, servicing another client, they were together. And while the closeness brought a degree of intimacy between them, a bonding forged through their shared experiences, they were never close to one another.

In many respects they were a family now. But it was a family Raven would have gladly discarded to return to how things were before.

Raven soon found it unbearable spending time alone. Sitting by herself in the sparsely furnished hotel room gave her the opportunity to think, but thinking was something she preferred not to do. She needed to be around others. It reduced the feeling of isolation.

Many times, when she could no longer stomach her own company and felt the urge to be with someone else, Raven would turn to Jasmine.

Of all the girls Slick had assembled Jasmine was the only one Raven regarded as a friend. They spent many afternoons together. And though they often didn't speak – Jasmine invariably had her face buried in a book while Raven routinely watched television to fill the idle hours – it felt good just having someone in the room with her.

"Don't you get tired of reading all the time?" Raven asked one day.

Jasmine answered without looking up from the pages in front of her. "It relaxes me."

Then another thought occurred to her. She set the book down, looking around the room before turning her attention to Raven. "Plus it's an escape from this shitty world we live in. It helps me forget what's going on around me."

"Escape." Raven said the word slowly, considering the possibilities. "I'd love to escape. But not with a book."

Raven stood, walking toward the window. She looked out through the curtains, at the handful of cars in the hotel parking lot.

"There's got to be a way out of this," Raven continued, her mind focused on the possibilities.

"It's no good even thinking 'bout that, Sugar. And for

sure you don't want Slick to hear you *talking* like that."

"Don't you want to go home?"

Jasmine shrugged, a gesture Raven missed, and continued. "Don't really got nowhere to go home to."

Raven turned to face her. "There must be something. Anything's better than this."

"Don't be so sure, Sugar. When you got a father that beats you, and a mother that's strung out all the time where she don't hardly know where she is anymore, there ain't much to leave behind."

"You must have other family. Don't you got no sisters? Or brothers?"

"I did. Shit, I guess I still do. But they're gone from my life now. From way before Slick got a hold of me. How 'bout you? What kind a family you got?"

"My Mama's the only one left now. Tommy died a few months ago."

She paused, considering her situation.

"Maybe he was the lucky one."

Jasmine shook her head. "Is that what you want to go home to? Sounds to me like you got plenty of nothing waiting for you."

"Maybe. But it's still better than this crappy place. It's still better than what we got to do with them guys that come here to see us."

It didn't take long for Raven to learn to despise the men who availed themselves of her services. She thought back to her first conversation with Jasmine, the day they had met, when the two of them were discussing how Slick had turned on the teenager. She could still recall Jasmine's words perfectly.

That's how Slick thinks of us. As things. Fucking things to be used whenever the mood strikes him.

So many of the men she encountered were the same as Slick. It was obvious – from the way they looked at her, the way they treated her, the way they *used* her – that Raven was less than a person to them.

Their attitude was bound to have an affect on the teenager.

She too became hardened, like the other girls Slick had gathered. It didn't take long for her to become immune to the lifestyle thrust upon her, feeling no regard for those around her.

Raven lost track of time. Living isolated from the rest of the world, her only interaction with others the minutes and hours she spent each day satisfying the carnal desires of the men who came to use her, she became apathetic concerning everything in life. One day was no worse than the other, and none of them were good. There were no weekends. There were no holidays. There was only the never-ending quest to satisfy Slick's desire for more money.

Each encounter was different – different men, different faces – but each had a sameness to one another. After a while she barely noticed what the caller looked like, blocking such images from her mind as she reluctantly set upon her task.

One evening an opportunity came that was unique.

Raven took advantage of the situation on the instant.

The man stunk. She wondered if he ever washed. She could smell him the instant she opened the door to let him in. It was worse when he was on top, his body pressed down on her as he satisfied his desires, his flesh cold and clammy against her skin.

Thankfully it was over quickly. Once the act was completed he was no longer interested in her. He rolled off the bed, his corpulent body jiggling obscenely as he walked away, ignoring the young woman who had been the center of his attention moments earlier.

"I got to take a shit," he announced to the room as he headed into the bathroom.

Raven got off the bed and started to dress, donning her bra and top first, then looking for the panties the man had so expediently removed. As she searched the meager contents of the room she saw something out of the corner of her eye. It wasn't her underthings. Rather, it was something that interested her far more.

Raven was a changed woman now. She did things she would have never considered doing months ago. Some of the things had been forced upon her. Some of the things she had developed out of an urge to survive.

Without giving the matter another thought Raven picked up the man's discarded pair of pants, which had been thrown haphazardly into the corner shortly after entering the room, and began rummaging through the pockets. His wallet contained twenty-seven dollars, which she quickly appropriated. Raven thrust the bills into her bra for safe keeping.

Continuing her search she discovered an item that interested her more than any amount of money.

The man's cellphone was in his pants pocket.

She glanced toward the bathroom. She could hear sounds through the opened door. The man was for certain still sitting on the toilet, having yet to complete his duty, so Raven realized she would have to act quickly.

She mis-dialed the number the first time around, the voice on the other end announcing she had reached Mort's Deli. Fumbling with the buttons she attempted a second try.

Silence answered, a silence that seemed to linger forever, but finally the number rang.

Once.

Twice.

After the third ring a voice answered.

"Hello."

Raven held her hand to her mouth, afraid to speak. Tears were in her eyes. A flood of memories washed over her at the sound of her Mama's voice.

Part of her wanted to scream into the phone, to shout to her mother. Part of her was too embarrassed to speak, ashamed of what she had become and uncertain how to continue. She struggled over what to say, aware she had seconds only to speak.

Whatever decision she would have arrived at became a

moot point when the phone was ripped from her hands.

"What the fuck's going on here?"

He punched the phone, disconnecting the call, then dropped the device on the floor. Still completely naked he grabbed Raven, hauling her to her feet.

The slap on the face sent her across the room. Losing her balance, groping in desperation for something to break her fall but encountering only air, she slammed against a corner of the night stand. She landed on the bed and rolled onto her back, afraid to take her eyes off the man. She felt something wet on her face and reached up to determine what was going on. Her fingers came away covered in red.

She had been startled initially, astonished by the suddenness of his attack. But at sight of the blood – her blood – which coated her hands she felt something more.

Panic gripped her. Every nightmare she had experienced in the weeks since her arrival, every fear she had imagined late at night when she was alone in her bed, returned to her now.

Her assailant shouted over to her. "You fucking whore."

He stepped quickly into his pants, threw his shirt on, then moved closer to the bed. Raven shrunk back, fearful of what would happen next.

Strangely, he paid no attention to her. Instead he grabbed her purse, spilling the contents onto the floor. A folded wad of bills – the ones he had given her not twenty minutes earlier – came to light. He pocketed the money.

"You owe me more than this, you fucking bitch."

He leaned closer, his face inches from hers. Once more his body odor overwhelmed Raven.

"I should beat the fucking crap out of you. You know that, don't you?"

He drew his hand back but, at the last second, stifled the blow. Without another word he walked away, picked up his shoes and the cellphone, and headed for the door. He turned as he was leaving.

"You're fucking lucky I don't do more to you."

He spit on the ground then left the room.
Raven took a deep breath and started to cry.

Jasmine found her forty-five minutes later. Still laying on the soiled bed. Still crying.

Chapter Thirty-Eight:

"Hello."

Consuella waited for a reply, holding the receiver to her ear. For a moment she thought she heard a voice, as though someone was shouting in the distance.

Then, abruptly, the call was ended. Whoever it was had hung up on the other end.

Consuella shrugged. What difference did it make? It probably wasn't anything important, anyway.

She wandered back to the living room, sat once more on the couch, and slipped easily into her self-imposed isolation.

Chapter Thirty-Nine:

JASMINE ONCE again attended to Raven's needs, washing the young girl's face with a damp cloth. She dabbed at the injury with short, gentle jabs.

Raven winced in pain but said nothing. The cut above the girl's eye was superficial. It bled profusely, but once the bleeding stopped it seemed obvious there would be no serious complications from the blow.

Upon completion of the task Jasmine stepped back, presenting her patient to the group assembled in the room.

"There you go. Good as new."

All the girls were present excepting Diamond, who was currently entertaining a client. They were gathered in Motorman's room, which was larger than the one each girl occupied and often served as an assembly place for the group. Raven had resisted the suggestion to leave her own room – she didn't want to face the rest of them and have to explain what happened – but had lacked the strength to put up a fight.

She still felt weakened, her stomach queasy, as she surveyed the others.

Slick was there as well, looking on the scene with an obvious trace of anger on his face. He had just arrived with Shasha, who had momentarily left to retrieve him.

Motorman sat quietly in the corner, content to be forgotten for the moment, hoping not to catch Slick's notice.

"How do you feel?" Vi asked, a trace of concern in her voice.

"Okay. It's not as bad as it looks. Really."

Slick drew closer. "How the fuck did this happen?"

Raven shrugged but said nothing.

"That's not an answer."

"I don't know. Things got out of hand, that's all."

Raven thought back on the event. She knew she couldn't reveal what had caused the disruption. Slick wouldn't like it. It was better to just plead ignorance.

She was just grateful things hadn't gone worse.

"So did you do something to piss the guy off?" Slick asked, not content with Raven's answer.

"No. Of course not."

"What did I tell you?" Jasmine asked, addressing the teenager. "You can't let them guys take advantage of you. You got to show them you're in charge."

"I don't like this," Slick added, then turned toward Motorman. "And where the fuck were you?"

"I was right here, Slick." Gone was his usual bluster, the bravado he displayed around the women he was in charge of. "Keeping an eye on things like I'm supposed to."

"Sounds like you was doing a fucking lousy job of it."

"It wasn't his fault," Violet remarked.

Slick turned on Violet, his voice raised. "Did I ask you what the fuck you thought about it? Did I?"

Her voice quieted. "No, Slick."

"When I want your fucking advice I'll ask for it."

Shasha, who stood beside Slick, stroked his arm lightly, attracting his attention.

"It weren't no one's fault, Baby. These things happen. Sometimes they can't be helped."

Her words seemed to sooth him somewhat. "I just don't like it."

Noticing a softening in Slick's attitude, Motorman took the opportunity to speak up. "I'll keep a better eye on things," the big man promised. "This won't happen again."

"It better not. Or maybe I'll have to install some more security measures around here."

Without another word he left the room, which relaxed somewhat with his departure.

Raven was the first to speak. "I'm surprised he was that concerned about me."

"Don't fool yourself, kid," Violet told her. "He weren't concerned about you. Slick just don't want no damaged goods. If one a us gets hurt we might not be able to turn as many tricks, and that's no good for business."

Motorman stood, his confidence returned now that he was alone with the girls. "Don't you worry about things." He addressed Raven directly. "I'll keep an eye on you."

Shasha shot him a scathing look. "You better. Because I'll be keeping an eye on *you*. Understand?"

Raven returned to her room an hour later. At first it had felt almost good, receiving the attention of the other girls. It made her feel important.

But the novelty of the event eventually wore off, like it was bound to do, and things returned to normal. Violet left for an assignation. Jasmine resumed her book. So, with nothing else to do, Raven retraced her steps to the room she occupied at the hotel.

It felt cold inside, though she suspected it wasn't merely the temperature of the place. Her eyes were drawn to the bed. The blankets lay wrinkled in a heap on the floor. The pillow sported a dark red stain. She tried to avert her eyes from the sight but failed at the process.

She needed to remember what had happened here, to make certain it never happened again. This was part of her education; one of the experiences that would teach her to survive in this new world of hers.

That's what her life had become now. Nothing more than a question of survival. She needed to take each day as it came in order to make the most of the lousy deal that had been handed her.

Her purse still lay on the floor, the contents strewn about on the worn carpeting. She knelt down and began replacing her meager belongings in the bag. A tube of lipstick. Some eye shadow she had burrowed from Vi. A wadded clump of tissues.

Something white attracted her attention. It had apparently fallen from the purse, but it lay now partially under the bed. She picked it up, examining the item. It was a white business card. The name on the card read MELANIE POWERS, followed by the legend CASA/GUARDIAN AD LITEM.

It surprised her to find it with her belongings. Apparently Slick had missed it somehow while ransacking her purse weeks earlier.

For a moment Raven's mind flashed back to that day, so many months ago now, when she had sat in the bedroom at her foster parents' house and spoken with Melanie. She had been through so much pain, agonizing over her brother's death, looking on her future as a bleak prospect with no chance of salvation. She had wanted a way out, had hoped desperately for a way out, and thought she had discovered it when she met the smiling young man in the shiny red Firebird.

How could she have ever imagined how screwed up things would become?

She grabbed the business card with both hands, intending to tear it in half and dispose of it.

At the last moment she stopped. It was all she had left. All she had left of her former life. All she had left to remind her that her name wasn't Raven, and that she hadn't always been forced to prostitute herself each day.

She nearly returned the card to her purse, then thought better of it. Slick had missed it once. That might not happen again. Turning around, she tucked the card under the mattress at the head of the bed.

She then resumed cleaning the room, getting things back

in order, preparing herself for the coming of the next man she would have to satisfy.

Chapter Forty:

 THINGS RETURNED to normal after that, or at least as close to normal as it could for Raven considering her situation. Her recent encounter had scared her. If things had gone further that night, if the man had continued his punishment....

She didn't want to think about the consequences.

She learned to be more wary. She adopted a meek attitude, a subservient nature, to set the clients more at ease. She didn't enjoy what she was doing – she knew that would never be the case – but she played the game. She went through the motions, called the men "Honey" and other terms of endearment, and became the playful thing they expected her to be.

She hated her life. She hated what she had become.

Life had never been easy for her. In her former life there had been struggles. Her Mama's constant criticisms and lack of regard had destroyed her self-esteem years ago, leaving her to question her worth.

Her brother's death – and the horrible fact that she had been there to witness the event – had devastated her still further.

Her life had been difficult. It had been a struggle for the teenager to make it through each day without succumbing to total despair.

But it had been nothing like what she was going through now.

Raven soon took to drinking.

At first it was beer. There seemed to be a constant supply of the stuff in the place. Slick allowed this, even encouraged it to an extent, as a tactic to keep the girls more malleable. Weekends they were expected to stay sober, so as not to interfere with their duties, but during the week things were more relaxed.

But even then there were restrictions. Two of the girls were required to refrain from drinking each day, so there would always be someone available to tend to the needs of the never-ending supply of clients. Demand for their services never disappeared; it merely slowed down during the week.

There was a release to be found when drinking. It provided the opportunity to escape for a time from the hard truth of what life had become. It allowed a freedom, albeit a temporary one, from the loneliness and sorrow that accompanied Raven constantly.

It didn't take long until the teenager from Toledo had disappeared entirely, her youth stolen from her and now remembered only as a thing of the past. She had grown up quickly since meeting Slick.

Life would never be the same again.

Chapter Forty-One:

ROCHELE HAD no qualms about speaking her mind. Melanie had barely begun talking with the teenager when that fact became evident.

"I know my mother drinks too much sometimes," the young girl admitted. "But it doesn't happen that often." She shrugged, causally dismissing the matter. "It just happens once in a while. There's nothing wrong with that."

The two of them were sitting together in a living room that was crowded with family pictures – hanging on the walls, propped up on the television – every available space filled to capacity. It was her Aunt's house, where the teenager had lived for the last two weeks following separation from her mother by Children's Services.

The sound of voices reached them from another room, the girl's cousins playing a game of some sort. Rochelle looked anxious to join them.

Their game had been interrupted by Melanie's arrival. It was the first visit from the CASA volunteer, the first opportunity for the two of them to talk since Melanie had taken on her new case.

"Doesn't that bother you?" Melanie asked. "Your mother's drinking?"

"Why should it? She's not hurting no one."

"That's not always true, is it Rochelle? Didn't she get violent with her boyfriend a few weeks ago?"

"Things weren't really that bad. They made it sound like she flipped out. She just got mad at something Larry said. That's all. It was no big deal. I don't know why the neighbors had to call the cops."

"They were concerned about what was going on. They were concerned about you."

"They were just sticking their big fat noses in where it don't belong. Me and Mom do okay. We don't need them."

"Are there ever problems between the two of you? When your mother's had too much to drink?"

"Like I said, it's no big deal. She just needs to relax once in a while. We all do, don't we? So I just go to my room when she's drinking. You know, to give her some space. By the next day things are back to normal again."

"Does this happen often?"

Rochelle hesitated, as though considering the proper response.

"Not very much," she answered at last, managing to avoid the question.

Melanie leaned back in her chair, considering the young girl sitting across from her. She couldn't help comparing the child to Rosaletta Guiterrez.

Rochelle was younger than Rosie – though she seemed big for her age – so, physically at least, they could have passed for classmates. There was a certain amount of similarity between their situations as well. They had both been removed from their mothers, following an altercation that had brought the police to their doors.

Though at least Rochelle had the luxury of having family in town. An Aunt had been willing to take her in while they waited for the court hearing that would determine what would happen next in the teenager's life.

Beyond these basic facts there was little the two girls had in common.

Rochelle was talkative. She was friendly and outgoing, and as Melanie had discovered from the onset ready to voice her opinion on matters.

This was in marked contrast to the withdrawn girl Melanie had met so many months ago, the troubled youth that huddled in a corner of her room and stared at the world with eyes filled with pain. Rosie had been so alone, and through so much, that even on their first meeting Melanie knew the teenager had a struggle ahead of her.

Melanie's current case was the opposite. Rochelle seemed anxious to return home. She accepted her mother for who she was and felt comfortable with her world and her place in it. She could barely comprehend the concept of changing anything in her life.

Whereas Rosie had desired change so much that she had fled, leaving everything she knew behind in a bid to start over again.

Or at least that's what Melanie kept telling herself, refusing any other possibilities.

The CASA worker couldn't help wondering if Rosie still felt she had made the right decision.

There were so many troubled children out there, Melanie considered. She knew this for a fact, as evidenced by the volume of emails sent out from the CASA office each day. But each case was different. Each case was unique. Every child had their own lifetime of experience behind them, with their own set of issues they were dealing with.

It brought home to Melanie how challenging it could be, to advocate for children with family issues. Every situation had to be looked at on its own, weighing the pros and cons to determine what was best in the child's interest.

And even more importantly, Melanie realized she couldn't let what had happened with Rosie influence her future cases. She needed to be cognizant of what she learned in the past, but prepared to meet the future with whatever was needed for the task at hand.

"Are we done now?" Rochelle asked, interrupting Melanie's thoughts.

"Unless there's something else you want to talk to me about. Regarding your situation at home."

She shook her head in reply.

"Then I guess we're done."

The teenager stood to leave, then stopped a moment, something else on her mind. "My mother's a good person," she said. "She takes good care of me. I don't know why they even sent me here."

She disappeared to the other room, and moments later Melanie could hear the child's voice mingling with those of her cousins.

Her Aunt entered the room then and sat down across from Melanie.

"Rochelle is a good kid. And she loves her mother."

Melanie smiled. "I sort of got that impression."

"There's nothing wrong with the way my sister raises her child. She takes good care of her. She don't do nothing wrong. I don't see why there's all this fuss about things."

"There is the matter of the mother's drinking."

"So she drinks once in a while. So what? She's an adult and she's entitled to do what she wants. This is still a free world, isn't it? That doesn't mean she isn't a good mother. Rochelle should be back home with her."

"It's not really my decision to make," Melanie admitted. "That will be up to the courts to decide."

"Well, you just tell them they made a mistake taking that girl from her home. A young girl like that, she belongs with her mother. My sister looks after her. Makes sure nothing happens to Rochelle.

"There's a lot of bad out there, Miss Melanie. A young girl like that, she can get into a lot a trouble if someone's not looking out for her. Know what I mean?"

Yes.

Melanie knew exactly what she meant.

Chapter Forty-Two:

IT HAPPENED on a Tuesday afternoon.

Slick was progressive in his techniques at acquiring new clients. In his room at The Majestic Hotel – a room none of the girls but Shasha had ever entered – he spent a large portion of his free time on the Internet. Slick ran a website offering an escort service, reaching out through cyberspace to make his girls available to anyone who chose to take advantage of them. Slick was non-discriminatory that way. As long as their money was good nothing else mattered.

The site was simple, featured no nudity, but left no doubt as to the services that were being offered. It even showcased specials from time to time – coupons, two-for-one offers, and similar gimmicks. It was a good way to reach customers who wished to remain anonymous, which meant any of the men who came to call. All they had to do was email their requests and Slick would respond at his earliest convenience.

The site even included descriptions of each of the available girls, so the client could choose who they wished to spend time with before their arrival.

On this particular afternoon the client had emailed to set up an appointment with Jasmine. He was given specific instructions on where to go – the hotel address, the room of the girl he was to spend time with – as well as a formerly prepared menu detailing how much he would be expected to pay for the services rendered.

The client arrived about ten minutes early, apparently anxious for his visit. Motorman, watching from his room across the parking lot, saw the man approach Jasmine's room and knock on the door. Jasmine greeted him, the false smile she used with all the customers gracing her face, and the door closed behind them.

Motorman, watching the activity from the comfort of his room, had no idea what would happen next.

Jasmine's voice was at its sweetest as she greeted the client, enforcing the little-girl-persona her body exemplified. "Come on in, Sugar."

He entered, a smile on his face, apparently content with what he saw.

No little girl would dress like this.

Jasmine wore a sheer white negligee with no bra, her tiny breasts clearly revealed beneath the flimsy material. Her panties matched the top, and likewise failed to hide what was between her legs. She held one finger to her mouth, provocatively, and twisted slightly from side to side.

"You must be Chuck?" Jasmine asked.

"That's me."

"I'm Jasmine."

She leaned forward, offering the simplest of hugs, and caught a whiff of alcohol.

This didn't alarm her any. Many of the men who showed up on her doorstep seemed to find the need to fortify themselves before stopping in for a visit.

"I believe you have something for me," she continued. This wasn't posed as a question. Rather it was a statement of fact, anticipating the payment the man would have with him.

He seemed momentarily confused, as though he wasn't certain what she was referring to. She noticed then that he was carrying a plain brown paper bag, which he set on the room's dresser. He then slapped at his pants pockets, as though searching for something.

A comical expression clouded his features. "Looks like I left my wallet in the car," he admitted, the words slightly slurred.

"No problem."

Jasmine kept her voice cheerful, and indeed was feeling content with the chain of events. The man was more drunk than he should have been. It would be easy to take advantage of the situation and worm some more cash out of him.

In his current condition she wondered if he'd even be able to perform properly. But that was his problem. As long as he had the cash. That's all that mattered to her.

It might be an easy score after all.

She turned around, provocatively swinging her hips, then walked over to sit down on the bed.

"Tell you what, Sugar. You just get that wallet of yours. And I'll be sitting here waiting for you."

He seemed uncertain what to do next. So he reached for the paper bag he had brought with him, removing a half-empty bottle of Jack Daniels.

"Why don't we have a drink together first?"

"I'm not really thirsty, Sugar."

"But I am. Let's have a drink."

She shook her head no. "Maybe later. Why don't you get your wallet first? We can have a drink after we've had our fun."

"I want a drink now."

He advanced closer, and suddenly Jasmine realized something wasn't right. The humorous expression on his face had disappeared, replaced now with a look approaching anger. It was obvious he had no intention of being denied.

He removed the cap from the whiskey bottle, tossing it on the floor, and held the bottle out toward the girl on the bed.

"Have a drink."

Momentarily speechless, concerned she might upset the man further, Jasmine made no reply.

He moved closer, offering the bottle a second time. In his

haste he spilled some of the contents onto Jasmine. The brown liquid dribbled onto her chest, soaking her negligee as it ran between her breasts.

"Shit!" she exclaimed, feeling a slight burn from the alcohol against her skin. "Now look what you've done!"

She tried to stand, but he was directly in front of her and she had no room to maneuver. He pushed the bottle forward yet again, and again she resisted, shoving him away.

Chuck's arm offered no resistance, his intoxicated state leaving him limber. The force of the blow sent his arm behind him. The bottle in his hand smashed against the dresser, spilling the brown liquid on the carpeting. Shards of glass cascaded downward, scattering to the floor.

Silence followed for several seconds, both participants too surprised to react. Jasmine stared in wonder, uncertain what to do next.

In a surprising move, considering the man's condition, he reacted first.

"You fucking bitch!" he bellowed.

His intention was obviously to hit her. But, in his haste, he neglected to release the portion of shattered bottle he still held in his hand.

The blow caught her on the left cheek, slicing a wicked gash from beside her eye down to her chin.

Jasmine screamed in pain as the blood poured forth, clasping her hands to the side of her face.

Her shout further enraged the attacker. He dropped the shattered bottle. One hand he clamped over her mouth. With the other he started shaking her, violently, causing the bed to moan and squeal with the motion.

"You shut your mouth! You hear me?! You shut your fucking mouth!"

She struggled against him, writhing on the bed as her open cheek leaked a steady stream of blood onto the hands that forced her down.

Eventually her struggles ceased, but it was only after

passing out from lack of breath.

He shook her a few more times, unaware of her condition, then stepped away.

He ran his hand over his forehead, as though to wipe away the exertion he had just been through, leaving a streak of red above his eyes. He surveyed the room, checking the contents, making certain no one else was around.

Panic gripped him.

"Oh, fuck. Oh, fuck."

He stood there in uncertainly for another ten seconds. As addled as his brain was he still, somehow, understood the ramifications of what he had done.

With motions intensified by fear he rushed to the bathroom. Staring at the mirror he detected the blood on his face. Impulsively he moved his hand up, to wipe away the smear, and succeeded only in making things worse.

Reaching for the sink he turned the faucet to high, plunging his hands into the cold stream without bothering to wait for the water to warm up. Blood – Jasmine's blood – ran from between his fingers, making a red swirl as the liquid made its way to the drain.

For several seconds he watched, mesmerized with the design the flow made. His breathing was beginning to slow down, his initial excitement abating slightly.

He grabbed a towel from the rack beside the sink, yanking it off the wall, and attempted to dry his hands. But, lacking the patience to do the task properly, he accomplished little. He discarded the cloth, leaving it in a heap on the floor.

He stepped back into the room, his eyes avoiding the still figure on the bed, and took a quick look around. Satisfied he was leaving nothing behind he bolted from the room, leaving the door open behind him in his haste to depart.

Motorman was watching television, the sound turned low so he could still hear what was going on outside.

The sound of squealing tires, of someone making a hasty

exit from the parking lot, reached clearly into the room.

Violet sat on the bed, braiding Diamond's hair. Raven, cross-legged on the floor, was watching the television. All three turned toward Motorman who, closest to the window, had the best opportunity to see what was going on outside.

"What was that?" Diamond asked.

Motorman pulled back the curtain to look out the window. The car he had seen arriving moments earlier was gone now. He just caught a glimpse of its taillights as it left the parking lot. Jasmine's room beckoned, the door flung open in invitation.

"Fuck!"

The big man was to his feet in seconds and out the door, racing across the concrete. The girls were only slightly slower in following him. By the time they reached the room Motorman had Jasmine in his arms, shifting her position to lay her fully onto the bed.

Blood seemed to be everywhere. It ran down the girl's cheek, coloring the top of her nightie, then dribbled onto the bedspread. Jasmine was breathing – slow, shallow breaths that hardly seemed sufficient to sustain her. Her skin was pale.

Motorman addressed the three girls in the doorway. Violent looked nearly as pale as the girl on the bed, as though she was about to get sick.

"Vi, go get Slick," the big man barked. "Now!"

She turned away instantly, relieved to not have to view the sight further.

"What are you two doing just standing there? Get your asses in here and close that fucking door."

They had barely completed his commands when Motorman continued. "Raven, get some fucking towels from the bathroom. Run a rag in some fucking water. Now!"

Diamond moved closer, afraid to touch anything but even more afraid to turn away. "Is she okay?"

"How the fuck should I know? Am I a fucking doctor? Get your ass over here and help me with her."

By the time Slick arrived things had calmed down some, but just barely.

Jasmine looked moderately better, laying asleep on the bed. The other girls had managed to remove her soiled clothes, replacing them with a simple pair of shorts and a t-shirt. The blood had been washed from her chest and arms and neck. Diamond, sitting at the head of the bed, held a bloody towel to the injured girl's cheek. From time to time she would remove the rag, checking the cut beneath. It still oozed blood, the red flow commencing as soon as the towel was taken away.

"She needs a doctor," Diamond advised.

Slick's answer was immediate. "No. No doctor."

"But look at her!" Diamond withdrew the towel completely, exposing the jagged tear that ran down the side of the girl's face. "She needs stitches."

"No doctor!"

He turned away, pacing the room a moment, all eyes on him. They were assembled together, all of the girls along with Motorman, each of them focused on what Slick had to say.

"Shasha and me will go to the drug store," he announced. "There's a Walgreens just down the road. We'll get some bandages."

"And Tylenol," Shasha added. "She's gonna have one hell of a headache when she wakes up."

Slick nodded in agreement before continuing. "The rest of you get back to your rooms."

"You can't leave her like this," Raven pointed out.

"One of you stay with her. Diamond, you stay."

"Why do I have to stay?"

"Because I told you to stay, that's fucking why. I don't need this shit right now. I'll send one of the other girls over later."

He moved for the door, then turned to see the rest of the group remaining where they were. "Now get the fuck out of here. All of you!"

As a group they followed him out the door, none of them saying a word.   Diamond alone remained behind with the injured girl.

Chapter Forty-Three:

NIGHT HAD fallen. Light from the parking lot outside invaded the hotel room, casting odd shadows on the walls. The overhead light was off, as was the lamp by the bedside. The single-bulb fixture in the bathroom was turned on but added little illumination to the scene, other than a rectangle of dim light that colored the carpeting just outside the opened door.

Jasmine lay on the bed, breathing heavily, occasionally snoring with a tone that was less than ladylike. Her face was bandaged now, lengths of gauze wrapped around her head and held in position with strips of white tape. The cloth was stained pink with dried blood. Occasionally Jasmine would twitch in her sleep, the action accompanied by a slight grimace of pain.

Raven sat at the girl's side. She too was asleep, slouched in a wooden chair, leaning against the wall to prevent herself from slumping to the floor. She had tried to stay awake. She had wanted to stay at her friend's side, maintaining a constant vigil over the injured girl in case Jasmine awoke and needed anything, but it had been too long of a day. In spite of her good intentions slumber had overtaken her.

Jasmine shifted slightly under the covers, the movement accompanied with a moan that sounded unnaturally loud in the quiet of the room.

Raven awoke on the instant, senses alert, and leaned closer toward the bed.

"It's okay."

Her voice was barely above a whisper. She reached her hand out, to stroke her friend's hair, but halted, fearful of inflicting pain.

"You're okay," she repeated, in an effort to convince herself of the fact.

"I don't feel okay," Jasmine replied.

The injured girl forced her eyes open and slowly turned her head. She seemed to recognize who was sitting next to her. She attempted a smile, but the action apparently caused more pain than it was worth because the expression refused to linger.

"What time is it?" Jasmine asked.

"Late."

"How late?"

"Don't worry about it. It don't matter. You just need to get some sleep so you can start feeling better."

"My face hurts."

"I'm not surprised."

"Isn't there anything you can do? Can't I have something? For the pain?"

Raven reached for the bottle of Tylenol on the nightstand. She paused, trying to remember the instructions she had received earlier in the evening. Diamond had been watching the injured girl before Raven had arrived. She had mentioned giving some of the medication to Jasmine, but Raven couldn't recall the time or how much.

Was it too soon to give more? Maybe she should check with Diamond?

Jasmine moaned again, which decided the issue for Raven. She couldn't just sit there while Jasmine was in pain. She went to the bathroom, returning with a glass of cold water, then removed two of the pills from the bottle.

"Can you sit up?"

"I think so."

With Raven's help Jasmine managed to sit up in bed, though it was obvious from the way she performed the procedure it was a maneuver fraught with pain. She took the offered medication, gulping down the entire glass of water after swallowing the pills.

"Do you want to lay down again?" Raven asked.

"No. I think I'd just like to sit here for a while."

"That's okay." Raven returned to her seat beside the bed. "I can sit with you. I'm just glad to see you awake."

Jasmine once more attempted a smile but again found the expression too painful to complete.

For several minutes the two of them sat there, each involved in private thoughts of their own. Raven broke the silence.

"This isn't right. What you're going through."

"It's my own fault." The words came slowly. "I should have realized that guy was trouble the minute he walked in the door."

"That's not what I mean." Raven stood, finding it easier to talk while moving about the room. "We shouldn't be here. None of us should be here. It's not right, what Slick makes us do."

Jasmine sighed. "What we gonna do about it?"

"I don't know. But there must be something."

"You may as well stop thinking like that, Sugar. Believe me, I've tried. I found out the hard way you don't want to get on Slick's bad side."

Raven refused to accept Jasmine's answer.

"Maybe, if we worked together...."

She stopped, uncertain what to say next. What could they do? Even working together, what could they do?

Raven sat down again. She leaned closer to the bed, lowering her voice to a whisper.

"You know, some of these guys don't seem too bad. I had a guy, the other day, didn't want to do nothing but talk. So that's all we done. Just talked."

"They're lonely, Raven. They ain't got nothing in their lives. That's why they come to us."

"Yeah, but maybe they could help us." The suggestion, now that it had occurred to her, raised Raven's enthusiasm. "Maybe if we told them what was going on they could get us outta here."

"They wouldn't care. To them, we're all nothing but a bunch a hookers. A quick fuck to get them through the day and then we're forgotten. Why would they bother to help us?"

"Maybe, if they felt sorry about what we're going through...?"

"No." The simple word spoke on the finality of the situation. "Ain't nobody gonna help us, Sugar. They don't want to get involved. And they don't want to get themselves in trouble. By helping us they'd have to admit what they was up to here. And they're not gonna do that."

"It wouldn't have to be that way."

"Forget it." Jasmine turned away. "We're stuck here, Sugar. That's all there is to it."

"But it ain't fair!"

Raven's voice rose again as she stood from her chair and stormed across the room, pausing in front of the window. What she said next was spoken softly. Chances are the girl on the bed didn't even make out the words.

"It ain't fair."

Raven stood there, fighting back the tears of frustration and hurt and anger, staring into the darkness but seeing nothing. Suddenly a light caught her eyes, of a car pulling into the parking lot. Something concerning the car attracted her interest. There was something different about it.

A moment later Raven felt a surge of energy. She ran over to the bed and bent down toward Jasmine.

"It's the police."

Jasmine exhibited no reaction. Her eyes were closed, as though she had drifted back to sleep.

Raven felt the urge to shake her, to tell her what was

going on, but decided there would be time later to talk to Jasmine. Now there wasn't a moment to lose.

Stepping out into the darkness, Raven was surprised how cool the night was. The temperature had dropped considerably since when she had entered the injured girl's room. Raven wore shorts and a tank top only – she had forgotten to even slip on her shoes when she exited the hotel room – and the air felt cold against her exposed skin. The concrete she stepped on in her bare feet felt like ice, sending a shiver through her body.

But it didn't matter. Salvation was at hand. This was an opportunity Raven couldn't afford to pass up.

Chapter Forty-Four:

Dwayne SHERMAN had been a patrolman for seven years, all of it with the Franklin County Police Department. Dwayne was an adequate cop. He would never have been accused of being anything more than that. He performed his duties as required, followed his routines as expected, and invariably tested as average when it was time for reviews. He avoided the spotlight. He neither sought, nor received, advancements, content with his position in the ranks.

For the most part his time on the force had been uneventful. There was the occasional domestic violence summons that got out of hand. Or the belligerent drunks that had to be dealt with, incidents he resolved as expediently as possible. He avoided giving traffic tickets except when absolutely necessary, so as to escape the disgruntled looks of the people on the receiving end of the procedure. But even that unpleasant task he accomplished without a hitch.

He accepted it all as part of the job, though when it came right down to it he preferred leaving the police work to others.

He liked being alone, and seemed most at peace when by himself. He enjoyed driving the city streets at night, cruising serenely past the deserted offices and empty businesses. He felt important then, as though he was watchdog to the entire city. He imagined the world coming to pieces if he wasn't there to keep an eye on things.

The Majestic Hotel was on his designated route.

Most nights he settled for a drive-by, slowing down as he passed the establishment and taking a quick look at the place. He had little time to do much else. Had he bothered to linger at each business he passed he would never have gotten through his shift.

Sometimes he changed things up by pulling into the parking lot. He would pilot the police cruiser slowly past the vacant cars, in a bid to make his presence known for at least a few seconds. Even such a rapid perusal could be an effective deterrent to crime.

On one such night he was surprised to see a young woman come running from one of the rooms. She was young – obviously still a teenager – with long black hair that shined from the glow of the overhead lights. She was barefoot, which seemed odd considering the chill in the air. She wore an obscenely short pair of shorts and a tank top that seemed to be threatening to explode at any moment from the sheer volume of what was packed inside.

She was screaming something, but the words were unintelligible from where Sherman sat in his patrol car. He maneuvered his vehicle into the closest parking space and had just rolled down the window when she reached the car.

"You have to help us!" Hysteria controlled her voice. "Please!"

"What's the problem, ma'am?"

"I'm being held here. Against my will."

"I don't understand. Who's holding you?"

"Slick. Todd." She seemed confused, unable to get her facts straight. "I don't even know anymore. But you've got to help me."

She reached into the car, grabbing his arm, urgently prompting him into motion. Tears were in her eyes. Her chest heaved as she gulped the nighttime air, catching her breath.

The police officer shut off his car and opened the door, stepping out into the night. He towered over the young girl beside him.

"You say someone is holding you here? Against your will?" His voice was sympathetic. Yet, at the same time, it managed to contain a trace of anger just below the surface, as though he was not pleased with the present situation.

She nodded in reply to his question.

"Why? Why is he doing this to you?"

"It's not just me," she admitted. "There are five of us. He keeps us here. Makes us do things...."

Her words trailed off, as though afraid to continue the explanation.

Dwayne Sherman looked around, scanning the parking lot, looking for signs of others in the vicinity. There was no one to be seen. The night was quiet, save for the crying from the hysterical girl beside him.

He put a hand gently on her shoulder.

"It's okay," he reassured her. "There's nothing to worry about now."

She looked into his eyes, gaining confidence by his words and the manner in which he spoke, and managed a slight smile.

"Where is this man?" the policeman asked.

She pointed to a room across from them but said nothing.

"I'll take a look. But you'll have to come with me."

"No!" She shook her head in denial. "I can't."

"It's okay. You'll be safe. I need you to identify him for me. Understand?"

She considered his words and reluctantly nodded her head.

"Good. Come along, then."

They walked across the parking lot together, in short little steps, her reluctance to confront the man she accused of misusing her obvious. But as they drew closer she seemed less hesitant, as though drawing strength from the man beside her.

Patrolman Sherman removed his Glock 22 pistol from the holster at his side as he leaned closer to the girl. He held the firearm with both hands, steadying himself. He addressed her in a low voice. "Knock on the door. Tell him you need to see him. Once he opens the door I'll take over."

She nodded in agreement, and when they arrived at the correct room the young girl did as instructed, knocking on the panel.

A gruff voice answered from the other side. "Who is it?"

"It's Raven," she squeaked. She swallowed hard, trying to control the panic that gripped her voice. "I need to talk to you."

"Come back in the morning. I'm busy."

"I really need to see you." There was no reply this time, so after several seconds the black-haired girl continued. "It's important, Slick. It's about Jasmine."

The two people standing outside the door waited, and after a few seconds they were greeted by the sound of a chain unlatching from the other side of the panel. The room was dimly lit, the only illumination coming from a computer monitor, but it offered enough light to make out the person who greeted them. Slick was dressed in a pair of sweat pants only, wearing no shirt. His expression betrayed his aggravation at having been interrupted, but the look on his face changed abruptly when he saw the uniformed officer standing outside.

Sherman made a gesture with his pistol, indicating for the room's occupant to step back.

"What's going on here?" Slick asked.

"Please move back into the room, Sir." The tone of the policeman's voice offered no room for discussion. No doubt the Glock 22 in the officer's hand contributed to Slick's reaction as well.

He had no choice but to comply. He slowly backed up, his gaze alternating between the gun in the uniformed man's hand and the young girl beside the officer, who betrayed a look of confidence that seemed unusual on her.

Raven seemed more at ease now. It was as though a burden had been lifted from her. She glared at Slick with disgust in her eyes.

As they entered the room a computer came into view. It displayed the website Slick had set up, featuring images from the escort service he managed from the hotel. A list of names ran down the left side of the screen.

Shasha.

Diamond.

Jasmine.

Violet.

Raven.

Each name was coupled with a face shot of the girl. Raven had no recollection of when the pictures had been taken. They must have been candid shots Slick had managed without them realizing it.

The teenager was horrified at seeing herself so blatantly displayed online. Her body had been subjected to the most embarrassing use the past several months. But this latest affront was a violation such as she had never imagined.

Her anger intensified.

She glared at Slick once more, and only then did she notice something. His face held an utter lack of concern, as though there was nothing out of the ordinary going on. Then she heard the sound, of the door closing behind her, followed by the metallic clink of a chain being fastened.

She turned slightly, to look at the police officer, who now appeared rather amused with the entire situation.

Slick stepped toward them. "Good job, Dwayne."

"Only doing what you asked me to do, Slick. You told me to keep an eye on things over here."

"I'm glad you did." He scowled at Raven. "We almost had a fucking problem on our hands."

The reality of the situation finally occurred to Raven. She lunged at the police officer, pummeling his chest with her hands.

The attack lasted for less than three seconds.

Sherman lashed out, his pistol catching the girl across the

cheek.   She fell to the floor, hitting hard against the worn carpeting.   When she looked up the trickle of blood from her split lip was already dripping on the floor.

Fear was in her eyes.

Slick sat down in the desk chair in front of his computer, his actions casual.   He swiveled in his seat, then spoke to the uniformed man.

"She's all yours, Dwayne. Have your fun."

Slick pulled out a cigarette.

"You've earned it."

Chapter Forty-Five:

EVENTUALLY THE uniformed man had his fill, though it took a long time for him to reach his saturation point. His sexual appetite seemed unquenchable. And the more Raven struggled against him, the more she fought his attention, the more aroused he became.

She was helpless to resist. Early on in the encounter – after removing her tank top but before pulling off her shorts – the officer had handcuffed her arms to the top of the headboard, effectively preventing her from fleeing. The position was excruciating. The metal cuffs dug into her each time the man on top moved, resulting in a constant rubbing against her wrists. They were scrapped raw and bleeding long before he was done with his entertainment.

Her pleas for compassion had been answered with brutality. A filthy rag from the bathroom had been tied around her mouth. She could no longer complain because she lacked the ability to do so.

Sherman enjoyed the young girl's discomfort, relishing the feeling of power he gained by being in total control, using her with the reckless abandon that comes from knowing there could be no possible repercussions for his actions.

Slick, for his part, observed the episode with the same amount of interest as others would display while watching a dull sporting event. His eyes remained glued to the scene – as though fearful of missing something should he look away – but he exhibited no sign of emotion. He sat calmly, occasionally puffing on his cigarette, while the police officer worked himself into a frenzy and Raven fought back the agonizing pain that washed over her from the punishment she was receiving.

When it was over, and Officer Dwayne Sherman moved away from the bed, Slick drew closer.

Raven was breathing heavily, fighting back the tears while she tried to control the pain that radiated across her breasts and between her legs. Her arms felt as though jolts of lightning were coursing through them. She tried to shift position, to relieve the discomfort, but all she managed was to scrape more skin from her torn wrists as the shackles that bound her dug further into her flesh.

"I'm disappointed in you, Rosie."

For a second she lay there, not realizing what was being said to her, but then her eyes snapped open. It was the first time she had heard her name – her real name – in months. It should have been a pleasing sound, a return to normalcy, but instead it brought a chill to her. It was worse than the cold air against her naked skin. A feeling of foreboding overwhelmed her.

Slick's voice was devoid of inflection as he continued. "I sheltered you, Rosie. I offered you a home when no one else would have you. I took care of you."

He sighed.

"And this is the way you reward me."

Had she been able to speak she would have pleaded with the man standing over her, promising anything to appease him and thus end her ordeal.

But she couldn't speak.

She couldn't plead.

And she couldn't do anything to stop what happened next.

Slick lifted his hand, displaying a leather stick of some kind. Part of Raven's mind recognized it as a riding crop.

He leaned closer, whispering in her ear. "I need to punish

you, Rosie. I don't want to do it. But I have to. You understand, don't you?"

She shook her head, her eyes imploring him to let her be. He never noticed.

"I don't enjoy this." His hand reached out, stroking the side of her breast that was closest to him. The touch was cold, icy, against her skin. "I can think of other ways to spend time with you. Other things I would enjoy much more than this. You have.... ...so much more to offer."

He sighed once more.

"But you leave me no choice. And what's really frustrating...!"

His voice had started to rise, anger attempting to burst loose, but he managed to get himself under control. He continued once more, speaking softly.

"What's most frustrating, Rosie, is the unfortunate timing of what you've done. Considering what Jasmine has just been through, it looks like I may be one girl short for a while. I really have no wish to have two of my girls out of commission at the same time."

He pulled away, standing up beside the bed. Raven closed her eyes, breathing a sigh of relief.

The first blow caught her just below the left breast. She tried to scream out, but the rag around her mouth prevented the action. Her eyes snapped open.

Slick was poised to hit her a second time.

"You need to be taught a fucking lesson, you bitch."

Seeing the strike coming did little to prepare her for the shock. She attempted to draw back at the last second, to lessen the force, but there was nowhere to go. Her body contorted in pain, as she struggled to alleviate the sensations.

But in the process she only managed to pull on her arms. She felt the handcuffs digging into her wrists, further cutting off the circulation to her already numbed limbs.

Slick was screaming by now.

"I don't need no fucking bitch fucking up the good thing I got going here!"

Another blow landed, catching her on the hip.

"I worked too fucking hard to let a slut like you fuck me up!"

The frequency of the hits increased, as the man wielding the riding crop worked himself into a passion. Red welts were raised on Raven's skin, standing out in stark contrast to the white of her flesh. She struggled, squirming for relief from the attack, screaming soundless screams that never escaped her throat.

Even after she fell unconscious the rain of blows continued.

Chapter Forty-Six:

W HEN MELANIE arrived home from work the house was dark. This didn't surprise her any. It was late – she had stayed over at the end of her shift at the hospital to catch up on some paperwork – and she hadn't expected Andy to be awake. She understood that he still had to get up in the morning for work.

She was worn-out, had been on her feet all day, and the thought of crawling into bed beside her husband was an attractive proposition. But, as tired as she was, she didn't feel she could fall asleep yet. Most nights were like that for Melanie. She needed some down time when she got home to unwind after the stress of dealing with demanding patients, who seemed to feel she was their personal nurse and couldn't understand she had other tasks to keep her busy besides attending to their wants.

Melanie turned on the computer in the dining room, waiting the few seconds it took for the monitor to warm up, and logged onto her internet account. She spent a few minutes on Facebook – checking out the latest news from friends and family – but she quickly bored of the activity. There was so much useless drivel out there, so many nonsensical posts and bickering opinions on politics and such, that she generally found it a waste of time to spend too long on the site. Once she determined she had her fill she logged off.

She checked her e-mails next, scanning the latest messages from the CASA office. There seemed to be a steady barrage of pleas, looking for volunteers to take on additional cases. The need never lessened. There were always children out there who needed help.

Another message was a reminder to Melanie that she had a hearing coming up in a couple of weeks. This involved her new case with Rochelle, the thirteen-year-old who had been removed from home following a Domestic Violence report involving the girl's mother. The Adjudication Hearing would determine whether the teenager would remain at her aunt's house or return to live with her mother.

Melanie suspected the child would be going home. She obviously missed her mother a lot, and seemed anxious to return to familiar surroundings.

As far as the mother, Melanie had to admit she was doing a great job. She hadn't balked at the idea of taking parenting classes, nor had she refused the substance abuse counseling program Social Services had set up for her. She appeared to be doing what was necessary to bring her family back together.

It was reassuring to Melanie to be involved with such a case. It made her feel like she was doing something worthwhile, contributing to a program that accomplished positive results.

It almost made up for the way things had ended with Rosaletta Guiterrez.

Melanie seldom thought about Rosie anymore. And when she did it bothered her to think the troubled girl was little more than a passing memory. Melanie was still concerned, and curious about what had happened. She naturally hoped everything would work out for Rosie.

But she could no longer dwell on it.

Time had moved on. Melanie had her life with Andy, and her work at the hospital, and now her case with Rochelle. These were all things that occupied her time and kept her busy. There wasn't anything she could do now to help Rosie. That part of her life was gone now, the door closed those many months ago when the teenager disappeared.

She sometimes wondered if she would ever know the truth; if she would ever find out what had happened.

People come and go. That was part of life. For a moment Melanie reflected on the friends she had known years ago, the girlfriends she had spent time with, the boyfriends she had dated. So many of them she couldn't even remember anymore. Their faces were barely a blur, their names largely forgotten. It was hard to believe that someone could be so important to you one day and gone the next.

Life was, after all, such a transient affair.

A memory. That's what Rosie was now.

Melanie suspected someday she would be forgotten completely.

Chapter Forty-Seven:

IT HAD been a long day already. Annie Klume had testified before a hearing at Juvenile Court, refereed an unruly visitation session between a set of parents recently divorced, and attended a staff meeting with her supervisor. She had answered a slew of e-mails and fielded half-a-dozen phone calls. All this and her day wasn't even halfway over.

She had just returned to her office from her meeting when the phone rang. She considered letting it go – after all, what was voice mail for? – then decided against it. It could be a matter that needed her prompt attention.

"Hello. Annie Klume here."

"Miss Klume. This is Consuella. Consuella Alegredo."

For a second Annie hesitated. The name was familiar, but it took a moment to place the caller. She hadn't spoken to the woman for several months now. After her daughter Rosaletta's disappearance they had kept in touch for a while. But the child neglect case became a moot point when the child involved wasn't anywhere to be found.

"Yes, Consuella. How are you doing?"

Annie nearly inquired about Rosie, thinking maybe Consuella had heard something and that was the reason for the call. But upon reflection she decided not to mention the missing girl. There was no point bringing up matters best left unsaid.

The voice on the other end of the line continued.

"I'm leaving, Miss Klume."

"I don't understand."

"I'm leaving Toledo. I need to go."

"Are you sure that's what you want to do?"

"Yes. I am. There's nothing left for me here. Tommy is gone. And Rosie...."

She stopped abruptly, choking back a tear.

For several long seconds neither woman spoke. The silence lingered between them, like a wall that each was afraid to cross.

"Where will you go?" Annie asked at last.

"I have family. Down in Atlanta. My cousin Juanita. I'll be staying with her. I don't belong here no more. It's no good for me here. The apartment just reminds me too much of...."

She took a deep breath, to strengthen herself to continue.

"Too many memories. I need to get away."

"I understand. And I'm sorry things have worked out like this for you."

"I'm sorry too. I'm sorry I didn't treat my Rosie better. I realize it weren't her fault. What happened to Tommy."

"Life has a way of treating us rough sometimes, Consuella. I'm sorry for everything you've had to go through."

"Don't be feeling sorry for me. It's my own damn fault. But I just wanted to thank you. For trying to help us the way you done."

"I only wish I could have done more."

"You done enough. More than I deserved."

"That's not true."

"Don't lie to me, Miss Klume. I know I done a lot of bad in my life. I have to live with that. Wherever I am. But I just wanted to ask you.... If you see Rosie.... If you find my baby some day...."

She was in tears by now, but forced herself to continue.

"Just tell her, tell her Mama's sorry about the way she treated her. You'll tell her that, won't you?"

"Yes, Mrs. Alegredo. I'll tell her."

"Thank you. That means a lot to me."
And then the line went dead.

Chapter Forty-Eight:

T HINGS CHANGED for the young women at The Majestic Hotel following the attack on Jasmine. Each of them had a history, a story that told how Slick had insinuated himself into their lives, and each kept that to themselves. They realized there was no way to ever return to their former ways. They had come to accept this, and learned with time to make the best of the horrendous situation they were trapped in.

But the attack on Jasmine, the brutality that had been unleashed against her, brought into sharp focus for each of them just how precarious their existence actually was. What happened to Jasmine could have happened to any of them. And each time they met a stranger in one of the hotel rooms, each time they closed the door to shut themselves in with a man they knew nothing about, they put their lives in jeopardy.

They didn't talk about it. It wouldn't have done any good to discuss the matter. But it was obvious from the way they reacted afterward that it was on each of their minds.

It took a long time for Jasmine to recover. Had she been given proper medical attention it undoubtedly would have gone easier for her. As it was she lingered in bed for much longer than she should have, the pain from the slash in her face contributing to multiple headaches that further perpetuated her suffering.

For days she burned with fever, slipping in and out of consciousness. She was unable to eat; even the simple act of chewing brought her so much pain that she declined anything offered to her. When she finally began to recover, when it became obvious the worst was over, she was so weak from lack of nourishment that it further prolonged her sick time.

Eventually she did recover enough to go back to work. But she was never the same. She lost interest in the things that had mattered to her before. Never one to socialize, she isolated herself even further from the others. At first they tried to console her. But with time they realized the futility of attempting to reach her. Eventually they gave up on the attempt entirely.

As a reminder of the event – as though she needed one – the slash across her face never healed properly. The white streak that graced her features would undoubtedly remain for the rest of her life.

All the girls suffered vicariously through Jasmine, but for Raven it was even worse. Her punishment at Slick's hands, following the brutal way she had been used by the police officer she had turned to for help, altered her way of thinking.

She still hated her life. But she realized more than ever the importance of breaking free from her predicament. She had learned from the experience as well, in a way Slick could have never imagined. She became docile, obedient, apparently content to follow every command she was given.

But it was all just a ploy; a trick, to conceal her true feelings. She became more devious in her way of looking at things, determined that whatever would come she would benefit from the tough lesson she had been given.

She was patient, knowing time was on her side. She forced her mind to go blank whenever she was with a man, performing the motions she was required to perform while she distanced her thoughts from the acts. She learned to fake enjoyment, giving the clients a semblance of excitement, while in truth she loathed each second she spent with them.

None of the men she spent time with appeared to be aware of her performance. Each was so content in his own quest for gratification they paid no attention to the young girl called upon to service them.

Raven knew salvation would come someday. She couldn't begin to imagine how deliverance would present itself, but she never doubted it would arrive. Because of this she was determined not to miss any opportunity that came her way.

Chapter Forty-Nine:

THE OPPORTUNITY Raven awaited came on an evening that began much like any other.

The commitment she was hired for was performed in the typical manner; as expediently as possible. With time she had become an expert at gauging what was required to satisfy the appetites of the men who came to see her. She completed the task simply and quickly, expending the smallest amount of effort necessary.

After all, she wasn't paid by the hour. It was more of a piece-work arrangement.

Afterward Raven sat on the bed, dressed in nothing other than a bra, watching as the man she had just satisfied finished putting his clothes on and slunk from the room. No words passed between them. There was nothing left to say.

As she was slipping into her pants she noticed something resting on the floor.

Raven's excitement grew as she picked up the object.

He must have dropped the cellphone from his pants pocket while he was undressing. No doubt he would notice it was missing and return looking for it. She knew she had seconds only to react.

Recalling her earlier mistake, so many months ago, she realized she would have to be more discreet this time to avoid any repercussions.

She slipped the phone under the mattress, placing it as far underneath as her arm would reach, then hurriedly finished dressing. She was just donning her top when the knock came announcing his return.

She tried to remain calm as she opened the door, hoping her nervousness wasn't obvious.

The man stood there with a dumb look on his face, like he felt uncomfortable being there and didn't know what to say. It struck Raven that he had exhibited no such hesitancy when he had first arrived on the scene.

Raven flashed him a smile. "Well hello there, Honey." She kept her tone flippant, hoping her voice wouldn't betray her. "I wasn't expecting to see you back so soon."

"I think I left something here."

"You mean you didn't come back here to have some more fun?"

He made no reply, attempting to look past her into the room.

"Well come on in, Honey."

She moved aside, allowing him to enter, then closed the door behind them She leaned against the panel, making no attempt to get in his way, trying her best to convince him she had nothing to hide.

"I'm flattered you're back so soon. But it's gonna cost you more if you want to continue the party."

He ignored her as he made a quick circuit of the room.

"What you looking for, Honey? Maybe I can help you find it?"

"No." He stopped, a disgusted look on his face. "I must have left it somewhere else."

Apparently satisfied, he let himself out the door. He never bothered to look back. Raven stood in the doorway, watching him get in the car.

"You come back and visit me again sometime."

He left, and Raven closed the door and sat down on the bed. She finally felt able to breath normally again.

She was tempted to grab the cellphone instantly, but she fought the urge. She had made mistakes in the past because of haste. She had paid the price for her indiscretions. This time she would be more careful.

Nights were generally long for the stable of girls sequestered at The Majestic Hotel. It wasn't unusual to be awake long past midnight, performing their duties, and this day was no different than so many others. Morning was approaching when Raven eventually turned off the lights in her room.

But she didn't sleep.

Reaching under the mattress she retrieved the hidden cellphone. For a moment she stared at the device. It was hard to believe the end of her suffering could be obtained through such a tiny device.

She never hesitated on what to do next. She knew who she had to call. She did pause, however, to contemplate what she would say.

Would her Mama still be mad at her? The last time they had spoken anger hung between the two of them. They were both hurt, still dealing with the agony of Tommy's death, and neither could see beyond their own pain.

But time had passed since then. Surely things had changed by now?

Would her Mama refuse to talk to her daughter?

The young girl couldn't accept such a possibility, not after all she had gone through. She had no one else to call. She was depending on reaching out to the only person she had left in her life.

She dialed the familiar number, holding her breath while she counted how many times the phone rang. After four rings a metallic voice answered.

"The number you have reached is no longer in service."

There was more to the message, but by then Raven wasn't listening.

Her arm fell to her side, the cellphone dropping to the bedspread.

It wasn't what she had expected.

Part of her wondered what had happened to her Mama. Had the woman simply gotten behind on her bills and had her phone disconnected? Or was there more, something tragic, behind the explanation for why the call couldn't go through?

Raven couldn't deal with it now. She had anticipated all evening hearing her Mama's voice. She had expected to reach out to someone that could help her, and bring an end to her ordeal. She felt defeated, her hopes crushed.

She lay back on the bed and stared at the ceiling, racking her brain for what to do next. She contemplated calling 911, reaching out to the emergency services for assistance. But when she considered the last time she had approached someone in authority, and how the incident had backfired on her, she dismissed the notion from her mind. She couldn't go through that again.

She wouldn't go through that again.

She was fairly certain Slick would be less forgiving this time around.

So Raven lay there, and the tears came, and she wondered again how life could turn into something so miserable.

She must have fallen asleep. Panic overtook her when she awoke to the sight of sunlight peeking through the edge of the curtains. She sat upright, searching, and found the cellphone where she had dropped it. She couldn't risk being seen with it. She would need to hide it again until she could determine what to do next.

She bent down and returned the phone to its former hiding place, under the mattress of the bed. As she reached her arm in to conceal the device her fingers encountered something. She withdrew the object.

The small white card glared at her. For a few moments she stared, trying to recall the significance of it, then everything came back to her.

Perhaps there was someone else she could contact after all.

Chapter Fifty:

"THINGS ARE going so much smoother with my second CASA case, " Melanie admitted.

"That's good to hear," Andy replied.

The two of them sat across from each other at the kitchen table. They had just finished dinner – a simple meal of hamburgers with mac and cheese – and were finishing a conversation they had started earlier.

"The girl's mother really isn't a bad person," Melanie continued. "I think she cares for her daughter. She just has issues of her own."

"What kind of issues?"

She shrugged. "I'll probably never know. It seems like everyone anymore has issues of some kind. She's been going to therapy the last couple of months. I only hope it's doing her some good."

"How about the other problem?"

"Her drinking?"

Andy nodded.

"She claims she's given it up."

"And you believe her?'

Melanie considered. "Yes I do. She's been sent for testing twice since I've been on the case, and both times came back negative. And whenever I've met with her she's appeared to be sober. So, yes, I believe her."

"You're too trusting, Mel," her husband replied.

"And you're too negative," she shot back, though the comment was delivered with a smile on her face.

"I just think some habits are hard to break," Andy commented.

She nodded in agreement. "It is a shame how some people get hooked on things. Sure, I've seen it in the hospital. It's nothing new to me. And I know there's physical – as well as mental – reasons to explain why people get addicted, whether it's alcohol or drugs or whatever. But it just doesn't make sense. To ruin your life that way..."

"It's the world we live in," Andy surmised. "People just don't know how to handle stress. The pace of life gets to be so fast sometimes that they turn to something, anything, for an escape."

"I think it's more than that. I think so many of these people come from homes where their parents didn't know how to function with things. The children never learn proper coping mechanisms, and as they grow up they pass those poor habits on to *their* kids. It's a vicious cycle, really."

"So how do you break the cycle?"

"I'd like to think what I'm doing now will help. By being involved with CASA, and helping to insure that these kids have a good life, maybe we can turn things around for them."

She would have continued, but at that point the chirping of her cellphone interrupted. The number on the display was one she was unfamiliar with.

"Hello. This is Melanie."

"Miss Powers. Thank God I reached you. This is Raven. I need your help."

"Who?"

Melanie was racking her brain, trying to recognize the voice on the other end of the line. The name didn't sound familiar to her. The girl on the phone had addressed her by her CASA name – Miss Powers – which meant this had something to do with one of her cases. But none of it made sense to her.

Melanie continued. "I'm sorry. Who is this?"

"Shit." The voice on the other end reprimanded herself. "It's Rosaletta Guiterrez. Rosie."

It all came back to Melanie then.

"Rosie! Where are you?"

"I don't know. Somewhere near Columbus, I think. I don't know. I'm at a hotel called The Majestic, but that's all I know."

As she listened to the panicky voice coming over the line Melanie shifted in her seat, looking around, then spotted a pen sitting on the counter. Grabbing a napkin she wrote down the word MAJESTIC, followed by COLUMBUS???, which she underlined.

Meanwhile Rosie was still talking.

"Slick keeps us isolated from everything. He don't ever let us leave."

"Who's Slick?"

The young girl chose to ignore the question, her mind preoccupied with other things.

"Please help me. You've got to help me."

"Of course. Anything. Rosie, what's going on? You're scaring me."

"I'm a prisoner. They watch me all the time. And they make me do things...." She stopped in mid-sentence, her voice wavering. "I don't want to do them things no more. I'm sick of all these men and what they make me do."

Images flashed through Melanie's mind. She forced the thoughts aside, concentrating instead on what the young girl was telling her.

"Rosie, wherever you are, you have to leave. You need to get out of there."

"I can't." She was crying now. "They'll hurt me if I try to go."

"Then get help. You have a phone. Call 911."

"That's no good. The police are part of it. They look out for Slick. Last time I talked to the police...."

She stopped abruptly, as though they had been cut off.

"I can't go through that again," she finally managed. "Please help me. Please."

"I will Rosie. I will. Don't give up. I am going to help you. I promise."

"I gotta go. I think someone's coming."

Then the line went dead.

Chapter Fifty-One:

Detective BENJAMIN Tuppelo sat in the back seat of the unmarked police car. The man in front, sitting next to the driver, turned to address the Toledo police officer. He was older, graying at the temples. The look lent him an air of authority, as did the commanding voice he used to speak to the detective.

"I want to remind you, Tuppelo, that you're out of your jurisdiction here. Allowing you to come along is just a courtesy from the Franklin County Police Department."

"And I appreciate it, Captain Lukas. But it's like I told you. Considering the nature of things, I think it's best that I'm here."

"I still don't believe one of my men can be involved in any of this."

"I'm just going by what I was told."

Tuppelo looked out the window, as though attempting to see beyond where he sat. It was dark. Night had fallen, descending on the city like a cloak. The street lights in the vicinity worked at their task, striving to turn the darkness into light, but failed at the attempt. They managed little other than accenting the black shadows, those pockets of night left undisclosed by their glow.

There were three other police cars nearby, like this one all unmarked. Tuppelo could see the figures within, waiting with the patience developed from years of police surveillance. Ahead of them, about a block away, the structure they were watching beckoned. The word MAJESTIC glowed in neon blue. The HOTEL was apparently burnt out.

Tuppelo turned back to face the officer in the front seat. "I've met the girl before. I think she'll trust me."

"She can trust any of us," Lukas replied.

Tuppelo made no comment, having no desire to further antagonize Lukas. He could understand the man's position, and appreciated that he depended on the loyalty and honesty of his officers. It must have been disturbing to have it insinuated that one of his men was involved in a sex trafficking ring.

Tuppelo thought back to the chain of events that had brought him here tonight. It had begun with a frantic phone call from Melanie Cox.

"I just heard from Rosaletta Guiterrez," the woman blurted out, after introducing herself.

"Please refresh my memory, Miss Cox," Tuppelo suggested. "What does this pertain to?"

"Rosie disappeared about six months ago. She left her foster home for school and hasn't been seen since."

The detective hesitated, searching in his mind for a recollection of the girl.

Melanie Cox continued from the other end of the line, apparently interpreting his hesitation correctly. "Her brother Thomas had been killed – here in Toledo – several months before Rosie vanished. An accident at the train yards."

"I remember now. The girl was thrown out of her apartment by her mother, following the boy's death."

"That's right. But I just heard from her. She needs help."

"What kind of help?"

"She said she's been a prisoner. And that they make her do things. It sounded like some sort of prostitution thing. Is that possible?"

"Unfortunately, yes it is. Sex trafficking is all too real of a thing."

"But Rosie is only fifteen. Surely girls that young aren't involved in such a thing?"

"Sadly they are. I just read a report that examined child victims in Missouri. Their ages ranged from twelve to sixteen."

"That's horrible. I had no idea it involved children so young."

"It's a rough world for kids, Miss Cox. And you think that's what's going on here? That Rosaletta is involved in some sort of sex trafficking?"

"That's the impression I got after talking to her."

"Did she tell you where she was?"

"She wasn't certain. She thought near Columbus. She mentioned she was staying at The Majestic Hotel."

Tuppelo's hands flashed to his computer keyboard. In moments he found the information he sought.

"It's in Dublin, Ohio. That's near Columbus. Thank you, Miss Cox. I'll contact the local police immediately."

"Wait!" An edge of panic was in her voice. "Rosie said something else. She said she couldn't go to the police down there. That they were involved with what was going on."

Tuppelo paused, choosing his next words carefully. "That's a serious allegation. Do you have any proof of police involvement?"

"No. I'm just going by what Rosie told me. She said the police were in on it. She sounded pretty certain of the fact."

"Then I'll need to proceed carefully. Just in case she's right."

"Isn't there any way you can go down there yourself?" Melanie suggested.

"That's out of my jurisdiction, Miss Cox."

"I understand. And I'm sure this puts you in a delicate situation. But didn't you tell me that you met Rosie once before?"

"I did. The night her brother died. I was the detective investigating the incident."

"Then she knows you. Or at least has met you. She wouldn't feel threatened if you showed up. She needs someone down there she can trust."

He paused, considering the suggestion.

The woman on the other end continued. "I just want what's best for Rosie. That's all. I can't imagine what she's gone through these last few months. I don't *want* to imagine it. I just want her out of that place."

"I'll see what I can do."

Tuppelo had talked to Captain Hulet, who had made a few phone calls of his own, twisting some proverbial arms in the persuasive manner he had. Five hours later, after the drive from Toledo and following a briefing at the Franklin County Police Station, Tuppelo found himself a part of the stake-out team at The Majestic Hotel.

A uniformed officer approached the car, keeping to the shadows so he wasn't observed. Tuppelo had been introduced to all the participants of tonight's action before leaving the local station. He was fairly certain the man's name was Sherman.

Officer Sherman had volunteered to approach the front desk, seeking information concerning a young girl answering to the description of Rosaletta Guiterrez.

"Looks like our intell may have been correct," the police officer informed them. "Room 232 has a girl that sounds like her."

"Was the desk clerk certain?" Lukas asked from the front seat.

"I showed him the photo. He said it was her."

"All right." The Captain faced Tuppelo again. "Go to her room. Identify yourself, make certain she's safe, then stay with her. Phone us any information she can give you regarding the people holding her and where they are. Also anything about the rest of the stable. If what you're saying is true I have to believe there's more than one girl involved in this thing."

Without a word Tuppelo got out of the car. He had barely taken two steps when Captain Lukas spoke up once more.

"No slip-ups, Tuppelo. I don't want anybody getting hurt. Especially not some out-of-county detective that shouldn't be here in the first place."

"I'll try to keep that in mind, Sir."

Chapter Fifty-Two:

THE TELEVISION blared in the corner of the room, filling the cramped space with sound. Raven sat on her bed, staring into space, ignoring the device completely. She couldn't get interested in the shows on TV, though she liked having the set on regardless. It made her feel less alone.

The knock on the door took her by surprise. She wasn't expecting anyone. Still, it wasn't unusual to have a client arrive unannounced. Slick was always ready to accommodate another paying customer.

She didn't bother to turn the set off as she went to greet her visitor. Her movements were lethargic, a slow plodding gait that exemplified the way she felt. She couldn't see the point in hurrying. Raven was fairly certain whoever was at the door wouldn't be going away.

The man was big, but not in a flabby sort of way. He was an imposing figure, standing in the doorway, towering over her by at least half a foot. His clothes appeared clean and well-cared for, not like the crap some of the guys wore.

It never made sense to her. You'd think if they could afford to pay for a fuck they could afford some decent clothes to wear.

For a moment Raven hesitated, fearful of being alone with the man. Then she decided she may as well get it over with.

"Come on in," she offered, hoping to put him at ease and not betray her apprehensions. The last thing she wanted to do was alarm him, and provoke him into doing something she would later regret.

He entered without a word, closing the door behind him.

"The money goes on the dresser," she instructed. "Then just get yourself comfortable."

"That's not why I'm here."

The fear returned with the man's words.

"What do you mean?"

"Hello, Rosaletta."

She caught her breath, gasping for air, and took a step backward. "How do you know my name?"

"I'm Detective Benjamin Tuppelo. Of the Toledo Police Department. We met before."

She examined him more closely then; the familiar look of his face, the earnestness in his eyes.

"It was the night Tommy died," she remarked, her voice quiet, as for a moment she recalled the incident.

He nodded. "I'm here to take you home, Rosie."

She sat on the bed. The tears came instantly, with heaving motions that shook her body.

Captain Lukas looked at his watch yet again. "Christ. It's been twenty minutes now. What's he doing in there?"

Officer Dwayne Sherman, still standing guard outside the car, spoke up, his mood flippant. "Maybe he figured he'd stop for a quick one while he was at it?"

The look he received from his superior sobered him instantly.

"Not funny, officer."

"I'm sorry, Sir. Just making a joke."

"One in poor taste considering the circumstances. Don't you agree?

"Yes, Sir."

They fell silent once more, the mood broken several

minutes later with the ringing of the captain's cellphone.

"What do you have?" Lukas answered.

Tuppelo's voice roared from the tiny speaker. "There are two men involved. Slick runs the scheme. He's in room 112. The other man is the enforcer. Goes by the name of Motorman. You'll find him in 142. From what I hear he's a tough one, so don't take any chances."

"Is he armed?"

"Miss Guiterrez informs me she's never seen either of them packing, but that doesn't rule out the possibility."

"Understood. And the girls? How many are there?"

"Five, including Miss Guiterrez." He rattled off four additional room numbers.

"You stay put, Tuppelo, until I give you the all clear."

"Yes, Sir."

They coordinated things to hit all six rooms at the same time. One policeman went to each of the rooms where the girls stayed.

Violet was entertaining when the officer arrived. The man with her was undressed down to his underwear when the knock came on the door.

"Christ!" He flashed a shocked look in the blue-haired girl's direction. "What the fuck did you get me into?"

She shrugged, casually approaching the door. She opened it just enough to take a peak outside as her client was zipping up his jeans.

"Franklin County Police Department," the officer remarked. "Are you in need of assistance, ma'am?"

She smiled at the thought and flung the panel open, revealing the room's contents to the outside world. She glanced at the shirtless man in the room with her, a smug look on her face.

"It's not what it looks like, officer," the man explained.

The policeman nodded, a knowing look on his face. "It looks to me like you should be leaving, Sir."

"On my way."

He slowed down as he got to the door, noticing the money he had brought with him still sitting on top of the dresser. He glanced at Vi, who slowly shook her head no. The smile never left her face as he came to the inevitable conclusion that it wasn't worth the effort after all.

Clutching his shirt to his naked chest he scurried out without a backward glance.

Shasha wasn't to be found in her room. They located her instead in Diamond's room. The two girls had been playing cards when the interruption came.

"What's this, then?" Diamond asked, having answered the door.

"Franklin County Police."

"Is that so? Is that supposed to mean something?"

"We understand you women have been coerced into staying here without your consent."

Shasha, standing up, was quick to respond. "We didn't do nothing wrong."

"We understand that, ma'am. It's not you we're after."

The two girls exchanged knowing glances.

Diamond smiled, the first genuine expression she had betrayed since she couldn't remember when.

For Shasha the reaction was more ambivalent. Of all the girls she had gained the most from Slick's arrangement. As such she also had the most to lose if things turned sour. But she was realistic enough to know that when an opportunity came – for good or for bad – the only intelligent decision was to make the best of the situation.

She approached the man in the doorway.

"Thank you for coming, officer. We are prepared to tell you whatever you need to know."

Jasmine was by herself, as she was wont to do anymore. Her expression failed to betray her thoughts as the officer at her door explained what was going on.

Months ago she would have reacted differently. She would have welcomed the arrival of the authorities, relishing the opportunity to be released from her situation. But things had changed since then, thanks to a drunken client and a shattered bottle of whiskey.

She knew enough about life on the streets to realize how precarious things could be. She had served her time in the jungle. She had no intention of returning to that life.

But what options did she have?

"Will you excuse me a moment, officer?"

The question was poised quietly; barely above a whisper.

Jasmine entered the bathroom, closing the door behind her, and leaned against the sink. She stared into the mirror, examining her features. The scar on her cheek glared back at her. Mocking her.

Who would want her now?

What good was she to anyone looking like this?"

She sat on the toilet and the tears began.

But unlike Rosie, who at the same moment was shedding tears of relief, Jasmine sobbed in anguish. She hated her life. She hated where she was at.

But she hated even more the thought of what life had in store for her next.

Chapter Fifty-Three:

MOTORMAN HAD just taken a swallow of Absolut Vodka – swirling the clear liquid in his mouth and savoring the slight burn as it trickled down his throat – when the world exploded around him. Three armed police officers burst into the room, accomplishing the procedure with the precision of a military drill. They fanned out as they entered, moving slightly away from one another while they inched closer toward the man they had come looking for, who sat on a wooden chair with an astounded expression on his face.

No warning had been issued prior to the invasion. Other than the sound of the door smashing inward there was no sound, save the trampling of boots and the rustle of clothing, as the team moved purposely forward.

Though caught unawares Motorman reacted immediately. He neither stopped to analyze what he was doing nor did he consider the consequences of his actions. He moved on the instant, his desire for self-preservation guiding his actions. It was a primal instinct that encompassed his body and guided his behavior.

He stood from his chair and, in one sweeping motion, grabbed the seat and threw it at the closest of the attacker men. The officer went down, bowled over with the projectile. In a move surprising for someone so large Motorman took two steps, then cleanly vaulted over the fallen officer.

A hand reached for the moving man, managing to grab him just above the elbow on his right arm. Motorman twisted, broke free, and lunged for the door, intent on making his escape. The panel was still open. He was outside in the cool night air in moments.

Instantly half a dozen lights shined on him, spotlighting him where he stood. Like a deer caught in the glare of headlamps he froze, assessing the situation.

He stopped short as the urge to fight evaporated.

The armed policemen facing him down were a definite deterrent to further resistance.

As strong as he was, he knew he wasn't bulletproof.

An unseen someone reached behind him, roughly pulling his arms back. He heard the metallic click as the handcuffs were locked into place. Hands pushed against him, forcing him to his knees.

There was little he could do at that point except bluster.

"What the fuck's going on here?" He spat to the side, demonstrating his disdain for those around him. "I think you got the wrong fucking guy."

"Is that so?" Captain Lukas strode toward him, projecting the authority he carried with him wherever he went. "The wrong guy for what?"

"Whatever the fuck you're looking for. I got rights, you know. I ain't done nothing fucking wrong here."

"If that's the case then I apologize in advance."

Lukas stopped short, inches from the captured man.

"But I sincerely doubt you're innocent of anything," the police Captain commented.

He motioned to one of the officers.

"Get him out of here."

They manhandled Motorman to his feet. He complied with no resistance. He seemed nearly complacent about the whole situation, as though he saw nothing serious with his circumstance.

As a group they led him through the parking lot. He

glanced around as they marched him forward, taking in the surroundings. A crowd had formed already, spilling out of the neighboring doorways to investigate the disturbance. He caught a glimpse of Vi, standing beside a uniformed officer. As their eyes met she flipped him the finger.

He laughed the matter off.

He looked toward the front of the hotel and his pace slowed. The officer behind him nearly collided with him.

"Watch what you're doing, asshole."

Motorman turned at the waist, flashed the man a smile, then leapt into action once again.

Those around him had taken his complacency as a token of surrender, having relinquished their vigilance once Motorman was cuffed. His actions proved them wrong as he appeared to go berserk.

He jerked violently to the left and right, upsetting the man on either side of him. The inefficiency of the tight-knit formation the officers had assumed became apparent when bodies began tumbling to the ground, arms and legs tangled together.

"Take that, you mother fuckers!"

His voice roared above the crowd, his enthusiasm evident as he crashed against another officer, sending additional bodies to the ground

By that point he had cleared a sufficient enough path to escape the melee around him. He ran from the scene, the boldness of the move taking everyone by surprise. He stumbled once or twice, finding it difficult to maneuver properly with his hands at his back, but made up for his lack of form with a singleness of purpose that drove him forward.

The representatives of the Franklin County Police Department had regrouped by this point. Several withdrew firearms, their intentions obvious from the looks of determination on their faces.

"Don't shoot!" Lukas advised, raising his voice above the pandemonium surrounding him. "Too many innocents!"

So the chase began, a mad scramble around parked vehicles and garbage cans.

Motorman continued, heading toward the back of the parking lot and the rear of the hotel complex.

But in his haste he made a fatal mistake. What looked to be an alleyway between two sections of the hotel was in fact a cul-de-sac, a discovery he learned the hard way.

Seconds later he was surrounded by a bevy of police officers, his back literally up against the wall.

He hung his head, dejected, and was led away again.

Slick's room was empty.

Or, at least, nobody was found within.

Officer Dwayne Sherman was first to reach the room, followed by several other policemen with drawn guns. While one of the men investigated the bathroom – on the off-chance that someone may have been lurking in the confined space it provided – Sherman bee-lined for the computer resting in the corner, switching on the monitor. It sprang to life and he pulled out the chair, settling in to examine what he had run across.

Revealed to the room was the home page of the escort service administered from the hotel. Pictures of scantily clad women beckoned from the screen.

Sherman grabbed the mouse and began scrolling through the website.

"What are you up to?" someone asked.

He didn't bother to look up. "Just wanted to get a look at this," Sherman replied. "Thought it might give us an idea what's been going on here."

"Better not mess with that," the other officer warned him. "Leave that to the tech guys to see what they can dig up."

The seated officer hesitated a moment, then realized several sets of eyes were watching his every move. Without a word he slid the chair back, stood up, and walked away.

"Yeah. You're probably right."

Chapter Fifty-Four:

"**S**ON-OF-A-BITCH!"

Slick disconnected the call and threw down his cellphone. At the same time he pressed down on the accelerator, increasing his speed to one clearly not intended for the road he traveled.

"Fuck."

His lips felt dry. He licked them, which failed to affect the situation in the least. His arms felt clammy on the steering wheel. He rubbed them against his pants, which also served no practical purpose.

He considered the phone call he had just received.

"Slick. This is Dwayne. All hell's breaking loose down here."

"What are you talking about?"

"What I'm talking about is four carloads of police, parked outside the Majestic. They're on to you, man."

"How the fuck did this happen?"

"How do I know? Listen, I'm in the hotel office now. Trying to stall things a bit. But if you want your computer, or anything else you got stashed away here, you better move your ass. You don't got much time."

So Slick raced down the streets, knowing he wasn't going to make it in time but knowing as well that he had to give it a try. Two blocks away he slowed down, so as not to attract attention. He was driving at a conservative speed when he reached the hotel.

Being of a naturally cautious nature, Slick decided to drive past before pulling into the parking lot. He was just in time to see Motorman being escorted from his hotel room. The man's hands appeared to be cuffed behind him. He walked with a slow, steady pace, as though having given up the fight.

Just then Motorman looked up.

Slick held his breath, not sure what to expect, wondering how things would play out. Slick was certain the bound man had seen the red Firebird. It was a hard vehicle to miss.

Suddenly Motorman went wild, pushing against his escort and screaming out loud. Figures from around the parking lot ran toward him as the escaped prisoner headed the opposite direction, leading the police away from the front of the hotel, away from where Slick sat in his sports car.

Slick smiled as he drove away. Good old Motorman. The man was all right. He'd have to do something for him one of these days.

It was a shame to leave behind his computer. And the money he had stashed away in the hotel room. But what the fuck? There were other cities. Other opportunities. He knew it wouldn't be long until he was back in business once again.

Chapter Fifty-Five:

Andy WAS in the bathroom, taking his morning shower. Melanie lay under the covers, willing herself to move but enjoying the comfort of the bed.

It had been a restless night. She had received no word from Detective Tuppelo since their conversation the evening before. All the anxiety she had felt following Rosie's disappearance, all the concern over the young girl's whereabouts, was nothing compared to what she was going through now. Because now she knew what had been going on the past few months, but she had no idea of what would happen next.

She felt helpless. As much as she wanted to do something to help Rosie, she knew there was nothing she could do.

So she waited.

And she worried.

And she hoped for the best.

The phone call came just as Andy was stepping into the bedroom.

"This is Melanie."

"Hello, Miss Cox. Detective Tuppelo here."

"How's Rosie? Did you find her? Is she all right?"

"She's fine. We're driving back to Toledo right now."

By now Andy had wandered over. He sat down beside his wife, the concern on his face obvious. Melanie voiced silent words for his benefit. SHE'S OKAY.

"When can I see her?" the CASA volunteer asked.

"We're still two hours away. We'll be taking her downtown, to answer questions and try to determine just what we were dealing with down there. We got some answers already but, as you can imagine, the girl's been through a lot. She hasn't been very talkative yet."

"I'm coming down to the station," Melanie informed him, determination in her voice. "Please tell Rosie I'll be here waiting for her. When she gets to Toledo."

"That's not really necessary, Miss Cox."

"Yes it is. I want to be there."

"Very well. I already spoke with Annie Klume, from Children's Services. You'll more than likely be seeing her at the station as well."

"Thank you, Detective. For everything you've done for Rosie. I really appreciate it."

She hung up, the smile on her face revealing to her husband that everything was indeed all right.

"So it's over?" he asked.

"Yes. She's safe now."

"But what happened? I mean, was it like you thought? Was she really involved in some sort of sex ring?"

"I don't know." She hesitated a few seconds, choosing her words with care. "I'm not sure if I *want* to know. When I think of the possibilities.... Of what the poor girl has gone through...."

She paused to collect her thoughts.

"How can these things happen? How can something like this go on? And practically in our own backyard?"

"There's all kinds of people out there, Mel."

"But can't they do something about it? Can't they stop it?"

"I'm sure they try. But it's all a question of supply and

281

demand."

"What do you mean?"

"I mean, consider what happened to her. It sounds like she was abducted, and forced to prostitute herself."

Melanie covered her ears.

"Please don't say it. It's bad enough to think about it. But to hear the words out loud.... How can people do that? To an innocent young girl? What kind of monsters are out there?"

"I think whoever did this *is* a monster. Just like you said. But consider this. These men, who corrupt these kids, they're just filling a need. As bad as they are, I think the real criminals are the men who pay to have sex with these young girls. Lets face it, Mel. If there weren't men out there, willing to pay for this kind of service, then maybe what happened to your CASA child would never happen to anyone else.

"Who's the real criminal here, Mel? The pimps that control these poor kids? Or the bastards who perpetuate the system by using these young girls to satisfy their own desires?"

Chapter Fifty-Six:

T HE BABY was crying again.

Sharon Daniels didn't really mind. It was a comforting sound, to know that an infant was in the house. It was what she and Neal had hoped for when they became foster parents; a baby to nurture and protect and fill up the emptiness in their lives.

Sharon thought back on the last year-and-a-half, and the road she and her husband had traveled together to reach their present destination.

Married life hadn't gone as either of them had anticipated. Things were still been good between the two of them. Neal continued to be affectionate toward her. They still did activities together, and enjoyed each others company. There was no doubt in her mind concerning their love for one another.

But things had changed since the miscarriage.

And the subsequent operation.

To discover they could never have children of their own had been devastating. A part of their life had been closed to them. There were experiences they would never be able to share together. Like going to a little league baseball game and watching their son hit a home run. Or watching their daughter in a dance recital.

So many life opportunities lost to them.

When Neal first mentioned fostering Sharon had balked at the idea. It seemed to her merely more chances for disappointment in her life. But with time, and upon considering the alternative, she warmed to the idea.

Their first experience as foster parents had been a disaster.

Not that Rosie had been a problem. The girl mostly kept to herself. She was quiet – unnaturally so – offering no resistance to anything her foster parents had to say. She picked up after herself, and even helped with household chores on occasion.

As she grew more comfortable in her surroundings Rosie seemed to open up to her foster parents. She laughed from time to time, and joined in family activities as though she enjoyed them.

Which made Sharon all the more distraught when the teenager disappeared.

It hadn't been easy for them. It was exactly what Sharon had dreaded all along. Having accepted a child into their lives – becoming adjusted to her presence, warming to the idea of nurturing a troubled youth, feeling the beginnings of a connection with Rosie – only to have that connection severed when the teenager ran away; this was the type of experience Sharon had dreaded all along.

Neal suggested fostering another child, but as before Sharon was hesitant. She had gone through too much already. She had lost one child through miscarriage. Now she had lost another.

She didn't need to set herself up for another disaster.

But her husband persisted, and when Timothy came along she finally relented. The child was born premature. Even now, at two months, he weighed barely seven pounds. His mother was an addict, taking prescription pain killers until the day the child was born. It was obviously the drugs that had affected his low birth weight and premature arrival but, fortunately, he had yet to exhibit lasting effects from his mother's drug use.

Sharon held Timothy in her arms, watching as he worked on the bottle she fed him. She smiled, overjoyed to think of what her life had become.

When the phone rang she reacted like a pro, as though she'd been handling babies all her life. Timothy never missed a drop of formula as Sharon answered.

"Hello. This is Sharon."

"Hello, Sharon. This is Melanie Powers, from the CASA office."

"Of course. Hello, Melanie. How are you doing?"

"Just fine. I have great news for you."

"What's that?"

"They found Rosie."

"Really? That is good news. Is she okay?"

Melanie paused. "I'm not sure. I haven't seen her yet. They're bringing her home now."

"Home? From where? Who's bringing her home?"

"She was down near Columbus. I'm afraid she got mixed up with the wrong type of people."

Now it was Sharon's turn to pause. "That doesn't sound good."

"Like I said, I don't know the details. I do know she was being held against her will, so I'm sure she'll be glad to get back to Toledo. And, hopefully, get her life back on track again. The poor girl's been through a lot."

"I hope everything works out for her. Thanks for letting me know."

"That's not the only reason I called. I haven't spoken with Annie yet, but I was hoping Rosie could return to something that was at least familiar to her. I think she was doing well with you and Neal, so I was wondering if there's a chance she could return to your care. I think it would do her a lot of good."

Sharon made no reply. The infant nestled in her arms continued with his bottle. His eyes were closed. He was nearly asleep, a picture of contentment.

Sharon smiled at him. She too was contented. This is what she had wanted from the foster care program. What her husband had wanted.

Melanie's voice spoke up. "Sharon? Are you still there?"

"I can't do it." The voice was a whisper, spoken more to herself then to the cellphone in her hand.

"What's that?"

"I can't do that. We can't do that."

"I don't understand."

"I was devastated when Rosie disappeared. It shattered my confidence. Made me feel like we had failed."

"It wasn't your fault, Sharon."

Sharon continued, as though she hadn't heard the reply.

"It took me a long time to get past that. But I did. We moved on, Melanie. Neal and I have another child we're caring for now. A baby boy. It's what we wanted when we first got into the program. I feel bad for Rosie. And I wish her all the luck in the world. But she can't come here. I'm sorry."

There was a long silence on the line. Finally Melanie resumed.

"I understand. And you have nothing to feel sorry for. You provided a loving home for Rosie when she needed one."

"Thank you for calling me. I'll let Neal know Rosie's okay."

Sharon placed the phone down. Timothy had finished his breakfast by now. She placed the empty bottle on the end table beside her and re-positioned the baby so she could burp him. She held him close, rubbing his back, and tried not to cry.

Chapter Fifty-Seven:

 THERE WAS a certain amount of familiarity to be found in the experience, sitting once again in the waiting room of the Toledo Police Station. It was hard to believe that, months ago, she had sat on the same bench and stared at the same walls. It seemed like so much longer ago than that.

Melanie couldn't help but wonder what Rosie had been through in the intervening time. She had been a troubled youth when Melanie had last seen her. How much more had she been affected by her recent experiences?

A few minutes later Annie Klume showed up. The caseworker seemed frazzled as always, carrying a folder of papers that she sat down on the bench beside her.

"Hello, Melanie. Is Rosie here yet?"

"No. They said they'd let me know as soon as she arrives."

"I talked to Detective Tuppelo. He told me a little of what happened."

"Then you know more about it than I do."

"Unfortunately, it's an all too familiar story. Rosie was in a vulnerable position following her brother's death. She's young. And, even with all she's been through, inexperienced.

"She got involved with an older man. All they know so far is he called himself Slick. He befriended her – or so she thought – and convinced her to run away with him. No doubt she thought it was love."

"But it wasn't," Melanie surmised.

"Far from it. This Slick had a stable of girls. Once he got his hands on Rosie he started prostituting her along with the others. She'd still be there now if it wasn't for you."

"What do you mean?"

"Detective Tuppelo told me what you did for Rosie. That was really great."

"What I did?" Melanie stopped to think for a minute. "I didn't do anything."

"Nonsense. If you hadn't contacted the authorities they never would have known where to find Rosie."

"Look. All I did was make a phone call. It was nothing. I'm just glad Rosie was able to get hold of me."

They talked some more, but there was really not much to say. Soon the conversation lagged. Annie opened her folder, began catching up on some work, while Melanie sat and stared into space. She tried not to think of what the young girl had gone through, but it was difficult to push the images aside.

The important thing, she kept reminding herself, was that it was all over for the teenager.

Melanie turned toward Annie Klume. "Does Consuella know her daughter's back? I tried calling but couldn't get through to her."

Annie placed her folder down, returning Melanie's stare with one of sadness.

"Rosie's mother isn't in Toledo anymore."

"What?"

"She moved. She said she was going to Atlanta. To live with family."

"Why would she do that?"

"I think life just got to be too much for her. Her son's death. Then Rosie taking off. The poor woman's world was falling apart around her and there was nothing she could do about it."

"Then she'll be delighted to learn Rosie is okay."

"If I can get hold of her. She never gave me any contact information for her family down south."

"Isn't there any way to find her?"

"I'll try. But it's amazing how easy it is for people to disappear when they don't want to be found. Maybe Rosie will have an idea where her mother went."

"I hope so. It's not much of a homecoming for the poor kid. But at least the worst is behind her now."

"You think so?"

"Of course. Why would you even ask such a thing?"

"Because I've been around enough to know some scars never heal. What Rosie has gone through these past few months....."

Annie sighed.

"It's not over, Melanie. It may never be over for her. How can she possibly lead a normal life after all this? Each time she's alone with a man she'll be reminded of what she's been through. Each time she tries to get close to someone, to build a relationship, she'll question motives and look for underlying issues. She may well be living this nightmare for the rest of her life."

When Detective Tuppelo entered the waiting room he looked tired, as though he had been through a long night. He hadn't shaved, and the stubble on his chin lent a fatigued look to his appearance. As he approached the two women they stood to greet him.

"How is she?" Annie asked.

"As good as to be expected. She hasn't said much. Slept for most of the drive up here."

"When can I see her?" the caseworker inquired. "There's so much to do. Find her a place to live. Start looking into services for her. I don't want to drop the ball on this, not after all she's been through."

"I can take you to her."

"I'd like to see her, too," Melanie spoke up.

Annie flashed a smile. "There isn't much you can do for her, Melanie. Not now."

"I know that. I guess I just need to see her. To know she's all right."

The detective nodded in understanding. "Of course. Follow me."

Rosie had been left in a large room by herself. It must have been a conference room of some kind. It contained a table and half a dozen chairs. A stand in the corner held a Keurig coffee maker.

The young girl sat on a wooden folding chair, intently watching the floor at her feet. She had lost weight since Melanie had last seen her. Her face was gaunt, her clothes loose fitting. Any spirit she had possessed before, any vitality of youth that had once animated her, was gone forever. She seemed older than her years, tired and worn-out from her experiences of the past few months.

Melanie choked back a tear as she entered the room.

Annie walked over and sat next to the girl.

"Welcome home, Rosie."

The girl made no reply.

"Is there anything you need? Something to drink? Or eat?"

She shook her head.

"We'll get through this, Rosie." Annie reached out her hand, to touch the girl, but at the last moment stopped short, hesitant to invade the teenager's personal space.

The caseworker continued. "We'll find you a place to stay. For tonight. While I look into getting you a permanent placement."

"I want to go home." Rosie's voice was hollow of inflection, empty of all feeling.

"I'm sorry, Rosie, but that isn't an option right now. Maybe later...." Annie paused, her voice choking on the words. "We'll look into it later."

Silence fell over the room. The young girl neither

questioned Annie's words nor brooked an argument. It was as though she had come to accept her lot in life and could see no point in saying anything more.

Melanie, standing near the doorway, spoke for the first time. "I'm glad you're back with us, Rosie. I'm glad you're okay."

The teenager looked up then, toward the CASA volunteer. Her eyes were dull and listless.

"Thank you."

She said the two words and nothing else.

Chapter Fifty-Eight:

SUSAN CHAMBERS was having a typically bad day. She had forgotten her book report for English and had to listen to a reprimand from her teacher. She had a test in math – a test she had neglected to study for – right before lunch, resulting in a subsequent loss of appetite.

So she sat alone in the lunchroom, playing with her food but not eating anything. She always sat alone. Once she looked up, glancing across the room at Trena and Stacey and the other girls from her class. They all sat there looking so smug and superior, like they always did. With their good looks they had no trouble attracting the boys, who hovered around the table.

It wasn't fair, Susan thought.

She knew she was overweight, and she tried to watch what she ate, but it never seemed to make a difference. All she did was starve herself and wish herself thinner but the extra pounds continued to come.

It was hopeless.

Somehow she made it through the afternoon. She could think of nothing better than to get home and leave school behind. To forget about it for the rest of the day.

As she left the building, burdened down with books, she tripped at the bottom of the stairs. She fell, her load tumbling to the ground, and scrapped her knee on the concrete step. It wasn't a bad bruise, but on top of everything else she had experienced during the day she felt like she couldn't take anymore.

She sat there, crying, until she heard a familiar voice.

"Susie cry-baby!"

Trena stood there with some of her friends, laughing at Susan where the teenager sat on the ground. Embarrassed, afraid to stand up for herself, Susan turned away.

When finally the other girls had left Susan fortified herself enough to look up. As she did so she caught sight of a young man approaching, a look of concern on his face.

"Are you okay? I saw you fall. Thought you might have been hurt."

"I'm fine." Susan stood, brushing herself off. She looked at her leg, bending her knee slightly. It hurt, a bit, but nothing she couldn't handle. "It's not that bad," she told him.

"Well, at least let me help you with your books."

The idea seemed foreign to her. Nobody ever offered to help her with anything. So she stood there, a dumbfounded look on her face, and watched him pick up the books and loose papers that were scattered nearby.

"Thank you," she said, as he handed the articles to her.

"And you're sure you're okay...?"

He left the sentence hanging, as though expecting a reply.

"Susan," she said. "My name's Susan."

"Glad to meet you Susan."

He smiled.

"My friends call me Slick."

THE END

Afterword:

THE COURT Appointed Special Advocates Program – CASA – began in 1977 in Seattle Washington. In the forty years of its existence it has grown tremendously into a truly national organization, with all 50 states now enlisting the aid of volunteers to help children in need. Nationwide, approximately 70,000 volunteers in over 1,000 CASA programs speak up on behalf of the nearly 280,000 abused and neglected children they worked with last year alone.

CASA volunteers deal with issues of domestic violence and child neglect. They work with families whose parents suffer from a dependence on alcohol, or struggling with addictions to prescription pills or narcotics. The children they serve come from all walks of life, covering the spectrum of society, though many of the children they deal with live below the poverty level. These are children who go to bed each day hungry. Or cold. Or alone.

The children CASA volunteers deal with are also prone to running away. Statistics vary, but it's been estimated that well over 2 million children run away each year in the United States. Many of these children feel they are trapped at home, and that the system doesn't accommodate their needs. They feel they have no alternative remaining to them but to run, in the hope of finding something better.

For some the only home life they've ever known has been one of neglect or abuse. They have failed to develop proper coping mechanisms, and the bonds they have with family members are tenuous at best. They need help, and programs like CASA offer them help, but many of these troubled youths are unable to accept the very thing that can assist them the most. Instead they turn to questionable alternatives that ultimately can ruin their lives.

The street beckons to them. They join gangs, from a misplaced sense of seeking connections with others. Often unable to support themselves they take to crime as a means to an end. Drugs are rampant on the street, and many runaways fall into a life of addiction.

Or into a life of prostitution.

Children are particular vulnerable to sex trafficking. They lack the life experiences necessary to prepare them for life on the streets. They often find themselves attached to an older person, an adult they look to for guidance and support. Unfortunately many of these adults utilize the children's naivete. They become friends to the youths, forging a false relationship, attaching themselves to the child. From there it's a natural progression to force the child into prostitution.

These are young children involved in this lifestyle, children that should be home enjoying their childhood. Research has shown that the average age of entry into prostitution ranges from twelve to fourteen years of age. Children as young as eight have been found drawn into this abhorrent lifestyle.

Though this story is a work of fiction, Rosaletta's experiences are common for many of the youths in this country. "The National Report On Domestic Minor Sex Trafficking," released in 2009, contains the following information:

One survivor's story of recruitment in Toledo, Ohio, illustrates how a trafficker uses psychological needs or vulnerability to recruit victims. An older male trafficker "romanced" this child by recognizing the emotional needs of the child were not being met. He presented himself as a boyfriend in order to gain the minor's affection and dependency. She explained that for six months, an older man pulled alongside her in his car every morning as she walked to a school for gifted children. He bought the 12-year-old small gifts and told her she was pretty. She finally agreed to a ride to school – and she was trapped.

What is even more horrifying to contemplate is the vast numbers of children involved in sex trafficking. It has been estimated that well over 100,000 children, right here in The United States, are trapped in this lifestyle. Some authorities fear the number is closer to 300,000.

These children have grown up under the most painful of situations, their youths stolen by the men and women that force them into this life of slavery.

Author bio:

DRAWING FROM nearly a decade of personal involvement working with troubled youth, author Keith Julius creates intense stories that pull readers into an emotional landscape of hopes, fears, and brutal realities.

Growing up in a large family, and raising two sons of his own, Julius has always had a compassion for children. Realizing not everyone has the stability he's been able to create for his own family, it has become his mission to provide a voice for the children in our society who need it the most. This led Julius to discover the CASA program. Founded in 1977, the program enlists volunteers to represent children in cases of child abuse and child neglect. CASA volunteers work closely with families to assure the children in these traumatic situations are placed properly and are well cared for.

In 2015 Julius released his first novel, the suspense thriller REMORSE BY DEGREE. This was followed by his series "The CASA Chronicles," which currently stands at four volumes, including the 2023 release A DECADE ABORNING. Each book focuses on a different family struggling with some of society's most challenging issues, including addiction, mental illness, human trafficking, teenage suicide, and childhood trauma.

Though his books are fiction, the writing brings a compassion and understanding to the stories that can only come from personal experience. These realistic portrayals allow the reader to join with mothers and fathers, and of course the children involved, as they face life's adversities. The author invites you to share in their triumphs, and sorrow in their failures, as they confront their struggles with dignity, determination, and the promise of a better future for their children.

Daniel Jameson was living the American Dream. With a secure job, a house in the suburbs, and a wife and two children, he seemed to have everything he ever desired out of life.

His storybook existence is thrown into turmoil when he witnesses a tragic accident at his workplace. Following the event Daniel begins to question aspects of his life he had long taken for granted. He manages to become separated from his wife Becky and on his own, aimlessly adrift and uncertain of his future.

A chance meeting at a restaurant introduces Daniel to Jackie Somerset, a younger woman to whom he is immediately attracted. His infatuation runs counter to the wishes of Jackie's boyfriend, Brad Wilkens, who unleashes a torrent of violence - beginning with a brutal attack against Daniel - that soon escalates to much more.

Daniel finds himself involved in situations and events he could have never imagined, fighting not only for his peace of mind but for the life of his family as well.

Aleisha Turner is young and attractive, a wife and the mother of three beautiful children.

Aleisha is also an addict.

Following a heroin overdose that nearly takes her life away her children are taken from her. Aleisha finds herself in a rehab center, the first step in what will prove to be a difficult recovery. She faces a long road ahead to restore normalcy to her life and bring her family back together.

Beverly Stone works as a CASA volunteer, a Court Appointed Special Advocate. Her responsibility is to see that Aleisha's children are living in a healthy environment conducive to their welfare while encouraging their mother to break the deadly habit that has come to monopolize her life. Along the way Beverly must immerse herself in a world far different from the one she is accustomed to, experiencing life from the perspective of the people who reside in inner city America.

When nine year old Aaron Reed has an accident at a local playground it seems like a routine emergency room visit. The case becomes more than routine when signs of child abuse are discovered. The young boy and his family find themselves embroiled in events that threaten to tear the household apart, as suspicion deepens and trust disappears.

Court Appointed Special Advocate Larry Kendall arrives on the scene to discover things are not always what they seem, as the secrets behind the family slowly begin to unravel. The truth, unsuspected by all, at last emerges. It is an ordeal that will test the bonds of family and the strength of faith.

A young girl's life is thrown into turmoil following the death of her older brother.

Fifteen year old Rosaletta Guiterrez finds things turning from bad to worse after witnessing the tragic accident that takes her brother's life. Estranged from the only family she's ever known – removed from a verbally abusive mother who has no concern for her daughter's well-being – Rosaletta is sent to a foster home, to live with a couple she can't relate to as she struggles to get on with her life.

Court Appointed Special Advocate Melanie Cox is assigned by the juvenile court to safeguard the child's interests, a task made more difficult due to the trauma that has infected the youth's thinking.

Desperate for change, seeking liberation from the loneliness that refuses to release her, Rosaletta runs away. But the escape she seeks becomes a nightmare, as the teenager becomes entangled with people and circumstances she could have never anticipated.

A suicide attempt by teenager Pamela Watkins leaves the young girl's family concerned regrading her state of mind and what could have driven her to contemplate such a drastic solution. No answers can be found from Pamela herself, who has withdrawn into doubts she refuses to express to others. As answers begin to reveal themselves Pamela's life spirals further downward, complicating the situation further and driving her closer to tragedy.

Beverly Johnson, a Court Appointed Special Advocate, is assigned to the case. Meeting with the teenager brings up unresolved issues form both of their pasts, with the clues to Pamela's mental health and Beverly's recurring doubts buried beneath ten years of family complications and unresolved issues.

www.ingramcontent.com/pod-product-compliance
Lightning Source LLC
Chambersburg PA
CBHW070306260626
47160CB00003B/731